THE LIFE THAT SITS BESIDE YOU

MARION COHEN

Copyright © 2018 Marion Cohen

ISBN 13: 9781726834032

Printed by Kindle Direct Publishing

Cover and interior design by Tami Boyce
www.tamiboyce.com

For all the women who

read the classic fairy tales,

and decided

they did not want to spend their lives

polishing a knight's shining armor.

Instead, they chose to gallop alone

along their chosen paths,

and for the most part,

lived happily ever after...

Passed years seem safe ones,

vanquished ones,

while the future lives in a cloud,

formidable from a distance.

The cloud clears as you enter it.

I have learned this,

but like everyone,

I learned late.

—BERYL MARKHAM

from *West with the Night*

APRIL 5, 1954

ON A GLORIOUS sun-filled day in Kings County Hospital, located in Brooklyn, New York, five babies were born.

The births came as follows:

3:12 a.m., Baby Girl: Alice Margaret O'Connell

7:04 a.m., Baby Girl: Amelia Rose Vernola

12:10 p.m., Baby Girl: Anna Susan Wittmer

2:32 p.m., Baby Boy: Alexander Marcus Hoffman

5:05 p.m., Baby Girl: Adina Claudette Saville

On the very same day in Stockholm, Sweden, Astrid Linn Karlsson was born.

CHAPTER 1

IT WAS THE 4th of May, 2004, fifty years and one month since Alice, Amelia, Anna, Astrid and Adina were born. They had all reached the age of fifty. Their mutual auspicious birth date, 4/5/54, a numerical palindrome, was always easily remembered.

Adina sat at her antique dressing table, the one piece of furniture that belonged to her grandmother, and was eventually passed down to her. It was mahogany with three drawers on each side, and ornate carvings across the perimeter of the top oval-shaped surface. As a child, Adina thought it to be terribly ugly. But now, she treasured it, and the memories it conjured of her own mother applying Helena Rubinstein's loose face powder and Flame Red Coty lipstick, so many years ago after her grandmother passed away. Her mother retrieved this salvaged piece of furniture, and had cherished it always. In one of the drawers, on the left side, Adina kept scraps from past times. A pale blue satin pouch was filled with unstrung pink pearls from a long-broken necklace that her mother had often worn. Also, there was a half-used matchbook from Lindy's Restaurant, a seafood restaurant in Sheepshead Bay that her family often frequented in their hometown of Brooklyn, New York. Next to the matches was the engraved Zippo lighter her father treasured. It was a gift from Adina and her sister Emma, for one of his birthdays. It always brought to mind the aroma of his fragrant pipe tobacco that lingered eternally in their apartment, in a high-rise building located in a lovely neighborhood. When he gave up smoking many decades ago, Adina held on to his lighter.

On the top of the dressing table was a brass, jeweled antique comb and brush set that Adina was given several years ago after her Aunt Sarah had passed away. As a child, when visiting her aunt's home, she always admired the set as her Aunt Sarah lovingly brushed Adina's hair, and told her stories about herself and Adina's mother when they were young girls. Also positioned on the top of the table were two Styrofoam head mannequins adorned with two wigs. One was a chestnut brown shoulder-length bob hairdo with bangs. The other was a lighter shade of auburn but had a baseball cap attached to the top of the shiny copper-like highlighted hairs.

Adina had been wearing both of these wigs for the past four months unbeknownst to her beloved group of friends that she would soon meet for their annual lunch. These cherished friends had been meeting once every year since they had graduated from college, in pursuit of maintaining their enduring friendships with one another. A few months after they met for their annual lunch the previous year, Adina was diagnosed with *breast cancer*. The diagnosis came in late October. She did not share this news for reasons perhaps still unknown to her today. Instead she faced the diagnosis and treatment without the support of her oldest and dearest confidantes. Why she chose not to reveal her predicament to these friends, was a mystery even Adina could not fully understand.

A year ago, when they had met for their annual lunch, the other members of this close-knit group of women openly shared their most difficult struggles. It was inevitable that the passing of time would in fact usher in new challenges for each of them, even though they all seemed to lead such uniquely different lives. Adina's life then was running fairly smoothly that year, and she just listened supportively as the others revealed their problems. However, soon enough she realized that none of them was immune to life's adversities, and that she too was subject to meeting life's cruel fate. Adina had come to realize that as always there were choices to be made. Ultimately Adina chose to focus her attention on managing obstacles, resurfacing after setbacks, and dashing gloriously toward that coveted feeling of triumph over defeat.

Adina knew, sitting at her dressing table, that her dearest group of friends would be shocked, and maybe even angry, that she had not revealed her illness to them. The group considered themselves a team of not ordinary friends, but a sisterhood in that they managed to remain in each other's lives for decades. In between their annual lunches, which always took place on May 4th, one month after their actual birthday every year, their individual lives unfolded. Although they certainly spoke on the phone to each other, and occasionally emailed each other as time transformed technology into an acceptable form of communication, it was their annual meeting for lunch that became sacred. It was indeed a requirement to rekindle the devoted friendships. They were a superstitious group of women. They believed in signs and thought there was certainly some divine intervention that had eventually brought them all together. There are some things in life that one should never question and simply accept.

Adina applied her usual make-up and positioned her chestnut brown wig on her now hairless head. She ventured out of her uptown apartment, into a cab, to reconnect with the women that she had shared so much of her life, until this past year.

CHAPTER 2

IT WAS IN junior high that Adina Claudette Saville met and became friends with Alice Margaret O'Connell and Amelia Rose Vernola. They had met in a social studies class, as it was called back then. Their teacher, Miss Saper, an attractive woman who dressed in stunning outfits every day, was well-liked by her students. Miss Saper wore her long brown hair in a French knot, as her overall appearance exuded such elegance. She sat her students alphabetically by their first names which was unusual. Most teachers usually seated students alphabetically by their last names. Adina was seated in the first desk in the first row, Alice in the second desk, followed by Amelia in the third.

Adina was living in a high-rise apartment building in Brooklyn where she shared a bedroom with her older sister, Emma. Adina's parents, Sophia and David Saville, were hard working, loving people who were both devoted to their two daughters. They prided themselves in their affiliation with their Jewish roots. Although they did not follow a very Orthodox existence, nevertheless, they were somewhat observant Jews. Her mother worked in an office in Manhattan and socialized with many gentiles. Her dad's clients in his law firm were quite diverse, and represented a wide variety of ethnic and religious groups. It was natural for Emma and Adina to understand the advantages and rewards of being in the company of people with multi-ethnic backgrounds, unlike many other children in the neighborhood, who were raised to only associate with children that had similar religious and cultural upbringings.

Although Adina became acquainted with Alice and Amelia casually, enough to exchange a friendly hello each day in class, it was not until Miss Saper announced a school project that their acquaintance would become more memorable. Each of the classroom rows were assigned a class project of a country to study. A presentation to the class about the country's culture was to be portrayed in any medium the group desired. The class had one month to research and prepare their projects. Miss Saper gave the class about twenty minutes of classroom time to organize themselves in small groups. During that time, Alice, Amelia and Adina, exchanged phone numbers. They decided they would need to meet afterschool the next afternoon, to organize and plan what they would do. The country they were given to study was France.

That night Adina received a phone call from Amelia. She told Adina that her mother suggested they meet the next afternoon at Amelia's house, and that her mom was inviting both Adina and Alice to stay for dinner. Then Amelia's mom asked to speak with Adina's mother, and they introduced themselves over a phone conversation. Mrs. Vernola assured Mrs. Saville that her husband would drive both Alice and Adina back to each of their homes after dinner.

Amelia came from a large family, having one sister and three brothers. Their house was a two-family home with a garage which meant they had a car. The interior was what Adina imagined a typical Italian family's home would appear to be. There were many Victorian looking pieces of furniture in bright colors, and crucifixes hanging on several walls. The dining room, though, was huge and the table could easily seat ten people. Mrs. Vernola did not work outside the home. Adina thought that was probably because there was plenty of work caring for a family of five children. Mrs. Vernola's welcoming voice greeted the three of them into her home. After all the introductions, they went into Amelia's bedroom to begin working on their project. Amelia shared a bedroom with her much younger sister, Josephina, who Amelia quickly shoved out of the room.

They sat under posters of Frankie Avalon and Fabian, and made up a schedule of which days they would all be free to go to the library together, and begin their research. Amelia's home housed the complete set of the World Book Encyclopedia, and so they began to investigate all that pertained to France. Amelia's father owned a bakery in Brooklyn in a different neighborhood, and so naturally she gravitated to information about French pastries. Alice Margaret O'Connell, who had attended a Catholic parochial school before entering the public junior high, had told them she sang in the church choir every Sunday. Alice said she loved the sense of security she always felt when she attended mass. Alice was mesmerized by pictures of the French cathedrals. Adina was intrigued by all the French artists.

There was so much to learn, and they were all overwhelmed. Eventually, the girls were summoned to dinner, not just by Mrs. Vernola calling to them, but by the heavenly aroma of tomato sauce permeating throughout Amelia's home. Mrs. Vernola made the most delicious lasagna Adina had ever tasted. She assured Adina that she had left out any sausage this time, in case Adina's family kept kosher. Adina thanked her for being so thoughtful as she slowly devoured the meat and cheese mixed together, hoping she was not committing a major offense to her Jewish upbringing. There was a wonderful salad after the meal which Adina was only used to enjoying before the main dish, but she consumed it just the same. Over the delectable aroma of baskets filled with garlic bread, there was much chatter at the dinner table, and Adina felt very much at home, as if she was with her own family. Two of Amelia's brothers, Anthony and Mario, were arguing over which of them would be allowed to borrow the family car over the coming weekend.

Mario said, "Anthony had the car last weekend and it's my turn."

Anthony presented his case by explaining, "My friends and I have tickets to the Yankees game this Saturday afternoon."

The conversation was loud and often argumentative which Adina delighted in immensely. Mr. Vernola was a pleasant man and had the look of someone who enjoyed his family completely.

Diplomatically he said, "Anthony can have the car on Saturday, and Mario you can have the car on Sunday, after we come home from church."

Alice seemed the quietest of them all, but Adina thought that maybe she hadn't been around a large boisterous family much. Adina thought they were very much like her family in their manner, and certainly in the volume of food that was served at dinner.

For dessert, each of them at the table was served a bowl of spumoni. Alice was not sure what that was, and Adina took it upon herself to explain that it was a combination of cherry, pistachio and chocolate gelato. Adina had eaten it before at a restaurant her parents had taken Emma and Adina to in Manhattan, and thought it was a wonderful treat. Once Alice tasted it, she was happy to be introduced to something new.

Mr. Vernola drove them home that night. He escorted Adina into her apartment that was on the tenth floor. He met with her mother and father. They thanked him and Mrs. Vernola for their kind hospitality. Mr. Vernola told Adina's parents what a nice, well-mannered child Adina was, and they were delighted to hear that. After he left, Adina told her parents more about the project, and how she was so interested in the pictures of the French painters. Her parents suggested that they take a trip to the Metropolitan Museum of Art, and that she could invite Amelia and Alice to come too. Adina was thrilled with that idea.

The following weekend Adina's parents took the three of them to the museum. They skipped up the many steps to the museum's entrance on 5th Avenue, and waited for her parents. The building was huge. They followed her father as he led them towards the left wing, and entered a gallery showing ninetieth and twentieth century European artists. The impressionist painters won Adina over immediately. Renoir seemed to be her favorite. Amelia favored the dancers painted by Degas, and Alice preferred Monet's landscapes. Finally, when they tired of walking around, Adina's parents took them into the gift shop before leaving the museum. They bought them each a few post cards of everyone's favorite paintings. The girls chatted non-stop on the subway ride home.

A few days later, Mr. & Mrs. O'Connell invited Amelia and Adina, and their parents for an evening of desserts on Saturday night. All the parents met, and talked about how their children had such a fine project to work on, and how lovely it was that they were all from nice families. What was truly amazing was that their mothers started speaking about the day each of the girls were born. It was that very night that they realized their daughters were not all only born on the same day, but that they were born in the same hospital as well.

Mrs. Vernola exclaimed, "Jesus, Mary and Joseph," once the realization was discovered.

Then Alice's mother said, "I only remember that there were several baby girls born that day. The other woman sharing the room with me gave birth to the only boy that day. I forgot her name. In fact, the nurse teased her about giving birth to the only boy."

Adina's own mother piped in stating, "How wonderful for them all to be re-united once again. It is *ba'shert*." Adina's mother then explained it was a Yiddish term meaning *meant to be*.

At that point all the parents wanted to get involved with the project, too, and offered to help in any way they could. The girls had all been working on the oral presentation, each writing a different part. Adina and Amelia decided that Alice would read the report to the class, as her speaking voice was the most delicate sounding. Each set of parents offered to do something extra to contribute to the project. On the day they were to present their assignment, Mr. Vernola had baked miniature eclairs for the entire class to enjoy. Alice's parents bought a record of Maurice Chevalier's songs to be played softly during the presentation, and Adina's parents purchased three black French berets for them to wear that day.

Not only did they all thoroughly enjoy doing this assignment for Miss Saper's class, but they found so much pleasure in the friendship that was formed with one another. "Let's be friends for life!" Amelia said, and Adina and Alice smiled.

"Let's promise to be in each other's weddings," came from Alice's lips.

Adina, on the other hand, thought they should all learn to speak French, and travel to Paris together one day.

Adina suggested, "Let's take a trip to Paris and visit all the places we just learned about. Let's go to the Louvre, the Eiffel Tower and for you Alice, the Cathedral of Notre Dame. You already told us how much you like to be in church."

Alice and Amelia both laughed at that suggestion. Even at that early time of their lives, their aspirations were decidedly moving in different directions. In the end, they all received an *A* grade on their joint project, which thrilled all of them to no end.

CHAPTER 3

ADINA'S FRIENDSHIP WITH Alice and Amelia continued throughout high school. Often, they were inseparable. They shared everything, except clothes. They were all built so differently. Alice was very tall and towered over Amelia's five-foot-two frame. Adina was somewhere in between, also considered tall but not like Alice. Amelia's hair was very dark brown, a contrast to Alice's dirty blonde color. Adina's chestnut brown hair always hinted of natural auburn highlights in the summer season. When they entered high school, none of them were in the same classes. And when it came to languages, Alice and Amelia both opted for Spanish. That disappointed Adina, since she was enthusiastically headed to master the language of romance, French.

They spent much time after school doing homework together in the neighborhood library, and many weekends in each other's homes with occasional overnight slumber parties. The four years flew by. Once they graduated, all three managed to be accepted into New York University. Alice was hell bent on becoming a nurse. She always envisioned herself married to a doctor, and that was the best path she thought to achieve that goal.

"I want to marry a doctor and live in a big house full of kids and work side by side with my husband," was her mantra.

Amelia was not quite as particular, and just wanted to have many children, and stay at home to care for them. As for Adina, well marriage was not a priority at that point in time of her life. There were trips to be taken and a world to see.

"Adina, what do you want to do after college?" Amelia would ask and Adina would respond, "I want to speak French and be sophisticated."

Alice would chime in, "But don't you want to find a husband first?"

"Maybe, if I fall in love in Paris that would be alright with me." Adina said smiling.

Alice added, "Adina, you are such a dreamer."

Adina didn't consider herself a dreamer at all. She just thought their plans seemed so predictable. Throughout her high school years, she had spent many evenings babysitting. Although some of the children in her care were adorable, she was not enamored by the daily responsibilities of seeing to their every need all day long. Of the many couples, whose children Adina cared for, the husbands seemed to be living the more fascinating life. One couple whose two sons she regularly babysat for lived in a wonderful apartment decorated with ultra-modern furniture. The walls displayed colorful works of art in bright, vivid colors. The wife was a sweet woman who was genuinely nice to Adina, and was relieved that Adina proved to be a conscientious caretaker of her two young children that were both under three years of age. Her husband had worked for Columbia records in some executive position, and Adina thought that was far more exciting than the daily grind of diaper changing, feedings and providing activities that would mollify the children's ever-changing moods. For Adina, clearly traveling into Manhattan for a day's work, seemed far more stimulating than a trip to a neighborhood playground.

But for Alice and Amelia, a home filled with the sounds of noisy fun-loving kids was their greatest desire. It was the 1970's and roles for women were rapidly changing. The campus life clearly exposed them to the struggle for Women's Liberation. Adina could not understand why Amelia and Alice were unaffected by all the new ideas that were being introduced to their young, female minds.

Sometimes Adina wondered if everyone's dreams were conceived very early on in their lives. Adina did not know why some women had different aspirations than others. Her own mother stayed at home to care for Adina and her sister, Emma. But eventually, when Adina was old enough to slip a house key on around her neck, Sophia sought to work outside their home, to continue the career she had abandoned once her first child was born. However, it was obvious by then, and Adina totally recognized that she and Emma were her mother's most important commitment. Sophia's career came second. But clearly, going to work every day made her mother a more interesting person. She came home with stories from her office that engaged discussions at their family dinner table. On their many weekend shopping excursions, Adina learned, too, the value of a simple black pump heel, to present an air of refinement. Her mother had taught her to *dress for success* before it became a fashionable buzzword.

Alice and Amelia continued to buy *Bride's* magazines while Adina would purchase *Apartment Life*. Alice and Amelia had insisted they all commit to being in each other's wedding, even before they graduated from high school. Alice had shown Adina and Amelia a special cloth covered box where she collected pictures from *Bride's* magazines of the dresses she liked for a bridal party.

As soon as they all received their acceptance letters to NYU they decided, and all of the parents agreed, that they would all share an apartment near the university. The university assisted them in finding a furnished two-bedroom apartment on the third floor of an old brownstone building. They would all be just a train ride back to their homes, and so their parents agreed they didn't need the supervision of dormitory life. The widowed landlady living in the first-floor apartment took on a motherly attitude towards the three of them, along with determining some house rules that they had to follow. Once they were settled when the academic year began, the three of them realized that their parents had planned a schedule amongst themselves to casually stop in to their apartment unannounced fairly regularly. They took turns, and whichever parent visited, they then provided a full report to the other two sets of parents. When Amelia's parents came by, their arms were full of containers of pasta and her mom's homemade tomato sauce, or gravy, as it's often known outside of Brooklyn. Alice's mom always brought a casserole of potatoes au gratin and Adina's own parents came with bags full of fresh bagels, lox and cream cheese. They certainly never starved.

During their freshman year Alice met Daniel McDermott. According to Alice, he was her dream man. He was three years ahead of them and a pre-med major. He was even an inch taller than Alice with a slim build, dark hair and truly beautiful blue eyes. They began dating right away, and Alice was convinced this was her destiny, to marry Daniel. She would often exclaim, "Daniel is the love of my life," even after their second date to a basketball game.

Amelia and Adina would exchange a look as they rolled their eyes and smiled. During their sophomore year Amelia had been dating a guy, Vinnie Fiore, that actually worked in an Italian restaurant around the corner from their apartment. The three of them occasionally would have a dinner there, whenever they would have some extra funds from the part-time jobs they had all managed to secure at the university library. Vinnie's dream was to open his own restaurant someday. Amelia was certain he would do this, and she changed her major from education to business. She was confident they would one day marry, and she would help with the business end of running the restaurant, while Vinnie became the celebrated chef of New York.

Adina didn't date that often, even though Alice would try to fix her up with Daniel's friends on the basketball team, and even later, pals from his medical school classes. After a second date with any of these perspective guys, Adina lost interest as she was not swept off her feet by any of them. Adina had been majoring in French and wanted to go to Paris, not down the aisle. And so, during the first semester of her senior year she was accepted into a student exchange program for the semester at the Sorbonne University. Nothing could ever compare to her excitement at the prospect of going to Paris, finally. Her parents, although concerned about Adina being overseas, were enthusiastic to see her fulfill the first of her dreams. Adina hoped she would so excel in the language, that she would eventually be able to obtain a teaching job in Manhattan upon graduation, and live in her own apartment.

When Adina attended her first meeting of students accepted into various exchange programs, it was there that she met Anna Susan Wittner. Anna was planning her studies in Germany for the same semester. She was also over the moon with the prospect of traveling internationally. After the meeting, Anna and Adina decided to go to the student cafeteria to have a chat about all they had just been informed of at the meeting.

As they sat and had their conversation, both looked at the forms and all the information they needed to include. Anna was living in one of the dormitories at NYU. She told Adina she was actually from Lancaster, Pennsylvania, and she came from a family of Mennonites. Adina knew nothing about this culture, and so Anna quickly summarized the basic tenets of that religion for Adina. Her description of her life in Lancaster was not presented to Adina in a good light. At least that was the impression Adina perceived as Anna spoke about her family, which consisted only of her mom and dad and herself. When Adina told her that she was raised in Brooklyn, a broad smile came to Anna's face. Laughingly Anna divulged that she was actually also born in Brooklyn. Adina then asked, "How did that happen?"

Anna explained to Adina that when her mother was pregnant, her parents went to visit a distant relative who had lived in Brooklyn at that time. Her father, a skilled woodworker, had crafted a huge piece of furniture for their cousin, and was delivering it to them. Unfortunately, her mom went into premature labor while the visit was taking place. Anna was born a month early, but fortunately with no complications other than having to remain in the hospital for a few weeks. Anna then proudly announced,

"I was born in Kings County Hospital in Brooklyn. New York".

Adina smiled and said, "Me, too, and my two roommates also."

The girls laughed and after a pause Adina asked Anna, "When?" She was shocked when Anna announced, "April 5, 1954."

"Anna, that is unbelievable. I was born that day too…and my friends Alice and Amelia also. All of us in the same hospital, the same day! How can this be?"

For a few moments, the two girls just sat smiling at each other appreciating the new discovery they had just unearthed. Adina said, "You must come over and meet Alice and Amelia."

A few days later they all met at the restaurant where Vinnie worked, and chatted away over a pizza celebrating the remarkable discovery that they were all born on the same day at the same hospital and another "A" appeared in their lives, which would be contemplated for many years to come.

Anna and Adina would always seem to have a slightly different bond than Alice and Amelia. Anna, too, wanted to see the world. Once they both left for their exchange programs, Anna for Germany and Adina for France, they would write to each other often. They even thought they could manage a visit, when Anna would venture to come to Paris one weekend. Their aspiring friendship was being cultivated, and their bond would grow even stronger during that time.

Anna did have a love interest whom she knew she would miss while in Germany. Peter Biddle and Anna had been dating for several years. He was two years older and working as an apprentice for an architectural firm. They were planning on getting married after Anna graduated. Unlike Alice and Amelia, Anna did not have a goal of filling a home with lots of children. She never spoke about that. When questioned about raising a family Anna would pause and eventually say, "…maybe sometime in the far-off future."

Peter's firm often designed office buildings for large companies and many of those buildings were located abroad. Anna hoped they would be able to live in many different countries, while these projects were being developed and implemented.

Finally, the day arrived when Adina would travel to Paris for her semester at the Sorbonne University. Adina's parents were excited for her with a touch of worry, of course. Her mother still thought of her as the baby of their family, and this was indeed a huge step, to provide Adina with the opportunity to study abroad, certainly out of arm's reach from her family and their unwavering care for her welfare. Her mother's words of advice at the airport,

"Remember that I raised you to always be a lady here in New York, and I expect you to behave the same way in Paris."

A moment later just before Adina was about to board the plane, her father gave her a black leather billfold, and told Adina to put it in her handbag. When Adina examined it more closely on the plane, in it she found two folded-up clippings from the *New York Times*. One was an article about a female French interpreter working at the United Nations. The other was the daily crossword puzzle. Her father always enjoyed working on every puzzle from the *Times*, with Adina and Emma from the time they each entered high school, although Emma became far more competent than Adina, at assisting their father with this task. Behind the article was a handwritten note on the back of her father's business card with the words, "*In case you need some extra cash, love, Dad,*" followed by several franc notes. Adina cried during the take-off, and realized how homesick she already started to feel. But the minute Adina stepped off the plane at the Orly Airport, the absolute excitement of being in Paris took over, and Adina knew the direction of her life was going to be altered forever.

CHAPTER 4

———————— ⟆ ————————

ADINA MANAGED TO find the baggage claim as she strolled around the airport in awe of the clatters of everyone speaking *en français*, in French. The sounds were like an exquisite lullaby to her ears. It was as if she was a voyeur eavesdropping on all the conversations of the native Parisians, and quickly translating in her mind what was being said. The ultimate thrill of this experience cannot be overstated.

At the baggage claim area, Adina found a short dark-haired man in a navy-blue suit carrying a sign displaying the words, '*Mademoiselle Saville*'. He must have observed the huge smile that came upon Adina's face and uttered the words,

'*Bonjour Mademoiselle, bienvenue à Paris.*' He was welcoming her to Paris.

Adina extended her hand and managed to utter the words, '*Merci beaucoup.*'

From that point on, as he started to speak in French, Adina was taken aback by the speed of his utterances. He soon realized she had a bit of difficulty understanding him, and he switched his announcements to English. Monsieur Dubois introduced himself to Adina as a representative from the Sorbonne, and his duty was to accompany Adina to the University, where she would be introduced to the foreign student liaison, Madame Perrot. Monsieur had two porters carry Adina's two suitcases and one carryon to a car parked outside the baggage claim area. He held the door as she got into the back seat and told Adina to relax and enjoy the views of the Paris streets. To say she was simply overjoyed, would not begin to describe the intense gladness Adina was feeling. She wished she could capture all the sights and immediately channel the images back to her parents; whose support made this dream of hers a reality.

Once they arrived at the University, Monsieur Dubois told Adina her bags would be taken to the living quarters and she would find them in her room. He then ushered Adina into the office of Madame Perrot, where Adina was told to take a seat by Madame Perrot's assistant. Madame Perrot emerged from her office and greeted Adina.

'Bonjour Mademoiselle Saville, comment allez-vous?' She asked.

Adina responded, ' Je suis heureux d'être ici à la Sorbonne,' meaning that she was happy to be there.

They exchanged pleasantries and soon enough Madame Perrot escorted Adina to the residence where she would be staying. The dormitory rooms were housed in a four-story building of beautiful architecture. Adina's room was on the second floor. Madame knocked on the door, and a voice followed that gave them permission to enter. There Adina was introduced to her roommate, Astrid Linn Karlsson. All of Adina's luggage had been deposited in the room. There were two beds, two chests of drawers and two desks with matching lamps.

Astrid had already arranged the furniture in such a manner that both students seemed to each have their own space. On Adina's desk was a folder that contained an orientation schedule that would begin the next day. Also, there was a list of her classes and instructions noting which buildings they were housed in, and the time Adina was expected to arrive at each class. Several textbooks were also piled on the desk for all her classes.

Madame Perrot left Astrid and Adina alone to get acquainted until they would be meeting other students for their first dinner together in the dining hall, a small walk from the dormitory. Astrid told Adina that she was born and raised in Sweden, but her parents now were actually living in New York City. Her father worked at the United Nations. Astrid had been attending Swiss boarding schools, and more recently spent time in New York City prior to enrolling at the Sorbonne. She seemed thrilled to have a native New Yorker as a roommate.

Astrid was what Adina imagined a typical Swedish girl would look like. She had shiny shoulder length blonde hair, which complimented her absolutely beautiful blue eyes. She was slightly taller than Adina and had a perfectly proportioned figure. Astrid easily spoke very naturally in English which was a relief to Adina. When Astrid asked Adina to tell her something about herself, Adina began by telling her that she was born in a Brooklyn hospital on April 5, 1954. Immediately Astrid's complexion began to show a reddened glaze. Before Adina could continue her own personal biography, Astrid placed her hand on Adina's arm and said, "No, that couldn't be."

Adina responded, "Why not?"

Astrid gave Adina a wide smile showing off her oh so perfectly straight white teeth, and said, "I was born on that same day in Sweden".

Adina was dumbfounded. She looked at Astrid silently while gently shaking her head.

"Astrid, not only was I born on that day, but two of my childhood friends were also born on that day. In fact, we were all born in the same hospital. And as it turned out another of my friends, Anna, who is now in Germany for a semester, also was born on that same day, in the same hospital."

Adina proceeded to explain how she had met Anna at NYU. "This is truly unbelievable," Adina exclaimed. Astrid just looked at Adina in amazement. From that moment on, Astrid and Adina were not just roommates, they became the best of friends. Their personalities were quite different as Adina learned in the next few weeks and months ahead. And Adina loved the differences between them.

For a longtime they were inseparable. Although Astrid was enrolled in mostly art history classes, and Adina in French literature, they managed to always set some time aside for long walks throughout Paris, and always met for dinner at the residence. Adina loved Astrid's wild spirit, and Adina assumed Astrid liked Adina's more serene personality. Astrid found pleasure in the most insignificant matters. She had a zest for life that captivated Adina. Astrid found Adina's quiet reserve mesmerizing. They were complete opposites, but they both genuinely admired their differences.

It didn't take long for Astrid to begin dating an assortment of male suitors. She was so pretty that men flocked to her wherever they went. Her vivacious personality attracted them like magnets. Astrid was certainly an accomplished flirt at this point in her young life. On a sunny day one Saturday afternoon when Astrid was out with one of her latest admirers, Adina decided to take a walk to Le Comptoir Pantheon, a lovely little café not far from the university. Adina ordered a coffee and a croissant. She took with her, the latest book she was reading for one of her classes. On the table she placed her copy of *La Petite Fadette* along with her French/English dictionary. Adina had come to rely heavily on that dictionary. Her few years studying French at NYU, although a totally comprehensive course of study, was not the same as being there in mist of everyone speaking in French, and at a rather expeditious rate of speed. When Adina read the French literature, she usually came across one word on every few pages that was new to her. Adina was learning there every minute of every day, and she was overjoyed with each new word she could add to her repertoire.

After a few sips of her coffee, a very handsome man approached and asked if he could share Adina's table. He actually spoke in English with the most enchanting French accent. Adina was so taken by surprise, that all she did was nod, followed a few moments later with "of course". He took a seat while uttering 'merci beaucoup'.

In this short amount of time Adina was so taken by his most intriguing blue-grey eyes and the soft wave of his dark, almost black hair. He wore a light blue V-neck sweater and carried a copy of the French newspaper, *Le Monde*.

Eyeing her books, he asked if she was a student at the University. Adina managed to answer that she was, and then he offered some information about himself. He was in his last year of studies at Paris-Sud University School of Medicine. He introduced himself as Tristan Orme, and Adina was immediately taken in by his charm. He asked about Adina's home, and he was excited to learn that she was a resident of New York. Tristan was also curious about her course of studies, and Adina told him about her hope to teach French in New York after graduation.

Their conversation was easy and there was something that drew her to him, and Adina felt he seemed drawn to her as well. After about 40 minutes, Tristan announced he had to get back to the University for a lecture and asked if they could meet again the next day at the café in the late afternoon. Of course, Adina agreed.

He shook her hand and said, "it was a pleasure to meet you Adina, and I look forward to learning more about you tomorrow." Adina responded, '*Et je suis enchanté de vous rencontrer, Tristan,*' meaning she was happy to meet him too.

He left and Adina sat with another cup of coffee as she watched him walk down the street as he headed back to the University.

That was the beginning of what was to be a very long association with Tristan Orme. Not only did they meet the next day, but for many days after that. Tristan's family lived in a small town outside of Paris. He was the oldest, with two younger sisters and a brother all living with their parents. Tristan was very devoted to his family, and he told Adina he felt responsible for them, being the eldest son. His goal, as he explained to Adina, was to study oncology and help cancer patients. Although his studies captured most of his free time, Tristan and Adina managed to see each other whenever time allowed. On weekends he took Adina on drives throughout Paris showing her all his favorite haunts.

One Saturday afternoon Adina was invited to visit his family. They enjoyed an afternoon meal outdoors despite the chilly temperature. His mother, Juliette, was an attractive woman with a warm smile and the same blue-gray eyes that Adina found so captivating when she first saw Tristan. His father, Arnaud, a pediatric surgeon, was as tall as Tristan, and had the same enchanting smile. They were very welcoming to Adina. Off the main house, which resembled a lovely little cottage, was a small structure that Adina found out to be Juliette's studio. His mother, Adina discovered, was a sculptress. She invited Adina to take a look at her work. Tristan had not mentioned this to Adina before, and so it was surprising that Adina had brought a book from the Metropolitan Museum as a hostess gift for his mother. Adina had brought several copies with her to give as gifts during her stay in Paris. Tristan's mom seemed truly happy to receive the volume Adina chose for her, that showed the influence of the Art Deco movement in the architecture of New York City. Adina spent a lovely day with Tristan's family. His sisters Cleo and Eleta were adorable and Jules, his brother, bore a remarkable resemblance to Tristan, although he was only twelve years old.

It had been a delightful afternoon and most of the day English was spoken with occasional short lapses into French. It amazed Adina how well they all spoke in English. Europeans, Adina observed, seemed so much more advanced in learning many languages. And more surprising was that when they did switch to French, Adina could clearly understand all that was being said even though the speed of their dialogue was so swift.

Tristan and Adina continued to become more and more involved in each other's lives. Astrid would tell Adina that she showed all the signs of being in love. Adina was not so sure, although spending time with Tristan was always thrilling for her. But in the back of Adina's mind she knew the day would come when she would have to leave Paris and Tristan behind, and maybe that colored her manner of thinking about their relationship. Adina surmised that Tristan seemed to be aware of that as well. He was applying for a residency program in a few US hospitals, but was unsure if that would ever materialize. So, they did not plan on that ever happening. The nights they managed to spend together at his quarters were wonderful.

When Adina's semester studies were completed, she was sad to be leaving Paris, but Adina did miss her family even though they wrote often, and Adina called every other week to speak to her parents. It had been an incredible opportunity, and Adina was leaving with so much more command of the French language, and also of the rich culture of France. Astrid and Adina vowed to keep in touch with each other, and planned to meet again when Astrid traveled to New York City to visit with her parents. What Adina also acquired was a love interest in Tristan, and she had no idea how she would feel leaving that behind.

On Adina's last night at the Sorbonne, Tristan came to pick her up and off they went for a light dinner at the very same café where they had originally met. For the first time their conversation was strained. Both of them were trying to find topics to discuss other than Adina's impending departure the next day. Tristan looked closely at Adina and said,

"I know I cannot ask you to stay longer. I am not in a position to make a commitment to you right now." Adina smiled a sad smile if that is possible and answered, "I must return to NYU and graduate next semester. My life is in New York…" But all the while thinking her lover is in Paris.

Afterwards they shared a delicious *Dacquoise*, a French dessert that held layers of almond and hazelnut meringue with whipped cream. Tristan reached into his pocket and placed on the table a small velvet bag, the colors of the flag of France, blue, white and red. He said, "This is for you Adina…*avec tout mon coeur.*" Slowly Adina untied the beautiful bag's drawstrings and in it was small box, and in that box, was a gold chain. Attached to the gold chain was a tiny gold charm of the Eiffel Tower. Adina accepted this token of Tristan's affection with complete joy.

'*Merci beaucoup Tristan. C'est tellement beau et je le chérirai toujours*'.

"Thank you very much Tristan. It's beautiful, I shall treasure it always."

Adina thought, there were moments in one's life that mark the passing of time or when one feels a year older, like blowing out the candles on a birthday cake. For Adina, this night marked a passage. Her experience away from home, family and friends had forever altered how she would see the world and her presence in it. The unanticipated connection Adina experienced with Tristan, gave her much to think about on her way back to New York. A fond connection to an amazingly handsome and kind man, was not at all expected. But all in all, it was thrilling to contemplate.

CHAPTER 5

ADINA RETURNED HOME with such mixed feelings. But as soon as she eyed her parents at the baggage claim area at Kennedy Airport, Adina knew she was home, where she should be. Adina's relationship with Tristan was like a dream that had been totally unexpected, and made the experience in France all the richer. Adina felt she was certainly too young to make decisions that would affect the rest of her life. Yes, as she'd always heard, timing is everything.

After many embraces with her family, they left the airport and arrived at her parent's apartment for a delicious meal that her mother had obviously been up since dawn preparing. Once Adina was totally stuffed with her favorite, delectable baby lamb chops, steamed French-cut green beans and oven-browned potatoes, her mother brought out the traditional strawberry shortcake. This family-favorite, Sophia always lovingly prepared for all their family's special occasions.

After dinner, Adina unpacked several wrapped gifts. The first Adina presented to her father. It held an oh so smooth chocolate brown leather tobacco pouch from *Tabac du Paris,* that instantly brought a wide smile to his face. He immediately pulled out his old tattered pipe tobacco case and filled the new pouch with the sweet aroma of his usual scent. Then he noticed in the lower corner of the front flap were his initials that Adina had engraved on the pouch in small gold letters. Adina just sat so thrilled to have given him this special souvenir. For her mother, Adina had beautifully wrapped a package containing a blue iridescent beaded evening bag, adorned with delicate embroidered flowers. Under the evening bag was a smaller package that Adina had wrapped carefully in pink tissue paper. Once her mother unwrapped it, she saw that it held a lovely cobalt blue Limoges candy dish embellished with colorful butterflies. Sophia was equally delighted with these presents from Adina, from Paris.

For Emma, who already had graduated from Columbia with a bachelor's and master's degree in art history, and was already married to her longtime sweetheart, Nathan, Adina presented her with two packages. One was a luxuriously soft navy-blue cashmere beret, and the other a bottle of Nina Ricci's *L'Air du Temps*, Emma's favorite scent. Emma was so pleased, and immediately placed the hat on her head to model for all of them to admire. For Nathan, Adina brought back a book from the National Museum of Natural History, located in Paris. Immediately he began reading the book's introductory pages with concentration.

Adina spent the night at her parent's home since it was so late in the evening. She would travel back to the apartment the next day to meet with Alice and Amelia.

While Adina had been away, both of her roommates had managed to get engaged.

When Adina arrived at the apartment, the taxi driver helped her bring her suitcases up the few steps to the building's doorway. Alice and Amelia rushed down to meet Adina and help with her suitcases. Hugs and kisses were exchanged immediately before entering their apartment. Once settled inside, both Alice and Amelia extended their left arms, so that Adina could see the rings on each of their fingers. Alice had a large Tiffany-cut marquis diamond. Amelia's was a more modest round stone with two baguettes, one on each side. After all the congratulations took place, Adina pulled two packages from her suitcase wrapped in identical paper. One was marked for Alice, and the other for Amelia. Inside Alice found a wooden box with a silk lid that displayed a picture of Monet's *Water Lilies*. The other, for Amelia had a silk lid showing Degas' *The Ballet Class*. Both were actually music boxes that played the beautiful French National Anthem, *La Marseillaise* with room enough inside to house their most precious jewelry. They both graciously thanked Adina for their lovely gifts.

Adina and her roommates continued to chat about her trip and most importantly they wanted to learn more about Tristan. From her suitcase, Adina pulled out a framed photograph of Tristan and herself, revealing the Eiffel Tower in the background. The girls swooned awhile hearing about her very French amour. Adina had also written them both about Astrid, and now was able to show them some photos of Astrid and Adina at some of the most picturesque sights in Paris. After a while, both Alice and Amelia disclosed each of their wedding plans to Adina.

Alice was planning an August wedding shortly after their graduation, while Amelia announced she would be an early December bride. Alice then exclaimed,

"Now Amelia has already consented and Adina you, too, will be a brides-maid at my wedding, right?"

Adina responded, "Oh Alice, you have many sisters and cousins, why don't I just come to your wedding as a happy guest? You know how I dislike all those traditional wedding rituals."

"I'll hear none of that. We promised each other in junior high that we would do this for one another and that's that." Adina glanced at Amelia but she was not to secure any support from her either.

It wasn't that Adina loathed weddings. In fact, they always brought such tears to her eyes as she watched couples exchange vows. As a child, Adina did imagine herself in a beautiful ivory-colored wedding gown with a lovely long train. But as time went by Adina began to think that the customs of a large wedding party, bridal showers, photographers, flowers and all the trinkets as-sociated with the event were much less important than to simply celebrate the glorious relationship two people found themselves enjoying. But at Alice's in-sistence, Adina was destined to be a bridesmaid. It was as if the women's move-ment of the seventies that Adina had witnessed, passed right over Alice's head, and her mind was still trapped in the 1950's of her childhood.

It was difficult for Adina to understand the big rush to get married. Adina knew Alice always had these grand plans since their high school days, but Adina really thought somehow those plans would get modified at some point in time while they were experiencing such new ideas at college, and living away from their homes. Maybe Adina thought, they were all meant to just lead different lives. When Alice spoke of her big wedding plans, Adina could still see the adolescent girl that she met so many years ago, and Adina could not deny Alice any of her well-organized dreams. Alice, Amelia and Adina already had a bond that could not be so easily shattered. Adina's bond with Anna was still forming, as they spent more and more time together after graduation.

Alice had secured a nursing position at New York Presbyterian Hospital on the pediatrics floor after graduation. Daniel was now an intern at the same hospital, and would hopefully soon be a resident there, too. They moved to a tiny apartment close by the hospital where both were working long hours each day.

Amelia and Vinnie planned to eventually move into an apartment in Brooklyn where Mr. Vernola and Vinnie might go into business together, opening an Italian restaurant. Alice would do all the bookkeeping.

Anna met Adina one day in the city for coffee. She had moved from the dormitory after graduation, and into an apartment with Peter. Anna had applied to the city school system for a job as a social worker, and was hired right away.

Adina was the last to secure a job. She had wanted to stay in Manhattan and applied to many schools. At the end of June, Adina received a call from Astrid informing her that Astrid was coming to New York to visit her parents. Delighted at this news, Adina invited Astrid to stay with her, as Adina had not yet moved out of the shared apartment from her days at NYU. She agreed, and a few days later they met at Astrid's parent's home on the Upper West Side. Mrs. Karlsson, clearly looking like a somewhat older version of Astrid, prepared a delicious meal, served at their exquisite rosewood dining table as Astrid and Adina recalled some of the antics they were involved in at the Sorbonne. Her father, still working at the United Nations, was most gracious to Adina, and Astrid explained the difficulty Adina was having securing a teaching position.

After dinner they headed back to Adina's apartment. Adina told Astrid, "Your parents are so charming and their apartment is lovely." Astrid said, "Yes, and they are very good to me, and I could tell they adored you too."

Miraculously, a few days later, Adina was contacted to be interviewed for a position teaching French at The Dalton School, of all places. She was stunned. This was such a prestigious institution. Adina never imagined she could hope to begin her career there. Adina suspected Mr. Karlsson had made a phone call to someone, and that started the ball rolling.

Astrid went shopping with Adina for an outfit to wear at the interview. They headed to Bloomingdales and spent a fortune that Adina really didn't have on a beautiful charcoal grey suit. After the purchase, they went out for a late lunch, and Anna met them at the restaurant. Astrid had already met Anna once, when she visited Adina in Paris while she was studying in Munich, Germany.

During their conversation at lunch they spoke about how unusual it was that they were all born on the same day, and also that they all had names beginning with the letter *A*. By now Anna explained, that she and Peter were making plans to leave for Amsterdam. Peter would be working on his next project in a few months' time. When they would actually tie the marital knot was still up in the air.

Adina's interview went flawlessly. Much to her surprise, the members of the search committee that asked the questions were able to converse in French. It had never occurred to Adina that it would happen that way, but by now she was so fluent in the French language, it was not an issue. Two days later Adina received a phone call and was offered the job. Adina did not hesitate to accept even before Dean McFarland discussed the starting salary.

To congratulate Adina on securing this new appointment as a French teacher, Alice, Anna and Amelia all met with Astrid and Adina that weekend. They gathered at their old haunt, the Italian restaurant near NYU, to share some pizza. Astrid told Adina later that night that she immediately felt at ease in the company of these other women. Adina knew they would all adore Astrid, as her personality was so infectious, and Astrid had a natural affinity to native New Yorkers.

With Anna's help, Adina found a small one-bedroom apartment on the Upper East Side in a much sought-after rent-controlled building, and moved in early August, a month before the school term began. Her parents bought Adina some basic furniture: a couch, a bed and a small chest of drawers to begin this new chapter of her life. Emma and Nathan gifted Adina with a beautiful painting of Paris along the river Seine.

When Nathan and Emma brought the painting to Adina's new apartment Adina said, "Emma, this is just beautiful!"

Emma explained, "I happen to see it on display at a gallery near where I work. Nathan met me there later that evening, and we both agreed it was the perfect gift for your new home. The artist is French and was having an exhibition in the city."

With warm hugs Adina thanked them both, then turned to Emma and said, "You always know what's in my heart."

"As you do mine."

On moving day, Amelia arrived with two sets of beautiful teal and burnt orange towels, and Alice arrived with two sets of ivory sheets. Anna arrived with six wine glasses and two bottles of wine, which were opened immediately. Astrid, the only one missing, was already back in Paris enjoying her life in a lovely little flat that had a terrific view of the Seine, located in the fourth arrondissement.

Clearly, Adina was flying high. Her own dreams, vastly different from Alice's and Amelia's, were about to be launched. This very small apartment would house all her hopes and aspirations for many, many years.

Alice made the first toast, which of course included a wish for Adina to meet a guy that would take her away from these very small living quarters. Anna was quick to defend Adina's introduction into single life in the city.

Anna said, "If I hadn't met Peter so many years ago, I would be doing the same thing as Adina. I think she will live the most exciting life. I am only marrying Peter so soon because he will be spending so much time abroad, and I want to travel with him. It will be easier for us to travel as a married couple. We'll probably just have a simple ceremony at City Hall a week before we leave for Amsterdam."

Adina smiled appreciatively. But Alice could not endorse either of their choices.

"Why wouldn't you want a nice wedding with all the trimmings?"

Anna said, "That's just it, they are all trappings. One day you will figure that out."

As the two bantered back and forth, Adina began to worry about this tension blossoming between these two friends. Adina was fond of them both, even though they seemed like polar opposites. They had been born into different worlds and Adina thought and hoped, eventually, that each of them might come to appreciate their distinctive points of view.

Like a perfect curtain call, the doorbell rang and there was Vinnie, carrying two cartons containing their favorite pizzas. No one was more delighted to see him than Adina. His arrival immediately changed the subject as Alice and Anna put their opposing outlooks to rest, at least for this day. In Adina's eyes, Vinnie was such a kind person. He was not complicated, and he adored Amelia, and that was his most admirable quality beside being an extraordinary chef.

This was the beginning of Adina's break with the kind of thinking she had always shared with these two dear childhood friends. Maybe it was her time spent in Paris that gave her pause to consider that these lavish ceremonial practices were becoming a bit outdated to her way of thinking. It was after all the seventies. More and more women were entering the professional work force, as a wider range of new careers became achievable. Divorces were becoming rampant, and thus many questioning the virtues of marriage anyway, or at least making the commitment at such a young age. But nevertheless, during the last week of August, Adina did march down the aisle for Alice, in a perfectly horrible unsophisticated, yellow, tulle gown, followed by Amelia right behind her in the same atrocious dress. The white and yellow rose bouquets were the only redeeming feature as four more of these dresses tramped down the aisle. Alice had everything planned perfectly, and all went according to her master plan that she had been perfecting since the age of thirteen.

A few months later, Amelia called Adina and asked if they could meet for lunch one day, just the two of them. Adina immediately agreed. Often, Adina had thought that when all the "A" girls were together, the conversations lacked any depth. They talked about the latest fashion fads, where furniture was on sale, and occasionally different types of birth control. Adina had always thought that if you want to have a genuine conversation, it has to be between two people, and two people only. So, the following Saturday, Amelia took the train from her parent's Brooklyn home, where she was now living till her wedding day, and met Adina at Katz's Delicatessen. This had always been a favorite spot of these friends when they were still in college.

Adina got there first and ordered a diet cream soda for herself and one for Amelia. Adina knew Amelia's likes having lived with her throughout their college days. Once Amelia arrived they ordered a corned beef sandwich, which they would split, and an order of fries. This was second nature as whenever they went to the deli, Amelia and Adina preferred the corned beef over Alice's all too often order of turkey and mayo sandwich. And every time they were at the deli, Amelia would always exclaim to Alice,

"Italians and Jews know how to eat."

By their last year at NYU, Amelia would add,

"Alice, have you learned nothing all these years?"

Alice would take the teasing in the spirit it was offered, but never deviated from her turkey and mayo sandwich, although once she acquiesced to have it on rye instead of white bread.

While waiting for their lunch, Amelia serenely began a conversation about the real reason for their meeting. It was late October and invitations already went out for Amelia's early December wedding. She would be married in their neighborhood church, and a reception would follow at a local Italian restaurant. It was not going to be the extravaganza like Alice's wedding was, but rather a more intimate affair. Adina had already RSVP'd that she would happily attend.

Amelia began, "Adina, I don't know why I put this off but I have something to ask you."

Adina was puzzled with Amelia's remark so she asked her what the matter was, and then very gently Amelia began to speak.

"Adina, you know I only have older brothers in my family and Josephina has just turned fifteen, but I have always considered you and Alice to be like sisters to me. I always envied your close relationship with your sister Emma. In addition to all that, I have admired you so much, and not just for traveling across the world as you did, but for the way you seem to evaluate what is important and what is not."

Adina sat back and just half smiled at Amelia, wondering where the full extent of this conversation might be leading.

Amelia continued. "Alice liked all the frills and fuss about her wedding. I am not so concerned with all those trappings. I simply want to make a life with Vinnie. You know he is a kind man, and I love him very much, and I think we can have a good life together. That is really all that matters to me. But I do need someone to stand up with me as my maid of honor, and I want that person to be you."

By now Adina had tears in her eyes. Adina took Amelia's hand and simply whispered, "I'd be honored." This was a very different conversation than when Alice made her demands for Adina's participation in Alice's elaborate wedding.

Amelia said, "You can wear whatever dress you like. It will be just you and Vinnie's brother as his best man. I want things simple."

Adina responded, "Let's go together for a dress. You can help me choose something you would like too."

Smugly, Amelia said, "Well it's near the holidays so we'll rule out anything yellow!"

They laughed and laughed until tears rolled down from their eyes.

When Amelia's wedding day arrived, it was a crisp cool day beckoning the beginning of winter. Adina marched down the aisle in a long-sleeved, velvet, hunter green gown. Peeking out from her wrist was a gold bracelet with a gold heart-shaped charm and engraved on one side of the heart were the words, '*Mon Amie*'. Amelia had given this gift to Adina the night before. Amelia's snowy white gown's neckline, outlined with pearls, was a stunning vision in simplicity showing off her charming petite physique.

Alice sat in a pew next to Daniel smiling, as both of her pals made their way down the aisle of this small Brooklyn church. Although Amelia did not want a large wedding party, she had asked Alice to do a reading during the ceremony, which qualified as Alice participating in Amelia's wedding. Alice seemed thrilled to have this spotlight moment thrown her way. The reception afterward was full of such joy as Amelia's family hosted a delicious dinner of several courses of Italian specialties.

There was a moment when Amelia, Alice and Adina sat together at one of the tables reflecting on this momentous occasion. Alice's parents and Adina's parents were sitting at a table chatting away with Amelia's mom and dad. Looking in that direction, Alice then said, "Can you imagine what they are talking about?"

Amelia answered, "Probably that day in the hospital so many years ago." Their mothers shared a unique bond, much like their daughters.

Alice then said, "Well Adina, you're next." Amused by that remark, Adina looked at Alice and said, "Don't go shopping for any dresses just yet."

They all shared a laugh after that. Dreams had been realized. Alice and Amelia were now married, and Adina had a coveted job in the city, and her very own apartment.

CHAPTER 6

WINTER SEEMED TO pass quickly. Adina was enjoying her teaching job at the Dalton School. She taught Introductory French to eighth graders. The dean promised that perhaps the following year she would be given more advanced students, especially once he observed the full extent of her command of the language. Adina was so elated not only to have a teaching position, but having one in such a prestigious Manhattan institution, was even more than she ever imagined.

Adina and Tristan wrote often to each other. They had an agreement that he would write to her in English, but she would respond in French. This would help both of them to continually improve their knowledge of each other's native language. Their letters were not usually of a romantic nature. Before she left Paris, they had come to terms with the fact that they would be living their lives in different continents. They both tried in all earnest to establish a friendship that both agreed would last their lifetimes. In the naiveté of their twenties, they assumed the promises made could be sustained evermore. But shifting any relationship, from that of passionate lovers to warm friends, was most often an unattainable proposition.

Alice, Amelia and Adina had always celebrated their mutual birthdays together even before Anna had been introduced to the group. But it was clear to them all that each of their lives were getting more complicated and it was difficult now, as time ushered new and significant people into their individual circles, to find time to all get together. Their birthday was on April 5th, the fifth day of the fourth month. Alice had the idea that they set aside another date that they would all meet to celebrate their mutual birthday and endearing friendship, that would not interfere with other more personal birthday celebrations. For a few seconds, they all thought about an alternative date. Amelia was the first to suggest, May 4th, the fourth day of the fifth month. Amelia had just reversed the order of their mutual birth date. Instead of the date 4/5, they could meet on 5/4. Immediately they all agreed that that day was easy enough to remember, and would be set aside for all of them to meet every year to preserve their special bond. They knew they might see each other at different times during the year, but that day, May 4th, would be reserved for all of them to meet together and catch up on the events of the year. The location was quickly decided upon: Grand Central Station, under the clock. They could have lunch at the station or at a neighboring restaurant.

Alice had mentioned that she would soon move to Long Island once her husband, Daniel was established, and it would be easier to come into the city by train. This was part of another of Alice's grand plans. She wanted to quickly get pregnant and wanted a huge house on Long Island. Adina wondered how they could all embrace such different dreams. These women had been so close in elementary school. Adina wondered, could it be that one's aspirations are formed at such an early age and remained unaltered? Didn't their collective university experience, and the changing times of the status of women in the seventies, have any effect on one's childhood dreams and visions?

Occasionally, Adina attended talks with guest lecturers at the university. She was moved by the ideas about women being independent, especially being financially independent. Adina listened as these representatives from the movement, Gloria Steinem, Betty Friedan and others, suggested, that all women could have choices, and numerous paths from which to choose. Motherhood, surely would always continue to be an option as it had been historically, but now a woman, if she desired, could view her life in another way. When Adina was able to hear Gloria Steinem give a talk one day on campus, she listened intently, and one sentence penetrated so powerfully. Ms. Steinem said,

"In order to make a choice, you need the power to see there is one."

That simple little sentence was then embedded in Adina's mind, and would color all her future decisions.

Adina remembered the day they had first met in Adina's new apartment. Alice had mentioned,

"Daniel's parents will give us a down payment on a house as soon as Daniel is in residency. I want to have lots of kids."

Adina had asked, "Don't you want some time with just you and Daniel?"

Alice responded, "Once I have a child or two or three, Daniel will be with me forever. There'll be plenty of time to spend together. I am certain of that."

Adina had looked then at Amelia, but neither of them had said a word.

When spring officially began, the city was in full bloom. Women traded their knee-high boots in favor of stacked heels in black patent leather and all the shades of beige, taupe and tan. Opaque stockings peeking out of the new length of mid-calf skirts showing various lengths of front or side slits, were all the rage. Denim was now not only reserved for bell-bottomed pants, but for long, straight skirts as well.

Amelia, the bookkeeper of the group, sent out postcards two weeks in advance to Alice, Adina, Anna and even Astrid, reminding them of the first official lunch to be held on May 4th. They were to all meet by 11:30 a.m. in front of the big clock at Grand Central Terminal. Fortunately, it was on a Saturday and Adina did not need to take off from school. Anna was back from Amsterdam by then, and even Astrid happened to be visiting her parents with her latest beau from Paris.

One by one they met each other with hugs and kisses under the infamous clock, even though some had seen each other only a month before. Since it had started to rain, they decided to dine at one of the eateries located in the station. As they were all seated at a large round table, Alice appeared to be bursting at the seams.

"Well I can't wait another minute to tell you all I'm pregnant. I just found out last week and decided to tell you all at the same time."

Astrid got up from her seat at the round table and walked over to where Alice was sitting, and gave her a huge hug. Amelia joined in hugging Alice from her seat to the right of Alice. Adina was on Alice's other side and placed her hand on Alice's and simply said, "This is what you've always wanted."

Anna just smiled from the other side of the table and didn't say much. Alice then announced she was due in early December and went on about how much there was to do before her delivery date. First on her list, of course, was finding larger living quarters.

"Daniel's parents and I will start looking for a house next week and once we find one I'll take Daniel to see it and we'll decide."

Amelia, the numbers person in the group asked her if they could afford a house so soon. But Alice was happy to accept the financial help Daniel's parents were offering. Amelia explained that this was something that Vinnie would never do. He and Amelia, since they married, were living in a small one-bedroom apartment in Brooklyn, not too far from her parent's home. According to Amelia, eventually they would buy a house near the restaurant he planned to open with Amelia's father, but buying a home was a long way off in the future.

Anna finally spoke up, and when she did she asked Alice if she was planning on giving up her nursing career so soon. Alice said, "Of course, maybe after all my children are grown I can go back to it if I ever get bored."

Anna couldn't imagine getting tied down by having children at their young age now of twenty-three. She had much on her to-do list before even entertaining the idea of getting pregnant, if she would ever consider it at all.

Their afternoon continued with the conversation centered around Alice's news. Once they finished their meals and ordered their dessert, all opting for a slice of cheesecake, Adina announced that she had some interesting news to share, too.

"Well in my school the language department takes a group of the older students to Europe during the summer vacation for eight days. This time they are going to Paris. One of the chaperones had to back out and the department chairman asked me if I could go instead. The transportation and hotel room would be paid for by the school. So, I am going."

Again, Astrid rose from her seat and put her arms around Adina. "This is wonderful. Will you have any time on your own?"

"I might. I think they, the other chaperones, take turns in the evening being with the students. And maybe I'll also have a free afternoon."

Astrid then realized and said, "You'll be able to see Tristan, right?"

"I hope so. I haven't yet mentioned it to him."

Astrid added, "If I'm still in Paris then, we can meet too, *oui?*"

"Of course, if there is time. I'll contact you before I leave."

Anna chimed in, "That's wonderful. I know how much you loved being in Paris and now you have a chance to go back. This is such good news, it's fantastic news!"

Anna was far more animated with the idea of Adina's trip, than with Alice's pregnancy announcement. Adina felt a little awkward about that. To change the subject, Adina then asked Astrid how long she would be in New York. "Long enough for Jacques to settle some business."

Amelia asked, "Who is Jacques?"

Astrid began to explain. "Jacques Gagnier is an adorable man I met in Paris. He came into the bookstore where I was working and we began to speak to one another. He was looking for a gift, a book for his five-year-old daughter. It was her birthday. I recommended one of my favorites, *Madeline and the Gypsies*, and the next thing I knew we were going out for a coffee. There he explained that he was divorced for a year and we have been going out since then. He had some business in New York and asked if I wanted to come along. Naturally I said yes."

Alice was first to ask what was on all their minds. "How old is he?"

"He is a very handsome man in his mid-thirties. He met my parents last night at dinner."

Amelia then spoke, "Your parents must be so different than mine."

Anna said, "Astrid's parents are European."

Amelia threw back, "My parents were raised by Italian Europeans and that would not go over well in their house."

"Well it's not like I am about to marry him. We are just having some fun."

"That's the part my parents would frown upon."

Anna declared, "Hey, my parents are still getting over that fact that Peter and I married so quickly before we went to Amsterdam. They act like we are living in sin, their kind of sin, even with a marriage license."

They all laughed at Anna's explanation. A moment later they realized how late in the day it was, and that they all should be getting back to their homes and their individual lives, each at a different location.

Astrid reminded Adina, "Remember to call once you get to Paris."

"Of course."

"And Alice be sure you send me an announcement once the baby comes. And Amelia, once that restaurant is open, I will return to New York for one of Vinnie's notable dinners."

This is what Adina loved about Astrid. Always, she was so full of optimism and vivacity. Her energy as always was contagious.

As it turned out, the first annual meeting of the April 5th birthday girls held on May 4th, was a very pleasant experience. Everyone departed to various subway trains that would take each one home. As Adina waited on the subway platform, she couldn't help but wonder what news they would all share the following year.

CHAPTER 7

WHEN THE SUMMER arrived, Adina was anxious for her chaperoning trip to Paris to get underway. Adina had examined the itinerary, and she saw it was filled with the wonderful places already familiar to her. Finally, the day came and a chartered bus took all fifteen students, and chaperones to the Kennedy airport in Queens, for their direct flight to Paris, France. The three chaperones; Robert Levin, the language department chairperson, Rhoda Gardner, an already seasoned teacher fluent in French and Spanish, and Adina, all took their seats. Rhoda and Adina chatted for most of the flight. They were still in the early stages of establishing a collegial friendship. They arrived in Paris, Saturday in the late afternoon. From the moment they deplaned, Adina was in her glory. Rhoda and Adina, immediately began speaking in French, and the students seemed so impressed. They tried hard to catch a phrase or two of what the chaperones were saying to one another. Most of these students had studied French for at least three years, and had only a moderate command of the language. A trip coordinator met the troupe at the airport. All the students and chaperones, were escorted into a bus, with their luggage already on board.

The group was taken to a lovely hotel on the Left Bank, and the students were given their room keys. All were on the same floor of the hotel. Each chaperone had their own room. The students were given an hour to unpack and organize, and then they were to meet in the lobby, in order to proceed to a small dining room for dinner, followed by an orientation meeting. The week was jampacked with sightseeing. The group would have a native Parisian, Mademoiselle Margaux, with them every step of the way. Each chaperone selected one day to have on their own without the group. Adina selected Thursday, the day the group was going to Versailles. Adina had been there many times, and decided that was the day she could possibly meet with Tristan.

After the dinner and orientation meeting, Adina phoned Tristan from her hotel room. Both were excited to hear each other's voice.

"Adina, when can I see you?"

"Tristan, our schedule is so packed. There is very little down time. But on Thursday, I have the entire day to myself, at least until the dinner hour."

"Well then, I will arrange to have that day off from the hospital. But how about now? Can I meet you in the hotel lobby for a drink? I want to see you."

"The students must be in their own rooms by eight, so I can meet you in the lobby, let's say a half hour later. I too, am anxious to see you."

When Adina entered the bar off the hotel lobby, Tristan spotted her immediately. He just stared at her for a minute until she saw him. He rose and ran to her as she ran to him. After a kiss on each cheek, they lingered in a long hug. They found a small table for two, and Tristan ordered a crème de cassis for Adina, and a cognac for himself. He had remembered her favorite liquor. They toasted to their upcoming day together on Thursday.

Tristan said, "Adina, you look wonderful. There is something different about you."

"I am a weary working girl now," Adina said and they both laughed.

Actually, Adina assured Tristan how much she enjoyed her teaching job. She also mentioned that she loved living in Manhattan, and having her very own apartment, much to her parents' worry. Adina then inquired about Tristan's family, and he filled her in on all the news about his parents and sisters, Eleta, Cleo, and brother Jules.

Adina asked, "How are things at the hospital going for you?"

"It is wonderful. I am learning so much. Next year I can select my specialty and I want to pursue the study of oncology, maybe pediatric oncology. I am hoping to get a fellowship in the field somewhere."

"Oh Tristan, that is fantastic. You will be such a caring doctor for patients with that horrible disease."

Adina was certainly his most fervent cheerleader. She was gratified to hear him speak enthusiastically about his admirable ambitions.

Tristan said, "I am applying to some places in the USA so maybe…who knows what might happen. Ah Adina, it is so good to have you here in Paris again."

Adina said, "It is so good to be here, with you."

Just then he moved his chair closer to her. She could feel his breath on her cheeks. His right hand extended over her shoulder. They kept moving closer and closer to each other, and finally they had to kiss again, a long satisfying reunion of their tongues. When their lips parted, Adina knew the spark had been rekindled, or perhaps, had never really dissolved during their long absence from each other.

They kept on talking for another two hours. Adina was thoroughly exhausted from all the traveling. As she yawned, Tristan could see how tired she was, and decided it was time he left her, until Thursday.

Adina said, "We better say good night here." Tristan moved closer to her again and kissed her in the most unfriendly manner. It bought back so many memories of their nights together when she was a student at the Sorbonne. When Adina entered her hotel room, she wondered how long would it take for Thursday to come around.

Adina enjoyed traveling throughout Paris with the students. They visited the Eiffel Tower, the Cathedral of Notre Dame and the Louvre. They went on a walking tour, and of course a few hours were dedicated to shopping on the Rue de Rivoli. Each location brought back so many wonderful memories of Adina's time in Paris. The students were in awe wherever they went. Many tried desperately to converse in French which delighted their teachers.

Finally, Thursday arrived. Adina rose early in the morning. After she heard all the doors of the students opening and closing down the hall, she decided to take a shower, and then get ready to see Tristan. She managed to dry her hair and apply a tiny bit of makeup. While still in her bathrobe, there was a knock on her door. Adina assumed it was the rather quick delivery of the breakfast she had ordered; coffee, juice and croissants. She opened the door but standing there, much to her surprise, was Tristan. *'Bonjour, j'étais impatient de te voir.'*

He was saying that he was anxious to see her. Adina smiled and told him that she also couldn't wait to see him.

She let him enter her room and then said, "But I am not even dressed yet Tristan."

Tristan then walked over to Adina and held her tight. He untied her bathrobe, took her by the arm, and led her back to bed. She lay there watching him slowly remove all his clothes, and then he slipped into the bed with her. For a long time, they just laid there with their arms around each other. Adina could not help but wonder about this new predicament she found herself experiencing.

Adina spoke first. "I thought we were going to be just friends from now on." Tristan responded, leaning on his side looking at Adina, "We are friends. We are friends who are also lovers. Neither one of us can deny that."

Adina told him that it has been difficult to be away from him. She even told him about two of the teachers she dated for a short time, and about the blind dates Alice had set up for her. "But none of them are like you," she told him.

Then he leaned forward and kissed her. It was a long kiss. They continued for about an hour being very friendly toward each other. It felt so natural for Adina to be with Tristan. She felt so electrified, to once again be the recipient of this thrilling, yet familiar love-making encounter. Tristan confessed that he was just as enthused to be reunited with her tender touches, and her intense desire to be with him. Adina thought it was wonderful to be sharing this special time with the man whom she obviously still had a strong connection.

Tristan finally announced, "Let's get dressed. I have the entire day planned. We are going to have lunch along the Seine River. I have reserved seating on the *bateaux mouche.*"

Adina was delighted. While she took another shower, the croissants and coffee arrived. Once they were both showered and dressed, they dashed out of the hotel happy to feel the warmth of a beautiful sunny day. For a while, they just walked hand in hand. Adina was overcome with two feelings. One was the sheer delight at being with Tristan, and the other was perhaps some regret that they had decided to allow themselves to be separated by the Atlantic Ocean for such a long time.

The boat ride along the Seine was pure delight. They enjoyed a lovely meal which Adina thought the best part was the charlotte russe dessert. Tristan took such pleasure in watching Adina devour her dessert.

"Adina, you enjoy your charlotte russe with such passion."

She responded, "Tristan, I enjoy many things with great passion."

"I've noticed," he admitted, while moving a few stray hairs from her forehead that the wind had misplaced.

Adina felt so contented as the boat journeyed up and down the sites of Paris that were so recognizable to her. When the boat reached the Pont Neuf bridge, Tristan held on to Adina tightly and kissed her. His kiss lasted until the entire boat had passed under this legendary structure.

Adina did not want this day to end, but she had responsibilities, and needed to be back at the hotel for dinner with the students. Tristan accompanied Adina back to her room, where they sat on a pair of burgundy upholstered chairs facing each other. They spoke of Tristan's future mostly, and he mentioned to her all the medical schools and hospitals, where he applied for a fellowship. Some were in the States but it was anyone's guess where he might be accepted.

As the dinner hour got close, Tristan inquired as to the time of their flight back to New York that coming Sunday. "I will try to meet you at the airport to say 'Adieu.'" She thanked him for the wonderful day they had just enjoyed, and he kissed her on both cheeks. Then Tristan left Adina's room only a few minutes before the bus full of students arrived back at the hotel from their day trip to Versailles.

Over dinner, instead of being elated about the wonderful day she had spent with Tristan, Adina was gloomy. This was a common reaction for Adina. Whenever she experienced fantastic joy, it was always trailed by unrelenting melancholy.

A few days later, while on the bus, the group was traveling to visit the Montmartre District and the bus happened to pass right by the Sorbonne. Mr. Levin mentioned to the students that this University is where Ms. Saville studied French a few years ago. It was so lovely a memory, especially when the bus passed the little cafe where Adina had first met Tristan. Totally impressed, the students immediately started to ask Adina many questions about her time there. This had been a wonderful opportunity for these students to have a glimpse of the University, and for Adina to savor her sweet memories as well. They came back to their hotel exhausted from an amazing day visiting Montmartre. They saw the Basilica of Sacre-Coeur, and passed by the Moulin Rouge briefly. The trip included a visit to the Musée de Montmartre, and later in the day, a final shopping trip for last minute purchases of tee shirts and other mementos.

The next day they all departed early for their flight home. The group arrived at the airport after a lovely farewell breakfast at their hotel, where their Parisian guide, Margaux, presented each student with a miniature French flag to bring home. The mood of the students was one of gladness to be going home, but also longing to remain in Paris for a few more days. Adina was in agreement with them all. Once at the gate most of this tired caravan took a seat, and Adina suddenly was stunned as she saw Tristan sitting close by. He got up and walked over to her. She introduced him to Mr. Levin and Rhoda. They exchanged pleasantries, and then Rhoda suggested that she and Mr. Levin go for a cup of coffee, giving these two friends some privacy. Adina threw her an appreciative look, and then sat down with Tristan.

"I cannot believe that you are here Tristan."

"I wanted to see you off, and spend a little more time with you."

Adina noticed that some of the students were eyeing them very curiously. She steered Tristan over to the group of students, and in French made the introductions. One of the female students attempted to respond in French, and Tristan took her hand and kissed it while telling her it was a pleasure to meet such exceptional students. Adina let this repartee between Tristan and the students go on for a while, and then excused herself and Tristan. They walked away from the gate area. Adina and Tristan found seats at an adjacent gate lounge.

Tristan said, "I wanted to give you this little souvenir of your trip here." He then pulled out a small box from his jacket pocket. "But I want you to not open this box until you are on the plane. Promise me this."

Adina smiled as she put it in her pocketbook, "Of course. *Merci beaucoup.*"

"Promise too, you will write me as soon as you arrive home."

"I will and I will miss you so much. It was such a joy to spend our time together."

"Adina, have faith in the future. Something will work out for us. I do love being with you, and there is still so much we should learn about each other."

Adina was in her glory. There she was in Paris, with Tristan, and for that brief moment her world was as perfect as it could possibly be, but only for that one brief moment. If she could find a reason to stay with Tristan and not return home, she would, but that reason was out of her grasp.

He said, "Well I must get back now to the hospital, but I wanted to see you one more time."

"I'm so glad you did."

And then, Tristan took Adina in his arms, kissed her forehead and both cheeks. They parted and Adina started walking back to the gate. She turned around, and saw Tristan watching her still, and she mouthed, 'Adieu'.

On the plane, she sat next to Rhoda. Once they were settled and the plane took off, Rhoda looked at Adina and said only one word. "Details."

Adina laughed and told Rhoda only a brief synopsis of how she had met Tristan when she was a student at the Sorbonne. Rhoda, a long-time tenured teacher at Dalton, listened intently. Adina then remembered the box, and reached into her purse and took it out. Rhoda said, "What's that?"

Adina told her Tristan brought it to the airport to give to her. She then took off the lid and removed some cotton. Inside was a Limoges replica of the boat where they had spent the day on the Seine.

Rhoda whispered, "Ah, the *bateau mouche*." Adina then told her that's how she and Tristan spent the day on Thursday. "I see…Adina, I think you have an enchanting problem on your hands."

A moment later Rhoda was engrossed in a French novel she had bought at the airport. And Adina was enthralled in the memory of her time with Tristan.

When they arrived at the airport in New York, many of the students' parents were there to greet them and take their teenagers home. The school had a van waiting to escort Mr. Levin, Rhoda and Adina back to their apartments in the city. When Adina entered her building in the late afternoon, she received a hardy welcome from Mr. Brooks. Mr. Chandler Brooks was the daytime doorman in her apartment building. He had a charming British accent and personified so much refinement. Adina and he became instant chums shortly after she moved into the building. Whenever Adina stopped at Glaser's Bake Shop on First Avenue after school, along with her own stash of black and white cookies, she always brought Mr. Brooks a cheese Danish for his afternoon tea. He came to adore Adina and her thoughtfulness.

Mr. Brooks helped Adina to the elevator with all her luggage, and when she finally arrived into her apartment, she simply plopped down on her couch. After a few minutes, she telephoned her parents again. She had contacted them from the airport to say they had arrived safely. Her mother, Sophia, was a worrier and was so relieved as soon as she heard Adina's voice, thankful that she was in her apartment, safe and sound.

Then she decided to phone Tristan to let him know she had arrived home. She also wanted to hear his voice, once again. Adina thanked him for the most marvelous time she had spending a day with him, and also for the precious gift he gave her at the airport. He told her that he hoped to see her again soon, and that he thought that might happen eventually. Then they said their good-byes.

Adina decided to unpack right away so she could spend the next day doing wash and getting organized. The gift from Tristan, she placed on her night table next to the picture of the two of them she always kept there. Eventually she fell into a sound and satisfying sleep.

CHAPTER 8

ADINA SPENT THE remaining summer weeks taking two classes at NYU. One was a contemporary French Literature class and the other was a secondary school teaching class. Both would be credited toward earning a Master's Degree which was required for all faculty at the Dalton School. Teachers were given five years to obtain the degree. Adina arranged it in such a way so that she could acquire the degree in three years. At least that was her plan. Anna was also taking classes at NYU that summer, so it was easy for them to occasionally meet for coffee or an early dinner.

Anna had mentioned to Adina that she thought she could travel with her husband, Peter during the summer, but as luck would have it, his office did not send him abroad. Instead, he was working on the construction of a shopping mall in Detroit. Anna admitted, that was the last place she wanted to visit in the summer, so she enrolled in some classes. Peter came home every other weekend throughout the summer which presented Anna with much free time, and so she and Adina could easily manage meeting for drinks or dinner some nights. On the alternating weekends when Peter did not return to New York, Anna and Adina visited a few museums and even managed to attend a Broadway show one Saturday afternoon. By summer's end they had bolstered their relationship. They spoke about their dreams, their childhood and of course the men in their lives.

Anna's childhood and family life were vastly different from Adina's. But after their conversations Adina began to understand why Anna fled to New York City. The farm country of Lancaster, Pennsylvania was not where Anna wanted to spend her life. Anna's parents were very simple and enjoyed their quiet life amidst the backdrop of the Mennonite culture. Anna articulated that she thought her dad's talent for cabinet making was being wasted in the Pennsylvania countryside, but he was quite content with his lot. Her mother, whom Anna explained was more open-minded in general, just went along with whatever her husband desired. This was exasperating, Anna admitted, who watched her mother, a gifted pianist stifle her talents.

Anna explained, "My mother was so in love with my dad and she gave up so much for him. And because of that he had all the power in their marriage."

Adina asked, "What do you mean by that?"

"Well I think my mother loved my father more than he loved her. When that happens, the person who seems to love more, loses the power in the relationship."

Adina, looking confused asked, "What if they both loved the same?"

But Anna was quick to respond. "That is not the way it is Adina. One person always loves more, and that person relinquishes the power in the relationship."

After a moment Adina said, "But then isn't it true that the person who loves more might also experience more joy from the relationship? What about your relationship with Peter?"

Anna said, "Peter adores me and always has. I knew I could make a life with him and he would always go along with whatever I wanted. Fortunately, our dreams of how we each wanted to live our lives were very similar. I am fairly certain if I wanted to pick up and move to Australia or Africa, Peter would gladly go along. Don't you have a relationship like that with Tristan?"

Adina frowned at the mention of her relationship with Tristan.

"We do seem to both love each other very much. The difficulty is that we both love our families as well. I cannot commit to moving to France for the rest of my life knowing I would rarely be able to see my parents and Emma. A yearly visit is not the same as witnessing their lives as it unfolds in the moment. Tristan is just as close to his family, and I could never ask it of him to disconnect from their daily lives."

"That is hard for me to understand Adina. If you two love each other..." Anna's voice trailed off.

Adina said, "It is because we love each other, that neither wants to ask it of the other."

"Then what will you do, Adina?"

"I guess live for the summers that I can maybe travel back to Paris on vacation."

Anna kept questioning Adina's choices, suggesting that it would be a lonely life for Adina, and that Tristan would probably meet someone eventually in France. Adina had thought of that possibility many times herself, but quickly dismissed such thoughts as she felt they were too painful to consider.

Adina said, "I know you, Alice and Amelia are all married now, but I really do not feel the pull of marriage at this point in my life. I still feel too young to even contemplate being married, even to Tristan. We are all so young and have a lifetime in front of us."

Anna replied, "Oh Adina, the longer you wait the more difficult it will be to find someone to marry that you can live with and enjoy a fond connection."

"Wow, you sound like my mother now. She tells me the same thing. I am only twenty-four. I feel so young. And don't start in about having children. I cannot even begin to imagine that. I know Alice is in a hurry but her motives were questionable. I do love children, but am quite satisfied bidding them farewell in the late afternoons and retreating to my serene little apartment."

Anna then asked, "What do you mean that Alice has motives? What sort of motives?"

"Well Alice believes that the way to keep a man married is to have his children, the sooner the better. At least that's what she always told me and Amelia."

Anna charged back, "That's ridiculous!"

"I agree. If a man doesn't want to stay in a marriage then I think children generate added problems. But you see, Alice has always had a vision of this happy home, only not so little. We all grew up watching these sitcoms that portrayed the happy little housewife with the lovely home and adorable children, and Alice always bought into that. I fear that after she manages to get Daniel to provide all that, she may still find herself somewhat unfulfilled to some degree."

Anna sat back and said, "That's interesting. Does she even love Daniel?"

Adina laughingly said, "She loves what she knows a cardiologist can provide."

"What about Amelia," asked Anna now so curious about these women.

Adina quickly pointed out that Amelia is very different. "Amelia is the most compassionate person I've ever known. Vinnie is truly her soulmate. They are unequivocally devoted to one another. Neither one is interested in material things. Vinnie will open his dream restaurant very soon, and Amelia will always be by his side cheering him along."

Anna observed, "I guess you've really known them a long time."

Adina couldn't miss the opportunity to lighten the mood and responded by saying, "Yeah, since birth." And a moment later she added, "We actually met in grade school and we ended up in the same social studies class. Once we unraveled the happenstance of our identical birthdays, we were drawn to each other and formed a cherished alliance. Even our mothers were drawn to one another once they met, realizing they had all been in labor at the hospital at the same time. Anna, maybe one day we could have your mother meet with mine and also Alice's and Amelia's mom."

Anna's expression changed. She looked closely at Adina and exclaimed, "My mother would never venture into New York City, and my father would not encourage it. I have wanted them to visit Peter and me on several occasions but they have an opinion of New York City in general that is not very pleasant. So, I've started to make the trip to Lancaster about once a year…mostly to see my mom."

"I'm sorry that is the case for you, Anna."

"Well now you know why I took advantage of having a semester abroad, and marrying Peter so soon after we graduated. But it's not like you described Alice's relationship. I love Peter very much, but maybe not as much as he claims to love me."

Then they began laughing. As they continued their chat. Adina had much respect for Anna choosing to work for the city school system as a social worker. She put in long hours, and the outcomes for the many children she worked with were not always very pleasing.

Anna and Adina had similar temperaments and that is probably why they tended to confide in each other so much.

In a thoughtful voice, Anna said, "What an interesting mix of us girls who were born on the same day in the same hospital. And what about Astrid? Is she really as flighty as she appears?"

Adina tried to explain to her that it is Astrid's exuberance that Adina admires most about Astrid. She described Astrid as having this remarkable zest for life. Adina recounted to Anna how Astrid eagerly took her all over Paris, and introduced Adina to a European style which Adina was captivated by. She encouraged Adina's relationship with Tristan at the outset.

Adina declared, "Astrid was always wise beyond her years. She knows a thing or two about reveling in what the world has to offer."

Anna asked if Adina thought Astrid would marry the man she accompanied to New York with recently, but Adina shook her head explaining that Astrid doesn't always see relationships as permanent. She relishes in having a great time with whomever she happens to be with at that moment. But Adina was quick to point out that maybe Astrid will at some point try her hand at a marriage arrangement. "One can never predict what Astrid will do in any situation, so who knows?"

Adina wondered in general what was the rush with getting married. They were still all so young, at least in Adina's mind. She questioned if any one of them could really make such a choice, to commit to someone for the rest of one's life, when they really all had just begun their adult lives. How anyone could make such a decision that would affect the rest of one's life, was actually quite terrifying for Adina. Her own parents did not marry so early. Her mother married at the age of thirty years old, which was actually considered ancient Adina supposed back at that time. Adina was convinced that the choices we make at twenty years old, for many, were probably not all that appropriate a prediction of what we can live with for the rest of our lives. She had to believe that. For that was the only way, in her heart she could accept not running to Paris to be with Tristan. Were the passions and desires they felt in their early twenties, sustainable for the rest of their lives?

When she posed this question to Anna, Anna laughed and cautioned Adina that she makes too much of love and passion. Anna asserted that marriage need only be a harmonious arrangement of two people, who can provide companionship and mutual affection for one another. For Adina, this characterization was unacceptable and lacked taking into account the divine desire two people should have for one another. When she tried to express her opinion to Anna, it fell on deaf ears and Anna told Adina she was a hopeless romantic. Maybe so, but for Adina, there was no other option. At twenty-four or twenty-five, one should be as idealistic and starry-eyed as possible anyway. There are a multitude of years ahead, too many, to subsist unsatisfied every day with the discontent wrought by one's youthful choices.

They were all products of the sixties, a time when all aspects of life were being altered. More than a seasonal change, something like a mental rotation of one's perceptions was in the air. But not everyone allowed themselves this

71

alteration. Adina had learned so much at the university. Her professors' every utterance was like a delicious meal to savor. Adina thought she was fortunate in a way that she had the stability of Alice and Amelia to share this experience with, because they never sought to experiment with any of the drug culture of the day, even though it was readily available. They kept one another grounded, and focused on their own dreams. Granted, Alice's was to stroll down the aisle, and Amelia's was to embrace Vinnie's dream of owning a restaurant. But Adina wanted Paris, while Anna longed to get as far away from her parents' lifestyle as possible.

It was amazing that one could be acquainted with some people for so many years and not know their true heart. Perhaps it was the nature of most individuals to keep their genuine inner thoughts private, so as not to show their souls to all, but just to some. Adina always felt that way around Anna. Close as they seemed to be, Adina suspected that Anna had an aspect of her life completely unknown to Adina. Adina hoped one day Anna would share that part of herself, but perhaps fear of disappointing or disapproval, keeps certain people from sharing their true souls. Such was the case for Anna. Although she always portrayed herself as a very independent and determined woman, Adina began to realize that was Anna's mask. Adina couldn't quite put a finger on what Anna's truth was, only that there was something she kept hidden at least from Adina, and maybe from also Peter. For Peter was a straight up kind of guy. He seemingly loved Anna and loved designing buildings. Both those missions took up most if not all of his time. If there was some hidden aspect to Anna's story, Adina did not know it and perhaps neither did Anna, yet.

CHAPTER 9

BY THE END of the summer of '77 Alice had experienced some sadness. She suffered a miscarriage and Daniel was adamant about them remaining in the city at least until his residency was completed. When Adina spoke with Alice on the phone she wasn't quite sure what was more bothersome to Alice, losing the pregnancy or her bid to have Daniel's parents help them purchase a house on Long Island. After all, Alice had a plan for her life, and she was beginning to get a bit behind the schedule she mentally carried in her brain.

Everyone had been enjoying their after-college lives as they all entered into true adulthood. They still met for their birthday celebrations, but also shared occasional casual dinners together at each of their apartments. But the most extravagant dinner party became an annual tradition once Alice and Daniel hosted an "after-Christmas" get-together. Anna and Adina often met in the city after the school day ended to swap stories about their impressions of working in a school system. Amelia did not come into the city that often, but she and Adina always managed a phone call during the week. When scheduling was possible, the four of them would attend a performance of the New York City Ballet at Lincoln Center. That was one activity that easily drew them together, as all of them had taken the same dance class during their last semester of their senior year at NYU. They had developed very little talent, but a huge appreciation for ballet. When Astrid was in New York, they all tried to meet on a Saturday afternoon for at least a few hours.

During the summer of '78, Adina's sister Emma gave birth to a beautiful baby boy, Joshua Isaac. When Joshua entered the world, he filled the Saville family with a unique kind of joyfulness. Adina was delighted to have a nephew that she could shower her affection on, and shop to her heart's content for baby toys and cute little outfits. Sophia and David Saville, easily embraced their role as doting grandparents. But more importantly, Emma and Nathan were thrilled with their sweet, precious son, as he provided such pleasurable moments for Adina's family.

The following year, on May 5th at the annual meeting of "the girls", Alice announced that she was pregnant again, and in search of a larger apartment close to the hospital where Daniel was now working. It seemed to be some sort of compromise between the two of them for the time being. Everyone wished her well and made a fuss which Alice thoroughly appreciated.

Adina said. "Speaking of apartments, I'll be moving into a little larger one myself."

Amelia shot her a quizzical look, "What's up?'

Adina explained, "Mr. Brooks, the doorman in my building, told me of an approaching vacancy, for an apartment somewhat larger than the one I'm in now. So, I inquired with the building manager, and *voilà*, I will be moving in at the end of June."

Alice demanded, "Just how big is it?"

"Oh Alice, not nearly large enough for you. It's still technically a one-bedroom apartment, but larger than the one I have now. It even has a separate space for an actual dining room table."

Amelia added, "That's great. The next time we come for pizza, we'll be dining in style."

They all laughed and then Adina suggested that once she was settled, perhaps she will prepare some authentic French cuisine for them all.

Adina said, "Actually, it's an apartment that I can see myself in for years to come. There is plenty of space and even an alcove, like a small den off the living room, where I can easily fit a desk and file cabinet to use for my school work."

Alice frowned and said, "Don't get too comfortable Adina. You'll never want to get married at this rate."

Anna interrupted and said, "And how are things with Tristan? Anything new?"

Alice said, "He probably has found a girlfriend in Paris by now."

Adina could always depend on Alice to say something hurtful when the conversation shifted to news about Tristan. Alice and Adina were such good friends, as long as Adina's relationship with Tristan wasn't the focus of their conversations. Adina thought that maybe it was Alice's distorted sense of concern for Adina's welfare. At times Adina thought Alice needed her friends to have and want the same type of life that she was assembling with Daniel. Alice needed some unilateral approval from this special group of friends, that her path was to be coveted by them all. Possibly she needed that affirmation from Adina, but Adina had her eyes fixed on a different lifestyle then the one Alice was so doggedly after.

"Well… I wasn't going to mention it yet, but it looks like Tristan may have a Fellowship at Sloan-Kettering beginning this fall."

Silence broke out as everyone exchanged a variety of looks as they sat at their table. Just then their lunches arrived, and Adina was quick to take a huge bite of her roast beef sandwich. With a full mouth, she could hardly respond to any questions. At this moment, Adina wished Astrid were there in New York and at their annual lunch. But Astrid had gone and married Jacques Gagnier a month ago and they were still honeymooning in Italy. Astrid and Adina had a long phone conversation the week before Astrid was married, and Adina was truly happy for her with only a little concern since Astrid hadn't known Jacques very long. But one thing that Adina knew for sure, Astrid would always land on her feet, whatever the future held.

Eventually Amelia, the diplomat, hearing this news about Tristan was first to speak. "How do you feel about this new development?"

"Yeah Adina. What's going on with that?" chimed Alice.

Adina turned to Anna and said, "What's your question Anna? Might as well get them all out at once."

Anna smiled, "I think we all know what will be going on with that. I think it's wonderful that you can get to reconnect with Tristan again. Maybe you two can settle on a more permanent relationship this time around."

Finally, Adina swallowed the last half of her sandwich and explained that Tristan would not be coming until the fall, so she had some time to think about it. Adina explained that right now she was just thrilled to be moving into a larger place, all things considered. They all knew how difficult it was to find an apartment in the city, especially in a rent-controlled building which Adina greatly needed considering her salary was not as grand as the reputation of the school where she taught. Trying to change the subject of Adina and Tristan, Adina asked,

"Who else has some news? Amelia, what is happening with the restaurant?"

"Actually, we are planning the grand opening on Labor Day weekend. Most of the interior has been renovated and we just need to decide what tables, chairs, plates and silverware to select, and have it all delivered sometime this summer. I was hoping Astrid could give me some ideas since she was spending so much time in Italy."

Adina told them that Astrid would be back in New York in early June.

"I'll call you once she arrives, and we can set up a day for you to speak with her and get some ideas about décor."

"Thanks Adina, that would be great. My father wanted to decorate in red, white and green. Can you imagine? The colors in the Italian flag. I put a nix on that right away. Vinnie and I want the restaurant to be comfortable but with some class and elegance."

"I'm sure it will be lovely" said Adina "and more importantly the food will be scrumptious."

Amelia then looked at Anna and inquired, "What is happening with you and Peter these days?"

"Well girls, we are off to Brussels as soon as school is out for me in late June. Peter begins an assignment there in mid-July so we have some time to travel a bit before he starts the job. It should be fun. Of course, I will come back at the end of August to get ready for the school year, but Peter may need to remain till the end of September. We'll see how it all goes."

Alice asked, "You really like traveling around as much as you do? When do you think you'll start a family?"

Anna took a breath and glanced at Adina before answering Alice's question.

"You know Alice, we are all still very young in the scheme of things. What's the big rush to be tied down by having children so soon? I love traveling with Peter, and I like my job as a social worker at the schools where I've been assigned. I'm in no way ready for diapers and dirty dishes. Just because we graduated from college, doesn't mean we are finished expanding our horizons. Plenty of time to contemplate a family later on."

Adina shot Amelia a look and then Amelia simply asked, "Adina, when are you actually moving into the new apartment? Do you need Vinnie to help move things for you?"

"Thanks, but I will hire movers this time. I don't have that much furniture and I'm looking forward to buying some additional pieces once I am settled in."

Chuckling to still lighten the mood, Amelia exclaimed, "Well at least you have a queen-sized bed. That will come in handy once Tristan arrives."

With that they all began laughing as the waiter arrived to distribute the dessert menus. This was a waste of time as each of them always ordered the cheesecake. Alice, Amelia and Anna ordered it with strawberry topping, and every time Adina opted for the plain. They always teased Adina about her selection, but she could never be swayed.

"I don't want anything to distract me from the delectable creamy texture of this delicious dessert. Any toppings would only detract from the pure essence of this heavenly indulgence." The others would just roll their eyes during Adina's declaration and continued to wolf down their strawberry-topped cheesecake. As they were all enjoying their luscious desserts, Alice remarked,

"Just think, by the time we meet next year our lives will be so different. I'll be a mother, Amelia and Vinnie will be restaurant owners, Adina will be hopelessly in love with Tristan, and Anna will be traveling who knows where by next summer."

Amelia then announced to the group, "I think Adina is already hopelessly in love with Tristan." Then Alice agreed, "I think you may be right, Amelia."

Adina knew she was smirking at her friends and decided it was time for them to leave the restaurant. Usually they all dispersed hailing different cabs since all of them lived in different neighborhoods. Amelia always opted to take the subway back to Brooklyn. The usual good-bye hugs took several minutes until everyone was on the way to their own residences.

Adina headed back to her apartment building. It was different for Adina to have her own space in the city. All her close friends were now married and living with their husbands. Only Adina had chosen to venture out on her own without a spouse or a roommate. Even though her apartment was small, it was all hers alone. It was located on the Upper East Side of the city. Although the building was rent-controlled it was nestled between buildings that were not, and Adina could only imagine how much the rent was in the neighboring beautifully architecturally designed structures. Her imagination went wild thinking about the occupants in these great buildings and what occupations their residents had, and how they came to live so grandly in this magnificent city.

Adina was always looking up when she strolled on the surrounding streets in her neighborhood. Adina's eyes would settle on a window in one of these buildings and examine the drapes or shades or blinds. Often decorative objects would be placed on windowsills, like a plant or some small sculpture, and in Adina's mind she would create a profile about who might be living within the walls of that particular unit.

Adina had started a collection of royal blue glass vases which she had placed on her own living room windowsill. In case any passerby happened to eye her window, perhaps that person could see the unusual shaped vases and concoct a story about who was dwelling in Adina's space. She started her collection when one of Adina's mother's dear friends had invited her mother, Emma and Adina one day for a Saturday afternoon. At the time Adina was about thirteen years old. Vanessa Clovis was someone her mother knew from her own childhood, and they were good friends. Mrs. Clovis worked as a buyer for Saks Fifth Avenue. She and her husband did not have any children. She was a tall, stately woman who wore her auburn hair in a bun, which always showed off an unusual pair of large earrings complimenting whatever glamorous outfit she chose for the day. Their apartment was filled with many treasures, as they had traveled to countless exotic places.

When they were all seated at the dining room table, there were two elegantly wrapped packages in beige velvet paper with a brown satin ribbon at Emma's and Adina's place settings. Mrs. Clovis said,

"Open your packages girls. These are gifts from our travels that Mr. Clovis and I want you both to have."

Adina eyed her mother who nodded affirmatively that it was okay to proceed. Emma opened hers first and found a small bowl of black, brown and grey etchings. Mrs. Clovis told them that it was Peruvian, and explained what the design portrayed. Emma was clearly intrigued. To this day, the Saville family believed that was the seed that grew and motivated Emma to pursue her career working as a museum curator. When Adina opened her package, she found a royal blue glass vase about eight inches tall. Surrounding the very top opening were tiny hand-painted pink roses around the entire circumference. It had been purchased during one of Vanessa Clovis' trips to Paris. That was the start of Adina's blue vase collection, and maybe her continuing fascination of all things French. Strolling down the street, mesmerized at the neighboring building's abundant windows and displays, always brought back fond memories and intriguing new curiosities.

Adina arrived at her building and was greeted by Mr. Brooks as she entered the lobby. She headed right to the mailboxes and emptied her box. She removed an issue of *Glamour* magazine, which she had been reading since her college days, and an issue of *Vogue Paris* that she would eventually bring to her classroom. Adina would share that magazine with her female students after she had read all the articles. It was a good exercise in reading comprehension for her more advanced students. Unexpectedly, Adina also found a letter from Tristan. Once in her apartment she hung her lavender sweater in the closet, and then went into her tiny bedroom. While leaning on several bright-colored throw pillows, she examined the envelope containing Tristan's letter. She so enjoyed looking at how he wrote her name. Before she opened the envelope, she smiled as she recalled Amelia's comment, that she might already be hopelessly in love with Tristan.

As her mind drifted off to thoughts of Tristan, she tried to identify her own feelings. Since her time at the Sorbonne, they had only reconnected when Adina traveled back to Paris with the group from school. Since then, they had written to each other frequently and occasionally spoke on the phone. Adina wondered how she could discern whether she was truly in love with a man living so geographically far away from her. But that was about to change, and maybe she would have the opportunity to discover her true feelings for Tristan, now that his arrival was imminent. Finally, she opened the envelope and unfolded the onion-skinned air mail sheets of paper.

Tristan's letter was filled with updates about his siblings' activities and special news about his mother. Madame Orme's latest sculpting pieces were going to be part of a group show in a gallery in Paris during the month of August. Everyone in their family was so happy for his mother's work to be on display. He also included more information regarding his Fellowship at Memorial Sloan-Kettering. Although he was due to report to the hospital immediately after Labor Day, he was trying to see if he could actually arrive in New York during the third week of August. He was unsure as of yet whether the housing situation would be available to him prior to the September date.

Adina knew immediately after reading his news, that she would write back and offer Tristan the opportunity to stay in her new, larger apartment, at least until his housing was available. She was fairly certain he would want to do that.

———— ❦ ————

At the end of June, Adina moved into her new apartment on the eighth floor of the building. What a difference the extra space provided. The move did not take long, as her apartment only housed a few large pieces of furniture. There were several cartons packed with dishes, cutlery and many files pertaining to her various lesson plans. It was an exhausting day and by the time the movers left it was three o'clock in the afternoon. Adina just spread herself out on her couch contemplating the job of unpacking all the cartons that were stacked all over the apartment. While looking at the boxes she was interrupted from her reverie when the doorbell rang. Adina stumbled around the many cartons to get to the door and once it was opened, there stood her parents, which took Adina by surprise.

Her father was carrying a large shopping bag that she correctly surmised was filled with food from their favorite deli in Brooklyn. Her mother also carried a shopping bag containing two loaves of rye bread, and three beautiful ceramic canisters. These items represented some old well-meaning customs, whose significance Sophia hoped would inhabit Adina's new home. Sophia believed in the traditions that were lovingly passed down from one generation to the next. One canister was filled with a small amount salt, and the other filled with sugar, and the third was empty. There was symbolism in these items. The loaves of bread ensured that Adina would not ever go hungry in her new home. The salt represented only the fewest of tears and sorrows. The sugar provided for a sweet life. The empty canister was her mother's own special addition to this ageless tradition. Although empty now, it was to be filled with pleasant memories in Adina's new home. The very bright blue and white canisters were placed on the kitchen counter. They were a welcomed offering that would always conjure the memory of this day, and of her parents' loving wishes for Adina's happiness in her new home.

Adina was so pleased that her parents seemed genuinely happy for her to be moving into this new, larger apartment. Sophia and David knew that Adina was not going to move back to the family's Brooklyn home, and wait for some marriage proposal to materialize. That, they realized after Adina moved into her first apartment. Their concerns lessened, knowing the building was in a good neighborhood and had a doorman, which provided some security for their youngest daughter. Her mother, the ever-hopeful member of the family, convinced herself that by living in the city, Adina had a greater chance to meet single, professional men, maybe even one of their faith. With that objective in mind, Sophia chose to accept Adina's flight from the family's Brooklyn residence, and her daughter's bid for independence.

Adina's father wove his way throughout the apartment and declared that the rooms were a nice size, and that the floor plan flowed nicely. By now, Sophia was placing all the food in the refrigerator and then she announced, "Change your clothes Adina. We are taking you out for dinner. You can start to unpack tomorrow, and you have food for the next few days."

Her mother knew she was not going to leave boxes around for too long. Adina liked things in order, and her mother was quite aware of that quality. Sophia also knew that Adina acquired that trait from her dad.

The Saville family walked up the street to a little Italian restaurant where they had dined once before and enjoyed the meal. After they ordered their meals, her mother then asked, "What are your plans for the summer Adina?"

"I will continue taking another two courses toward my Master's degree."

With a broad smile on his face, Mr. Saville said, "Excellent."

In his circle, a man was judged by how many degrees his children earned. Emma already had her Master's in anthropology, so he was happy to hear Adina's plans to earn her Master's degree in French literature.

The conversation continued and Adina told them the news of Tristan's fellowship, and how they will finally have an opportunity to make his acquaintance.

Sophia gave her husband a curious look and merely announced, "That will be very nice." Her father seemed more impressed and interested in hearing about Tristan's Fellowship at Sloan. By choice, Sophia did not know a lot about Tristan, only that he was a Frenchman, and indeed not of the Jewish faith. Adina knew she would need to start slowly dispatching more information about Tristan to her parents, since he was hopefully going to become a fixture in their daughter's life. At least that was what Adina anticipated.

In an effort to change the subject, Sophia had a suggestion for Adina. "I would like you to have my mother's dressing table." Adina was taken aback and thrilled at the prospect of having that beautiful antique piece of furniture in her new home.

"Oh my, I love grandma's dressing table. Are you sure you want to part with it?"

Sophia said, "Of course, I'd like you to have it. Your grandmother would have been so pleased to know that you appreciate something that was so precious to her. Besides you now have more room in the new apartment and it will fit in nicely."

Her father made a proposal. "We can have it delivered to your apartment next weekend. Our maintenance worker has a pick-up truck and would like to make a little extra money and can do it then."

Adina agreed that would be a good time. After her parents went home and she was back in her apartment, Adina decided where this distinctive piece of furniture would be placed. Her mother's dressing table, that originally was owned by her grandmother, always held a sentimental place in her heart, once Adina was old enough now to appreciate the beauty of the intricate carvings on the frame, and clawed legs of this very special antique mahogany gift.

Throughout the coming weeks Adina worked diligently unpacking all the cartons, and arranging everything she had into her new living space. The old dressing table had arrived and Adina placed it along the wall adjacent to her bed. Eventually she filled it with her various cosmetics, and in one drawer she arranged a space for her stationary and stamps. She found a lovely tabletop mirror in a vintage shop that fit perfectly on the table. It was a good spot to sit and write letters to Tristan. By mid-July the apartment looked as if she had lived there for a while. She purchased a small dining room table that comfortably would seat four, and even more if it were extended with the extra panel cleverly hidden underneath the table.

Tristan responded excitedly that he was more than receptive to her offer, and would plan on coming to New York in mid-August. The details would follow in a later letter. Adina's reaction was joyful and at the same time a bit terrorizing. She knew how much she cared for this man, but having him here in New York was beyond her dreams. She had tried dating a bit, but none of the prospective candidates ever held higher regard then her memories of Tristan.

When Adina tried to imagine Tristan in her apartment, she was a bit unsure about how they were going to relate to one another. She wondered if she should offer him the couch for sleeping, or whether he would still want to sleep with her. As self-assured as she seemed to project herself, like many women of all ages, she was insecure when it came to dealing with a love interest. She remembered a conversation with Anna about relationships. Maybe Adina already was loving Tristan more than he loved her. Maybe she was already relinquishing the power to him. She hoped in her heart of hearts, he would have the same concerns and feelings for her, as she had for him.

When mid-August arrived along with Tristan at Gate 5C at Kennedy International Airport, Adina was waiting with the happiest of smiles planted on her face. He spotted her immediately as he entered the waiting area and kissed both her cheeks and then the longest of hugs. '*Bonjour, bonjour ma belle Adina*', he announced.

The taxi took only forty-five minutes to arrive at Adina's Manhattan apartment, and immediately Adina introduced Tristan to Mr. Brooks. Once in her apartment, Tristan's eyes scanned Adina's home.

"Adina, you described your new apartment to me, but you neglected to note the pleasing feel of your home. Ah, I see the landscape painting of the Seine above your couch. It's lovely."

"Thanks. It always reminds me of my trips to Paris."

He walked into the dining room and commented on the one wall Adina had painted a pale aqua, which served as a lovely backdrop to several black and white pen and ink drawings, showing distinctive scenes of Central Park. When he moved towards the window in the living room, he smiled as he saw Adina's collection of blue vases placed on the window sill. Her collection now had grown to five such vases. Adina watched him gaze at every corner and every piece of art that she had on display. Eventually he found his way back to where Adina was standing, put his arms around her and said, '*Tout est si charmant.*' Adina smiled, happy to receive his admiring comment, and said, "Tristan, I am so happy that you are here."

In an attempt to impress Tristan with her culinary skills, Adina prepared her specialty dish of chicken piccata and pasta which Tristan devoured. He complimented her on the lovely table setting, and meal she had prepared. They spoke hurriedly about everything, forgetting that they now had time to savor their conversations since they would be in such close proximity to each other. Jokingly, Adina told him she was not a gourmet cook, and not to expect such a dinner all the time, as they had just enjoyed that evening.

Tristan said, "We will dine on wine, cheese, baguettes, and each other, from now on." Adina responded, "That's a deal."

They both conveyed such gladness being with each other. As the late of night approached, Tristan looked at Adina and said, "Show me your grand-mother's dressing table that you wrote me about in your recent letter."

Adina ushered him into her bedroom, and Tristan ran his one hand against the mahogany surface. "It's quite beautiful." When he turned around she was standing very close behind him. Silently, he stared into her eyes for a long moment, then lifted her chin and placed his lips on hers. Adina knew instantly that Tristan sleeping on her couch, was not an option.

That weekend, Adina and Tristan attended the customary Sunday brunch at her parent's home. There Tristan was finally introduced to Adina's parents and also to Emma, Nathan, and little Joshua. Adina's mother, Sophia, who had been somewhat skeptical of Adina's resolve to continue this relationship with Tristan over the past few years, was immediately beguiled by Tristan's charismatic personality. As soon as he admired the exquisite array of delicious platters of food, she was won over by him. When Tristan explained the ideas embodied in his research project to Nathan and her father, David Saville was most impressed by Tristan's devotion and enthusiasm for his work.

When their time at the Saville's ended later in the afternoon, Adina was sure that both of her parents were beginning to recognize what a special individual Tristan was, and that maybe they could begin to understand Adina's decision of choosing to be with a man who was not the conventional selection they had envisioned for her. Adina felt sure her mother was beginning to succumb to Tristan's charm. After all, Sophia was also a true romantic, and in time, Adina knew she would come around to accepting her daughter's attraction to this most appealing man.

On Labor Day weekend, Adina and Tristan attended the opening of Amelia's and Vinnie's restaurant. At last, Tristan was introduced to Adina's special group of friends. Adina was utterly delighted as Tristan mingled with all her friends. Even Alice seemed enthralled by his genuine and magnetically attractive persona. At one point, Amelia dragged Adina into the kitchen, away from the others and said, "Adina, he is such a good-looking man and very pleasant to be around. I am so happy that he is here for you."

Adina smiled contentedly and said, "Now you know what always enticed me to return Paris. I am very glad you can now all get to know him."

From behind one of the counters in the kitchen, Vinnie looked at Adina and said, "He's A-OK." She responded, "Just like you, Vinnie."

The opening was a huge success and many people were still coming to the restaurant even as Adina and her friends were making their exit. Outside the restaurant they all said their good-byes, and Adina was filled with happiness. Seeing Amelia and Vinnie fulfill their dream was amazing to have witnessed. To have watched it all with Tristan by her side, made the moment all the sweeter.

Tristan moved out of her apartment the following week, and into a studio apartment near the hospital where he was working. But it was more than evident, he would be spending the weekends at Adina's home, as they grew more and more committed to each other.

CHAPTER 10

WHEN THESE FRIENDS met on May 4, 1984 to celebrate their reaching the age of thirty, their lives were all beginning to form their own particular shape. Alice had given birth to her second child and first son, Jeremy, while her daughter, Fiona was now four years old. At long last Alice won the right to finally acquire that house on Long Island, in the community of Woodmere. Daniel had joined a practice of cardiologists that had one office on Long Island and one in Manhattan. The practice kept an apartment in the city for the doctors who did not live in the city, but saw patients there for one week every month. Alice was agreeable that Daniel would spend his one week a month rotation there instead of commuting from the Island. As long as she was able to spend her time decorating their four-bedroom colonial home, Alice was in her glory.

Amelia was content, and the restaurant that she and Vinnie now owned, enjoyed a good reputation in the neighborhood. She continued to have difficulty getting pregnant and starting a family. Amelia was planning on visiting a fertility doctor in the city to determine what the problem might be. On the phone, she seemed only mildly concerned when she told Adina about her plans to seek some professional advice in the near future.

Anna, the year before had given birth to a beautiful boy, Benjamin. She took a leave of absence from her job. With Benjamin in her arms, she followed Peter to Scotland while Peter was overseeing his firm's latest project for three months. Anna was a real trooper and had bounced back from a difficult pregnancy. She had been on bedrest for her ninth month. Anna's parents finally made their voyage to New York City once Benjamin was born, to see their first grandchild. Even though that warm April revealed the city's early blooms, her father could not appreciate the energy of New York. Her mother had sewn an exquisite quilt from swatches of Anna's childhood clothes. In his workshop, her father had built a rocking cradle. When the cradle did rock, there was a small box with a switch to the side of the cradle that, once placed in the "on" position, played a lovely German lullaby. It had been recorded at the piano by Anna's mom. The craftsmanship was superb. It probably served to melt some of the harsh feelings that Anna retained for so many years, when she and her dad had wrangled on so many issues.

Even though that warm April began to reveal the city's budding blossoms, her father could not appreciate the vibrancy or energy of New York, and the noise that came as a result of that liveliness. They visited for only two days, and returned to Pennsylvania the next morning. Peter had offered to accommodate them in a nearby hotel for a week, but Anna's father would not agree. Her mother, as usual, went along with his decision, and Anna said little to attempt to dissuade them. For as nice as the gifts were that they had made for their grandson, and how thrilled they were to become grandparents, Anna was relieved when they went home. She could never be completely unruffled in their company. Adina surmised that there had to be some undisclosed disputes that Anna chose not to share with any of her friends.

Early in the year Astrid divorced Jacques Gagnier, and was living again in Paris. Her parents were still in New York, which made it easy for her to visit every three or four months. She definitely wanted to attend this particular get-together as they all reached the age of thirty. Astrid's mood was quite up-beat despite her recent divorce. Adina knew that Astrid would take the divorce in stride, and that was the attitude she displayed at their lunch. Jacques, she discovered, was not the most faithful of husbands, and Astrid was not going to ever allow herself to be a victim of marital betrayal. She explained to the group, "There are many men in this world and Paris is full of them. I will just find myself another one that will only have eyes for me."

Alice's reaction was predictable as she asked, "Did you get a good financial settlement?"

"But of course, my friend. Jacques has a lot of money and now I have at least enough to live in a lovely flat overlooking the Seine."

Astrid was one of the strongest of women Adina knew. She always had the capacity to turn any situation to her favor. She was never given to self-pity or melancholy. Adina so admired that about her. Adina was so much more intro-spective, always deliberating if what she was doing at a particular time, was the proper thing in fact to do. Astrid went about her life with a clear head. It was as if she held her head so high, that the clouds danced around her to win her attention. Astrid was going to be just fine. Adina had no doubt of that.

As for Adina, she was probably at the height of contentment in her life. Tristan had been offered a staff position at Sloan-Kettering after his fellowship ended. He worked in pediatric oncology, which was so challenging. It was heartbreaking to see such young children riddled with such a devastating disease. But Tristan was determined to help the children, and his sweet, kind manner made him an excellent practitioner to manage their ailments.

Tristan kept a small apartment near the hospital. When his schedule allowed, they spent Friday nights and Saturdays together at Adina's place. They prepared simple dinners together on Friday nights, and Tristan always arrived with some French wine. He desperately tried to teach Adina the distinctive differences of various wines, but it was obvious that she would never become a connoisseur of the grapes. Adina was always more attune to the varieties of French pastries, rather than any alcoholic beverage, much to Tristan's amusement. One evening he said, "I've brought an exquisite Cabernet Sauvignon for us to have with dinner tonight."

Adina said, "Oh that's so nice." Tristan then poured some into a wine glass for Adina to sample. She tried as hard as she could to be delighted with the taste, as she exclaimed, "Mmmm, it's a good. Cabernet."

Shaking his head and a bit exasperated, Tristan said, "Adina, it is a Merlot." Adina sensed he was frustrated with her lack of concentration with the different wines. But nevertheless, he continued on his quest every weekend to educate her, and Adina tried her best to be a discerning student.

That night when they went to bed, Adina told him it was now her turn to teach him a few things, once they were lying naked. She said, "Tristan, close your eyes." As Adina slowly stroked his chest with a few of her fingers, she asked him, "how many fingers am I using?" At first, he said, "three", and then a moment later as she moved her hand further down his body, he said, "two". By the time Adina changed to only one finger, rubbing gently below his hip bone, he opened his eyes and threw himself on top of her.

They had gone to bed early that Friday night and the anticipation from not seeing each other all week, piqued their desire for each other. They were so passionately mad for each other. On Saturdays, they went out for breakfast and then planned their day. Sometimes they would choose a movie or an exhibition at one of the many museums in town. On a winter afternoon, they would occasionally spend some time skating at the rink in Central Park, holding on to each other, trying not to fall on their faces. They usually ended the day bringing back a pizza and Caesar salad to Adina's apartment. On Sunday afternoons, Tristan left to review his case load and Adina needed to spend time preparing her lesson plans for the week ahead. They had a nice rhythm. By Monday nights she was already missing him, but they spoke on the phone a few nights during the week.

Adina thought the fact that they did not see each other constantly, only served to enhance their great attraction for one another. When they did relax over dinner on Fridays, they had a lot to tell each other.

Alice was beyond patient with Adina's relationship with Tristan. She could not understand why they were not getting married. But Adina and Tristan were so enjoying their time as it were, and neither of them seemed at all discontented. One week slid to the next, and they never seemed to feel like they were missing something. Although at times Adina wondered if Tristan missed his family and Paris.

Alice asked at lunch, "What are you waiting for?"

Amelia was quick to come to Adina's aid saying, "Leave her be. She's having a delightful time with Tristan. Look at her, she's glowing, more so than anyone else at this table."

Is it any wonder that Adina loved Amelia so much?

"Well just how long are you going to wait Adina?" Alice demanded.

"Wait for what? I am living a life that I love with Tristan. I have everything I want right now. I adore Tristan, I enjoy my job, and I have a very nice apartment in the city, on the Upper East Side I might add. What could be better than that?"

Alice came at her, "You could be in a house and start a family."

This was when Astrid entered the conversation. She explained that she had had a house and that was clearly not a guarantee for a happy life.

"My husband had other lovers, so what good was the two-carat ring I had on my finger? Let Adina be. As long as I've known her, she has never expressed wanting a life like yours. This is the time of the 80's. Women have other choices and apparently, Adina is making hers, and it's not what you Americans call a biscuit-cut life. Is that the right expression, yes?"

Anna, who had been very quiet, suddenly burst out laughing.

"Astrid, it's cookie-cutter life, the expression you want to say. Adina would never be happy planting herbs in a small patch of land in a quiet neighborhood. She will always crave the spices of life she can find in Tristan's arms. Am I right Adina?"

Adina responded, "Alice, I know you have my best interests at heart, but what makes you happy is not necessarily the way I choose to live. Now let's talk about something else, shall we? Besides I find that the smaller the living space, the easier it is to fall into Tristan's arms."

They all laughed at Adina's remark, and as if on cue their desserts arrived to lighten the mood. While they enjoyed their slices of cheesecake, Alice passed around some pictures of her daughter Fiona, and her son Jeremy, that had been taken this past Easter. They were both adorable. As they all admired the photos, Adina did notice that Amelia was not as enthusiastic as she usually was regarding these photos of Alice's children.

When their afternoon ended all too soon, Alice took the train back to Long Island. Anna took the subway to the day care center where she had left Benjamin for the afternoon, and Astrid hopped into a cab headed for Bloomingdales. Amelia made no move to head to the train going back into Brooklyn. Instead she linked arms with Adina, and said she wanted to walk a while. Amelia explained that she needed to purchase some odd utensil for the restaurant that Vinnie had asked her to buy at a supply store on thirty-fourth street, just a few blocks away. Adina said, "Amelia, I'll walk with you to the shop. It's still a lovely day."

Amelia said, "That would be nice." Off they went arm in arm.

As they walked, Adina said, "Isn't it wonderful how we all manage to keep this date sacred, and meet each year? We all seem to have such separate busy lives now compared to our days at NYU."

They passed by a little boutique on the way and in the shop's window, was a mannequin wearing a pair of black leggings, bright red bulky socks, and a loose-fitting red sweater that hung off the mannequin's shoulders. Obviously, it was very much inspired by the movie *Flashdance*. The model was posed in a position with both legs straight, but with one arm bent up to the forehead touching a black beret. Amelia and Adina stopped at the window, looked fondly at the black beret, and then each other as they continued on their stroll up the street.

Amelia recalled, "Remember that day in Miss Saper's class?"

"Yes, that was so much fun. I can still taste the delicious eclairs your dad prepared for the entire class. Amelia, how is he?"

"Well, my brothers are running the bakery business. Occasionally my mother brings my dad to the bakery for a few hours. Since his stroke he still has difficulty walking. But he enjoys watching my brothers run things."

Adina said, "It is so hard watching our parents age. My mother turned sixty-five on her last birthday and she, too, like my dad, is on Medicare already!"

"Yes," Amelia said in agreement, "I see the passing of time in my mother's face. It's scary."

Amelia then turned to Adina and told her that the following week she had an appointment with a doctor at Lenox Hill Hospital, just to be checked out. The doctor specialized in fertility issues. Her appointment was at three o'clock in the afternoon the following Thursday. "Adina, could you meet me afterwards and we can go out for an early dinner?"

"I'd love to. I'll leave school by 3:30 and how about we meet in the hospital lobby by 4pm?"

"That sounds great."

They continued walking until they reached the restaurant supply shop. Shiny stainless-steel objects glistening on every display table, and hanging from hooks in mid-air could be seen even from outside the store window. There they parted and Adina hailed a cab to return home.

When Adina arrived in her apartment Tristan was there doing some paperwork that he had brought with him the night before. "How was the lunch with your friends?"

Adina answered, "It was good. Always good to see my old friends. And, it was so lovely that Astrid was in town. She is my most ardent supporter."

"What do you mean Adina? What kind of support do you need?"

"Oh well…Alice is always on my case for not having a… how should I explain this to you? A more traditional life, one like hers."

"I see. But *ma chérie*, you have the life you want, *oui?*"

"Yes. I certainly do."

By now Tristan had stood up from the desk where he had been working, and put his arms around Adina's waist. He hugged her tightly and asked what else was wrong. He could always sense when Adina was troubled by something.

Adina then explained that one day next week Amelia would be seeing a fertility specialist here in the city.

"She suggested I meet her after the appointment and we'll go out for dinner. Actually, I think she doesn't so much want to have dinner, as she wants to talk about what kind of problems she and Vinnie might be having trying to conceive. I feel so badly for her. Amelia would make a terrific mother and Vinnie would love a child as well."

"Well, there is much that can be done these days to assist a couple with that objective. Do not worry Adina, things will work out for them, eventually."

"I hope so. Amelia is so special a person to me, and so is Vinnie."

Tristan suggested, "Well how about I finish up a little of these cases and then we will go out for some dinner."

"Okay, I think I'll just go in the bedroom and call my mother while you are working. I haven't spoken to her all week."

When Adina phoned her mother, their conversation covered many topics. Her mother filled Adina in on all the little details of their family, and especially about their only grandchild, Joshua, from Emma and Nathan. Sophia then asked Adina if she and Tristan would come for brunch the next day. Adina told her mother that she would come for sure, but it depended on how much work Tristan had left to do.

Tristan decided he would accompany Adina to her parent's home for their Sunday brunch. He enjoyed the Saville's warm hospitality and most especially the bagels, cream cheese and lox, he knew was always to be served. After most of the meal was enjoyed Adina accompanied her mother into the kitchen to put away some of the food. Sophia placed the delectable pastries on a platter that Adina and Tristan had brought with them. Sophia liked that they all could still linger around the table for more coffee, dessert and even more conversation. While in the kitchen, Adina mentioned that she was concerned about her friend Amelia. Adina told her mother that she and Amelia had plans to meet after Amelia's appointment with a specialist in fertility. Sophia listened intently and then left the kitchen. She came back a few moments later carrying a bottle half filled with her favorite Oscar de la Renta Parfum. She reached into a cabinet and retrieved a small shopping bag, and placed the bottle in it. Sophia told Adina to pass her a piece of paper from one of the kitchen's cabinet drawers. On the paper, she wrote some instructions for Amelia.

The first suggestion was for Amelia to prepare a light dinner, explaining to Adina, "A man doesn't want to feel so full that all he wants to do is nap afterwards." Sophia asserted that the important part was to keep the meal light with no heavy meats or sauces.

The second suggestion had to do with Sophia's perfume bottle. Adina watched in awe as Sophia wrote down detailed instructions for Amelia. Over Sophia's shoulder Adina read some of these notes wide-eyed, somewhat stunned at her mother's frank advice. Sophia folded the note paper and placed it in the bag, with the bottle of her half-filled favorite scented perfume.

"Now give this to Amelia when you see her this week."

Adina just took the bag and put it in her pocketbook and returned to the table to enjoy some coffee and pastries with Tristan and the rest of her family. Joshua was already munching on a huge cookie with multi-colored sprinkles that Adina had bought especially for him. Shortly after that, Adina and Tristan departed to return to Adina's apartment.

On the train back to Manhattan, Tristan asked, "You must have had some interesting conversation in the kitchen with your mother. You looked quite flushed when you came back to the table. What was in the bag Adina?"

Adina supposed she did project an odd expression and only said, "It's my mother's suggestions for making a baby."

Tristan's expression was priceless. His faced portrayed a look of surprise and then distress. Adina said, "Now who's looking flushed?"

Adina waited a moment, and then explained that it wasn't for her, but for Amelia. Tristan then regained a calmer demeanor.

Tristan said, "Your mother is a force to be dealt with, for sure."

"Yes, and she is very fond of Amelia and Vinnie too, so if there is any advice she can offer to help them, she's willing to assist with her own special prescription."

For the remainder of the subway ride back to Adina's apartment, they just kept chuckling to each other as they recalled her mother's little antics.

Then Tristan said, "Adina, if we put the joking aside, am I right in assuming you are not thinking about children."

"Tristan, I think about children all the time. It's my job. But no, I am not thinking about having a child at this point in my life. After all, we are not even married."

"But you know we could be, if that was what you wanted."

A little surprised by Tristan's remark, Adina considered what he had just said and responded.

"Tristan, I love how things are between us now. If you are content with the way we live now, that is more than enough for me."

Tristan said, "I am very happy here in New York with you, and with my medical practice. I doubt getting married would change that. But let's not disrupt our life such as it is, if we are both now so comfortable."

Tristan put his arms around Adina and she sat quite contented for the remainder of the train ride back home.

CHAPTER 11

———————∽∾———————

THE DAY ADINA and Amelia were to meet was unusually gloomy. Maybe there were latent April showers wanting to finally be released during this second week of May. Her students' moods reflected the weather, as all seemed quieter than usual. Adina left school a little early to make her way to the hospital's lobby, where Amelia and Adina had planned to meet. In a small shopping tote, she carried Sophia's bag of tricks with her directions for conceiving a child.

Adina sat in the lobby of the Lenox Hill Hospital on the Upper East Side for only a few minutes until she spotted Amelia walking towards her. Amelia's expression was cheerful as she approached, offering up a hug and sitting down beside Adina.

"Is everything okay Amelia?"

Amelia smiled convincingly. "Yes, all is good. I liked the doctor very much. The exam she gave me did not reveal any problems or issues of concern. She just told me to keep trying, and to come back in six months if I still could not conceive."

"Well, that's good news. And to assist you in that goal, my mother insisted I bring you her very own 'fertility kit'".

Amelia looked puzzled as Adina held up the small tote. "Let's sit down in the restaurant, and I will bestow Sophia's special instructions, which she sends to you with the most loving of intentions."

Off they went leaving the hospital in search of where they might relax over an early dinner. About two blocks up the street they spotted Nero's Uptown. Adina had been there many times. They agreed it might be a pleasant spot for them to relax and have a good chat, as well as a nice meal. It was still early, and the dinner crowd had not yet arrived. They were seated towards the back of the dining area, away from the bar scene, which was agreeable to both of them.

When the waitress arrived, they each ordered a glass of chardonnay, a Caesar salad, and for later, a Margherita Flatbread Pizza to share. After the waitress left the table, Adina placed the small tote she had been carrying on the table and gave Amelia a broad smile.

"Well here it is, Sophia's recommendations for conception."

Amelia burst out laughing as Adina removed the smaller shopping bag from her tote and handed it to Amelia. First Amelia took out the piece of paper written in Sophia's handwriting. It read as follows:

1. *Have a light dinner for you and Vinnie. Make an omelet with some home-*
    fried potatoes and for dessert some fresh fruit and pour some Amaretto over

it. Second night have some broiled flounder with buttered noodles, no meats or heavy sauces.

2. *After dinner soak in a hot bath for at least 20 minutes.*

3. *Douse yourself with some Oscar de la Renta Parfum, neck, wrist, bosom and thighs.*

4. *Make love to your husband or better still wait till morning. Take the lead, men like that.*

Adina was a bit shocked as most daughters are when the subject of sex is a topic of conversation between mother and daughter. She hadn't read fully the specific instructions until Amelia read them aloud. Also, in the bag was her mother's half used bottle of her favorite Oscar de la Renta Parfum.

Amelia shook her head and said, "This is so precious of your mom to think of me in this way."

Adina responded, "If it works, we can set up our own fertility clinic."

Just then their wine arrived, which was much needed. "Well Adina, I will definitely take her suggestions to heart. What have I got to lose?"

"I hope it works for out for you and Vinnie. But even if it doesn't, sounds like a fun evening and an even better morning."

A few moments later their salads arrived and Amelia asked about Adina's day at school. She thought Adina was probably looking forward to her summer vacation that was coming soon. They chatted a while longer and then their waitress brought over the Flatbread. Adina glanced up while the waitress was placing the Flatbread on their table and as Adina's eyes skimmed the room she saw a most disturbing sight. Adina waited till the waitress left their table.

Amelia said, "What is it? You look like you just saw a ghost."

"Amelia, I think I see Daniel at the bar, and he's with some woman."

Immediately Amelia turned to see. The woman was sitting on a bar stool and Daniel was standing rather close to her side. They seemed to be effortlessly involved in their conversation. They were sitting far enough away, so that unless Daniel specifically looked in their direction he would not see them. Amelia turned back towards Adina away from the view of the bar.

"Adina, maybe it's someone that he works with from the hospital."

Adina's eyes were transfixed on them. They seemed a bit too comfortable with each other for it to be a professional consult. From that moment on Adina kept an eye on them, as Amelia and Adina munched on their Flatbread. Then Adina witnessed Daniel kissing this woman, and she almost choked on the bit of crust she was eating.

"He just kissed her." Adina exclaimed.

Amelia asked, "What kind of kiss?"

"Amelia, it looked like his tongue was halfway down her throat."

Amelia said, "What should we do?"

"I don't know. Poor Alice is sitting in her dream house on Long Island and Daniel is here having who knows what with who knows who."

Amelia asked, "Should we go say hello to him?"

"No way." Adina was convinced that was not the right thing to do. She thought he might just try to make up some excuse as to why he was in this restaurant with this woman, when clearly it was obvious that he was cheating on Alice.

Amelia then suggested that they better order some coffee and dessert to give them more time to monitor the situation, even though they were both rapidly losing their appetites. Despite how upset they were, they managed to share a slice of chocolate mousse pie with their coffee.

Adina then noticed another couple enter the bar, and they sat down next to Daniel, and the woman in question. "Amelia, now they're having drinks with this other couple."

Amelia wondered, "Don't they know he's married to someone other than that woman?"

Adina said, "Maybe that guy is cheating too. Who knows?"

After a moment passed, Adina said, "We cannot ever say a word about this to Alice. It would be so embarrassing for her. As angry as she sometimes makes me feel, I would not want to see her hurt."

Eventually, before their check came, Daniel and the woman left with his arm around her. The other couple left at the same time. Adina and Amelia tried to make excuses for what they had just witnessed, but it was more than obvious that Daniel was having a grand old time with his week rotation in the city. They wondered if Alice had any inkling that Daniel was possibly having an affair, or having something, with that woman. It was so sad. Both Amelia and Adina sat quietly, perplexed as to what to do, if there was anything to do at all.

The irony was not lost on either of them. Their dear friend Alice, who always planned out each step of her life, certainly did not consider that her marriage might not be as rosy as the picture she painted in her childhood dreams.

Amelia said, "Alice would be crushed if she knew what we saw."

"Oh, I'm not so sure about that Amelia. I was never sure that Alice loved Daniel. I mean really loved Daniel, like you love Vinnie. She loved what being married to a doctor could acquire for her in the scheme of things."

"Adina, that's so cruel. Do you really think that?"

"I didn't mean for it to sound cruel, but I think that Alice has always been interested in material things. She wanted the house, the kids, the cars and those silly garden club luncheons she's always attending. Then she goes on and on about how fashionable all the women look in their designer outfits."

"Yes, you're right. She does go on about that whenever we meet."

"I know she thinks my life is tragic because Tristan and I are not married."

"Well I don't think that, Adina."

"I know you don't Amelia. In your own way, you have always respected and understood my choices. And I have admired yours as well. The way you and Vinnie persevered to open a restaurant of your own, and how hard you work on the business end doing all the accounting work. You and Vinnie have shared goals, and that has made you both a couple I highly regard. Alice and Daniel were never a team. Alice was a force to be dealt with and Daniel went along. Looks like he might be tired of Alice's choices. He never wanted to move to Long Island. That was all Alice, remember?"

"Well, maybe you're right, but I hate to see Alice go through this problem."

Adina said, "Maybe it's not a problem. Maybe she knows and it's all right with her as long as that nice, big cardiologist paycheck arrives every month. I think there are lots of women who snag a guy just to be married, and have a husband to provide for them. But it would be hurtful if she didn't know Daniel was fooling around, and found out, especially from us. No woman likes to have that thrown in their face. I don't think we should ever mention this to her."

"I agree Adina. But it will be hard to not let on we know anything. I don't like keeping secrets, but this is one we will have to hold on to."

"Well, we'll just have to take it one visit at a time. It's a long while till our next birthday get-together. Let's not give her the opportunity to shoot the messengers."

Amelia asked, "Will you mention this to Anna or Astrid?"

"No, let it be our secret."

After that decision was made, Adina and Amelia left the restaurant. They got into a cab which dropped Adina off at her apartment's building, and Amelia at the subway for her trip back to Brooklyn.

About four months later, when the summer ended and Adina was starting a new term, she received a phone call from Amelia. Amelia was happily three months pregnant. That same day, Sophia received a beautiful bouquet of long-stemmed pink roses and a brand-new bottle of Oscar de la Renta Parfum, delivered to her door with a loving thank you note from Amelia, announcing her pregnancy.

The next two years passed uneventfully with the exception of Amelia giving birth to a beautiful baby girl, Angelina Rose. At the christening, a month after Angelina was born, Sophia, who Amelia was most excited to have attend, kept hinting how nice it was to give birth to a baby girl. Neither Adina, nor Tristan, who was sitting by her side, paid too much attention to the subtle suggestion hidden in her mother's remark.

Alice sat behind them, alongside Daniel. Amelia and Adina never mentioned to Alice the time they saw Daniel at the bar with another woman. Alice was in fact happily pregnant with their third child, Liam, and seemed to be merrily right on target for her plan to acquire a family consisting of four children. Daniel, though, still spent one week a month in the city making an even larger income. Alice had acquired a live-in housekeeper, a Jamaican woman, who took care of Fiona and Jeremy. She also prepared meals, leaving Alice time for her garden club activities, and tennis lessons at the country club where she and Daniel were now members.

Adina knew Amelia felt as awkward around Daniel as Adina did. When they all met at some social event, or just at a casual dinner out in the city, Tristan would engage in a conversation with Daniel, mostly about some new medical-related issue, but Adina, much like Amelia, kept her contact with Daniel to a minimum. They were cordial to him, but not overly solicitous.

Adina was still enjoying her time with Tristan up until the night he received a panicky phone call from his mother. Tristan's father was in the hospital in Paris, and had apparently suffered a stroke. They stayed up most of that night talking about his father. Adina could tell Tristan was very disturbed by this new situation.

"Tristan, I know you must be so worried about your father."

He said, "Yes, he always looked so strong and healthy. I am worried about how seriously this stroke will affect his ability to continue practicing medicine, not to mention his health in general."

"I know your mother will feel more at ease once you are there to speak to his doctors."

The next day Tristan nervously got on a plane for Paris. Adina wanted to accompany him, but Tristan insisted he go alone to assess the situation.

After he arrived at the airport in Paris, he went directly to the hospital and found his mother sitting alongside the bed where his father lay quiet and pale. He hugged his teary-eyed mother. She was immediately relieved that Tristan was home, at her side, and back in Paris.

Eventually Tristan had a consultation with his father's doctors, and the prognosis was not the best. The stroke affected his father's right side. Also, his speech, although, with much therapy there was some hope for improvement. Tristan swiftly comprehended the grave situation his family was now facing. That evening at midnight, Tristan called Adina in New York where it was only six o'clock at night. He knew she would already be home from school. He slowly explained his father's condition.

"Adina, it is not looking so good for my father. There are many complications. My mother is taking it very badly, and is understandably very upset."

Adina responded, "I know how difficult a time this must be for you and your family. I can fly out soon and be with you, and them for a while."

"I know that Adina, and I love you for wanting to come and be with me, but there is much here I need to figure out."

"Yes, I'm sure you will be able to determine what is best for your family."

"I will call you again when I have a better grasp of the situation here. I promise I will keep your informed."

"Okay Tristan."

"Good night Adina. Take care of yourself while I am gone."

That night she knew, deep within her heart, that her relationship with Tristan was being altered. It felt like the universe was shifting in some manner. Tristan called again a week later. That feeling was validated during their phone conversation when Tristan uttered these words.

"My father has a thriving pediatric practice, and one of his colleagues stepped up to see his patients. Since my specialty is pediatrics, I will attend to my father's patients too, for a few days a week."

111

"How long will you be able to do this?"

"For as long as it takes to see if my father will make enough progress."

"Will you call me next week to let me know what is happening?"

"You know I will Adina. In the meantime, also know how much I miss you."

"I miss you too, Tristan."

Soon several had weeks had passed, and Tristan told Adina that he discussed arrangements with his mother, sisters and young Jules, to bring their father home. Everyone was willing to help out with his care, and assist their mother with the Herculean task of caring for their father.

Tristan, too, made the painstaking decision to move back to Paris and assume his father's practice. He returned to New York to take a leave of absence and resign his position at Sloan-Kettering, and to discuss his decision with Adina. He proceeded to her apartment as soon as his plane landed in New York in the early evening. They sat in her living room and Adina had prepared a tray of finger foods for them to nibble. There Tristan reiterated his decision to move back to Paris, to help care for his father. He appeared so distraught as he explained his position to her.

"Adina, what choice did I have? My family needs me. My mother is devastated."

Adina felt devasted too, but she did not want to appear selfish in front of Tristan. She did not want him to think she was unkind. Adina did not want to be unkind, but she wanted Tristan to be with her.

"I can imagine, Tristan. I know the responsibility is falling on your shoulders. I know you have to do this, but I am heartsick at how this decision with affect us."

"Adina, working and caring for my father will take up all my time. I cannot ask you to come, nor do I think you would want to give up your life here in New York. You have your career, your family and your friends."

Adina said, "When we considered getting married a few months ago, maybe I should have been more agreeable to that. Then I'd be obligated to return to Paris with you now."

"But Adina, we both decided then that it wasn't necessary. It would not have altered my feelings for you, or I imagine, yours for me. We had the best of both worlds, at the time."

Adina frowned and seemed to simply study the design on the area rug on the floor below and then said,

"This has always been my fear. I knew one day something like this would cause us to have to separate...again." Tristan took her into his arms, "It's not forever. You can spend the summer in Paris with me. I'm not letting go of you, or of us. We'll find ways to be together, just not all the time."

Adina said, "I don't want to make this hard for you. I love you for the manner in which you care for your family. If the situation were reversed, I would choose to care for either of my parents, too."

"Adina, I know you would. We'll get through this time in our lives."

Adina asked, "When are you returning to Paris?"

Tristan answered, "At the end of the week. I'll stay here tonight with you, and then tomorrow return to my studio, and begin tying up loose ends and dealing with my patient files. There is much I need to do before returning home."

It was crushing for Adina to hear Tristan speak about returning "home" when he was referring to Paris. She had hoped by now he considered this apartment, as his home, as their home. But Adina knew it was necessary to not burden him with any of her sadness and her fear, her fear of losing him. It was an impossible situation.

The week passed all too quickly and Adina actually did not see Tristan as much as she would have preferred, as he had so much to do transferring his patients to other physicians. But his last night they spent in her apartment. He made love to her fiercely then later slowly touching every inch of her body, as if he was bidding his own farewell to every dip and curve from her neck to her breasts and further down until he was kissing her toes. When he looked up, he noticed tears moving slowly down her cheeks. He then put his arms around Adina, held her tightly, and whispered the words, "I'm sorry." Adina pulled back, looked directly into his eyes, those same eyes that had so enchanted her in that Paris café a very long time ago, and tearfully responded, "Me too."

Tristan slept for a few hours while Adina lay awake knowing that the course of her life was being changed. She wondered if she was making the right decision. Adina knew if she had wanted to marry Tristan and stay in Paris, that was possible. They had discussed that possibility only a few months ago. They even considered it while Tristan was still living in Paris. But leaving her family, her little New York apartment of her dreams, was a decision Adina could not embrace. She thought about her friends and how they would handle the challenge of her heart.

Anna, for sure would not hesitate to join Tristan, and enjoy a life far from her family, and spend her time traveling through Europe. She'd see it as a wonderful opportunity. Alice, Adina thought, would go as well if Tristan would provide her

with a sprawling French country home. Amelia, would go anywhere with Vinnie…
and Adina assumed she would advise her to pack up and leave with Tristan. Adina
wondered what Astrid would counsel her to choose. Maybe, Astrid's thoughts would
be more in line with Adina's. Astrid was her own true self, even as she flitted from
man to man. She was so independent, and always kept her small flat in Paris as if she
knew she could escape, and be on her own whenever a relationship soured, and love
took flight. She understood the importance of a woman ultimately taking control of
her life, and not expecting a man to be the sole source of her happiness.

Adina seemed to be choosing to let Tristan literally fly out of her life. Maybe
Adina thought, she wasn't so brave as Anna and hungry for adventure. Adina
certainly was not like Alice, who in trapping a man didn't realize he would never
really allow his heart to dwell in that over-decorated house. But Amelia's love for
Vinnie was so pure and true. She would pick up stakes and travel to Italy, if he
had wanted a restaurant there.

Hours passed quickly and Adina continued to struggle thinking of losing
this man that lay beside her. She knew deep down, once Tristan got on that
plane, their relationship would be forever changed. That morning Tristan and
Adina sat quietly as they sipped some coffee. Adina offered to make him some
breakfast but he was not interested.

"I better leave soon for the airport. I called the airlines and my flight will
be on time."

"Okay. Do you have everything?"

"I've packed everything but you, Adina."

"I wish I could fit into your suitcase. I wish I could fit in your pocket and be
close to you all the time."

"You would soon tire of that. I know you."

Tristan left for the airport, alone. Adina remained at home, choosing to avoid a teary airport farewell. They embraced, getting as close to each other as possible. His parting words,

'Je t'aime mon Adina. Nous serons toujours connectés. Ne soyons pas triste. Une jour, je reviendrai et je serai de noveau les cotês.'

I love you still my Adina. We will be connected always. Let's not be sad. One day I'll come back and be with you again.

And then the taxi drove off, and there went an enormous source of Adina's profound joy.

CHAPTER 12

TRISTAN DID GET in touch with Adina a few days after he returned to Paris. When he arrived at the hospital, he did not see much improvement in his father's condition other than the fact that it was obvious his father was more alert than when he had been there last. He told Adina that he and his mother were planning to bring his father home. They would hire a physical therapist to begin to help teach his father how to walk again, and regain use of his right arm. Eventually they would bring a speech specialist to their home, to assist in the task of trying to restore his father's ability to speak.

Although Tristan didn't want to make any decisions just yet, he did tell Adina that it might not be a good idea for her to visit so soon this coming summer. Adina was so distraught hearing Tristan say this to her, but she would not add any more burdens to his already overloaded responsibilities. Maybe he thought by August they would reevaluate the situation, and she could come for two weeks or so then.

And so, it began. She was losing him. No matter how many letters or phone calls she received steadily from Paris, Adina knew that bit by bit they would drift further apart from each other, as the distance from New York to Paris seemed to increase with each passing week. When Friday night arrived, Adina would be at her worst. She would recall how often Tristan came to her at the end of their work week, and they would enjoy such a wonderful time together. It must have been on Tristan's mind as well, since he began phoning her at midnight Paris time, as he still remembered she would usually be home in her apartment by six o'clock in the evening. He would tell her about his father's slow progress.

In letters that Tristan wrote to Adina twice a week, she was kept well-informed on what was happening in Paris. Tristan took over his father's practice three days a week and joined with a colleague to combine their offices. Eventually he began working at *Institut Curie*, a children's cancer hospital in Paris, the other two days. He lived at his parents' home, and helped his father get washed and dressed every morning before he left for work.

In another letter, Tristan explained that his mother decided to hire a young man, a medical student, to help with this task for a few hours in the morning before his classes, giving Tristan some more free time. In the evening Tristan assisted in getting his father ready for bedtime. Tristan's sister Cleo, was already married and lived about an hour's drive away. Eleta had her own flat in the city working as a fashion consultant for some magazine. Adina was kept informed about all the family dynamics.

Adina wrote often to Tristan too, always telling him how much she missed him, and letting him know that she understood his commitment to his father's care. In another letter he mentioned that Jules, who inherited his mother's creative nature, also remained at home. Jules was now sharing his mother's little cottage art studio where he painted to his heart's content. During the day, Adina knew that Jules worked with a computer company that created pictures for medical textbooks online. Tristan described so beautifully his brother's talent in a recent letter. *It is a blend of my father's medical background and my mother's creativity that led him to this professional path and enabled him to pursue his painting during his time away from his job.* Adina was sure Jules was probably more than pleased to have his older brother back home.

During their occasional Friday night phone calls, Tristan told Adina that he insisted his mother spend time in the studio sculpting, to hopefully relieve the pent-up tension that her husband's care initiated. She needed a break from the constant worrying about her husband's welfare. Sculpting was an ideal outlet to free her mind of this constant drain on her emotions. Hearing Tristan speak about his mother in this way, only served to reinforce Adina's love and respect for this man.

Adina tried to fill her summer days in the city. One week she took her nephew, Joshua, to stay at her apartment while Emma and Nathan went to an international meeting of museum curators somewhere in Peru. Joshua was a delightful and inquisitive seven-year-old. He was mild-mannered and was easily entertained with trips to the Central Park Zoo or a ride on the Staten Island Ferry. During a visit to her parents' home in Brooklyn, her father decided to join them for a trip to the New York Aquarium, which delighted Joshua. On another day, Joshua and Adina met with Anna and her son Benjamin in the park, for a day of hot dogs and ice cream. That week went by quickly, and it certainly kept her mind so occupied that she hadn't had that much time to think about Tristan, except in the stillness of the late-night hours.

Also, during the summers Adina worked part-time tutoring at The French Alliance Institute in New York City. Her hours were fairly flexible, and she was able to earn some extra money during the summer when no salary was coming in from the Dalton School. Her friendship with Rhoda continued to evolve, as they often met for dinner during the week. One time in particular, she noticed Daniel out with a woman a few tables away from where she and Rhoda were seated. Adina managed to ignore the view she had of Daniel once again, of possibly betraying Alice.

When August arrived, Tristan contacted Adina suggesting she forgo her trip to visit that summer. He said, "Adina I am so busy here working at the practice and then helping at home with my father. I really would not have any time to spend with you."

Immediately Adina felt ill at ease. "But Tristan, maybe I can help out in some way, and take some of the burden off of you and your mother."

"No, I am afraid that would not work. What I will do instead is try to come visit you in New York during your winter break from school. By then, I can use a little respite from all that is happening here, and maybe this situation with my father will be somewhat improved."

Adina had mixed feelings about this proposition. She had already missed Tristan so much, but having him back in New York, all to herself was irresistible. Adina agreed to his long-range proposal, despite the concerns she had about how a separation of a few months could affect their relationship. Adina had no desire to date other men, but she couldn't help but wonder if Tristan would be content not seeking the company of another woman, a Parisian woman.

The summer ended, and images of fall emerged, and Adina spent her time making additions to her furnishings so that her apartment would be even more comfortable and pleasant not only for her, but for when Tristan arrived. Adina's life took on a very nice flow. She often went out with other faculty members from school. Some days she and Rhoda would get together after school for a coffee, to unwind from the day's events. Astrid had visited in October, which always left Adina in an upbeat mood.

One day, just after Astrid's visit, Adina received a phone call from Alice.

She said, "I met this guy, a colleague of Daniel's at a dinner party the other night and he is new in the city, working in the same hospital as Daniel."

Adina's first reaction was met with anger, "So what does that have to do with me?"

"Well because Tristan is gone, an ocean away, you should have a social life of your own. I am sure Tristan is having a social life in Paris."

If Alice had been in the room with Adina, she would have seen the sheer annoyance her call was producing. "Alice, I don't need to meet another man."

"Adina, just go out with him. I'm not suggesting you marry him. He's a really nice guy."

Reluctantly, she agreed that Alice could offer the guy her number, anything to end this conversation. When he did call the next day, Adina was feeling in an odd mood, maybe a little bored, and agreed to meet him for drinks the next evening. Dr. Richard Turner, a fellow cardiologist of Daniel's, was tall and really quite handsome. He had come from Seattle to resettle in New York. He had been recently divorced but had no children. Richard was pleasant enough, and although they seemed to be able to carry on a conversation without any long, awkward moments, Adina had her doubts whether she even could entertain the possibility of getting involved with another man. Richard did ask how she had escaped not being married yet. Adina laughed, and then answered.

"I prefer being in love rather than being in a marriage."

Richard smiled, "You might be on to something there."

Richard asked if she would like to do something over the weekend on Sunday, maybe meet for brunch. Surprisingly, Adina agreed, but when the day came, and they sat down at their table, Adina felt she had to tell him her situation.

"I'm not in the market for a romantic relationship right now. You are new to the city and all I can offer you is friendship."

Richard smiled and said he had never before felt so comfortable and relieved around a woman.

"How did I stumble onto you? After the divorce I had, I am not looking for anything so serious either. Let's agree to be friends, and you can now tell me the real story behind your friendship proclamation."

Adina chuckled out loud and sure enough proceeded to tell him about Tristan and her odd relationship with him.

"I suspect this Tristan is a very lucky man. A pediatric oncologist, that's a difficult field of study."

"Yes, I seem to know many people in the medical profession."

Adina then explained how she knew Alice and Daniel. Richard was astounded by the fact that all of them eventually met each other at some point in their lives.

"Yes," Adina nodded, "its's really quite remarkable when you think about it. We just all take it for granted as something meant to be."

After her third cup of coffee, Adina looked at her watch and told Richard she needed to go home and work on some lesson plans for the coming week. She thanked him for the lovely time. Adina had mentioned that Tristan was about to visit the following month, and Richard told her he'd like to maybe meet the man who has won her heart. Adina smiled and told him that might be possible.

She offered, "In the meantime, if you are free one weekend before that, I'm happy to show you some of the sights of this magnificent city. There is no other place as lovely as autumn in New York."

Richard said, "I'll take you up on that. I'll give you a call." Both of them got up from their table and took a few steps out onto the street. Adina then extended her arm and hailed a cab to take her home.

When Adina spoke with Alice a few days later, she told Alice that Richard was indeed a very nice man. But she also let Alice know that she was anticipating Tristan's arrival in New York in December, and that she really didn't need any more male distractions.

Alice said, "I'm glad you spent some time with Richard, maybe after Tristan returns to Paris, you can see Richard more often."

"Alice, I'll never understand why you cannot accept my feelings for Tristan. But let's not talk about such things anymore. Agreed?"

"Yes Adina, agreed."

Richard had called Adina a few weeks later and explained he had been very busy getting settled in his new apartment, and had been working long hours in the hospital. Adina was friendly speaking to him, but explained that she too was tied up for the next few weeks, and maybe they might get together after the new year. Richard seemed fine with that.

When December finally arrived, Adina anxiously awaited the day Tristan would finally return to New York. It was the last day of school prior to the winter break. Adina was in such good humor that her students were in awe of her exuberant manner. They were thrilled when she announced that no assignments were being given during their winter break.

"Go and have '*des vacances agréables*'," she exclaimed as the bell sounded signaling the end of each class period.

Adina knew when she arrived home, Tristan would already be in her apartment waiting for her, if his plane had arrived on time. His flight was scheduled to arrive at ten o'clock in the morning and he planned to take a taxi back to the city, Adina's city, the place he had begrudgingly just left six months ago. By the time he found his suitcase at the baggage claim and went through customs, it was close to noon. At one o'clock in the afternoon he was greeted by Mr. Brooks, the doorman, with a hardy welcoming handshake. Mr. Brooks was delighted to see Tristan back in these familiar surroundings. Once in Adina's apartment, he still had the key to her place, Tristan breathed in the scent of Adina's home. Wherever he strolled in her apartment, unpacking his belongings, he could detect the distinctive fragrance of her Chanel No.5. When he entered her kitchen to get himself a glass of water, he smiled when he spotted the familiar photograph she had taken of him at the skating rink in Central Park, tacked on her refrigerator. His memory of their times together came rushing back, reminding him of days less complicated by his father's illness.

He stretched out on Adina's sofa, and in a short amount of time his eyes closed, and he fell into an unencumbered sleep for the first time in months. When Adina arrived at her building, Mr. Brooks smiled and told Adina that Dr. Orme had arrived and was already upstairs. She could only muster a broad smile as she then raced to the elevator.

Tristan was still in his calm slumber as Adina entered her apartment. Her eyes caught sight of him immediately as she hesitated, unsure whether to make a sound while he lay asleep. She took off her tweed winter coat and brown knee-high leather boots and tiptoed toward the couch. She bent down on her knees in the space between the couch and the coffee table, so that she was at eye level with his face, now resting on a throw pillow. Adina just looked at Tristan sleeping for a while. His dark brown hair fell a bit longer to one side than she had remembered. His cheekbones were somewhat more chiseled as well. For so long she had waited for his return, and there he was, finally. Then, as he sensed her breathing close to him, he opened his eyes, and within a matter of seconds, a broad smile transformed his sleepy facial expression. Neither of them spoke. He raised his one arm slowly and gently moved a few strands of her hair away from the side of her face. Then with his other arm, wrapped it around her neck as he brought her closer to him, and kissed her so gently.

Finally, he spoke. "Come off your knees and lie here with me." Adina did just that, and although they were not speaking, the room was filled with quiet moments of soothing communication, expressing the intense joy they were sharing locked in each other's arms.

Everything about Tristan's visit was particularly heart-warming for Adina. The little things were distinctively special. Whether it was just sitting at her dining room table having breakfast with Tristan, or watching his jet-lagged body napping on the couch, while she prepared a simple dinner, his presence in her home was irresistibly electrifying. Of course, she knew that it was their long absence from each other that was responsible for the ever-present feelings of relentless pleasure she experienced, whenever they were near each other. Adina knew too, this was not the case in most marriages. It was their separation from each other, even when he was living in New York, that engendered the endless passion that existed between them. And for that reason, she never needed to march down the aisle that Alice considered to be the entrance to heaven on earth. Adina was getting wise. She could weigh the pros and cons of a marriage contract. She was getting along fine on her own, and still was not at ease with the notion of following Tristan to Paris, marrying him, and living there in his world, even though at times he was her world. Adina thought if she could see him at her winter break and spend the future summers with him in Paris, that would suffice. After all, she knew, no one gets it all.

The day after Christmas, Alice had her traditional "after-Christmas" dinner party for these friends. Adina was thrilled this time to have Tristan with her. Maybe if Alice once again saw Adina with Tristan, it would end Alice's quest to introduce her to more eligible men in the city. Tristan and Adina arrived at Alice's home along with Anna and Peter, who had rented a car for the occasion. Peter and Tristan had always gotten along well. They, much like Adina and Anna, had similar temperaments. Peter spoke to Tristan about a medical research facility his company was involved in to be located in The Netherlands sometime in the near future. Needless to say, Anna was ecstatic about the possibility of spending some time there.

They all enjoyed a lovely evening, and Alice's extravagant hospitality was very entertaining. It was a soothing evening spent with the oldest of friends. Even Vinnie commented on the fine cuisine that was served, and that certainly was high praise. Alice was delighted that her dinner party was such a success, judging by the time they finally all left late in the evening. The only hitch was when Daniel received a phone call and when, upon returning to the dining room explained that there was some emergency in the hospital. None of his partners were supposedly reachable, so he left to head back to the city. Adina and Amelia couldn't help but exchange quizzical looks across the beautiful dining room table, as Daniel made his apologies to all of their guests. Adina felt so sorry for Alice who had meticulously prepared this lovely dinner down to every detail, and was ecstatic to be able to show off some new pieces of furniture she had recently purchased. This is actually what Adina admired most about Alice. She was so capable of creating an atmosphere in which all of these friends felt so comfortably at ease, and at the same time, so valued.

Adina sensed the only thing missing from Alice's soiree was Astrid's vivacious laughter. Last Adina heard, Astrid was now dating a man who was a Swedish

Baron, whose family was extremely well-to-do. Ironically, Astrid had met him at a gathering in New York that her parents insisted she attend at the Swedish Consulate on 2nd Avenue. Baron Henrik von Rosen happened to be an old family friend of the consulate's son and true to form, Astrid fell for him immediately. She returned home not to her Paris apartment, but rather to her family's residence in Stockholm. From Astrid's letters, Adina suspected that Astrid was quite serious about the relationship. Although the Baron came from a long line of Swedish royalty, it was only a title by blood, and didn't have any real function or power. But besides inheriting the title, he was also heir to a quite substantial financial portfolio, which Adina was sure Astrid would find very appealing as well.

Astrid's name came up in conversation when Alice inquired, "So Adina, do you think Astrid is serious about the Baron?"

Adina responded, "From our last phone conversation, she seems completely enthralled with Baron Henrik von Rosen."

Amelia spoke up and said, "Astrid is always living such an exciting life. I can just imagine her ensconced in the arms of some baron." Then Anna added to the conversation by saying, "We'll have to keep close tabs on this situation. The next time she comes to New York she'll have a lot to tell us."

Alice said "By the time of our next birthday lunch, Astrid might have quite a tale to tell, indeed."

The men, Vinnie, Tristan and Peter, just sat shaking their heads as they listened to the women go on about Astrid's love life.

Looking at Tristan and Peter, Vinnie said, "When I hear Amelia on the phone speaking with Adina, I can't believe how long they can remain on the phone chatting about Astrid."

Peter said, "Well they all are like that when they get on the phone with one another."

Tristan added, "They certainly are a devoted circle of friends. I find that so admirable, they are this way towards each other."

The rest of the week ended much too quickly. Tristan was scheduled to leave on New Year's Day. They decided to stay in on New Year's Eve wrapped in each other's embrace as the New Year arrived. During the week, he had returned to Sloan-Kettering to visit his former colleagues, and to consult with one of the doctors there on a case he was working on in Paris. Adina spent that day looking over preparations for when she would return to school. They did get a chance to speak about their timeworn relationship before New Year's, and it was decided that Adina would spend the next summer with Tristan. Adina would be good company for his mother, Juliette, while Tristan was at work. They would enjoy the week nights and weekends together.

This became a routine for the next few years. Tristan always came to New York during Adina's winter break, and Adina would spend her summers in Paris. His father's condition never really improved much, although there were more words added to his repertoire, and he was able to communicate his basic needs fairly easily.

Whenever her friends met for their annual lunch celebration, Alice was always Adina's biggest critic at how she was choosing to live. It took all Adina's strength to listen to Alice's lectures about how Adina should be married by now. If it wasn't for Amelia holding and squeezing Adina's hand under the table, Adina would have let loose to school her friend Alice, on Daniel's many affairs that he managed to have during his rotation in the city. Adina wondered how many women deluded themselves thinking their marriages were so wonderful. Instead, she simply told Alice,

"I am not interested in the kind of life you live, Alice. I enjoy having a career, supporting myself, and a man in my life that loves me, and who I love with all my heart."

After leaving this particular annual lunch, for their mutual thirty-sixth birthday, Adina had an odd feeling. On one hand, it was comforting spending time with these women that she had known for so long, but it also unleashed an array of self-doubts that she harbored about her own life, and whether her choices were made in her best interests. Her life was very different from the others. On the way home, she stopped in at the neighborhood bookstore. In the 1990's there were still little quaint book shops that housed a range of volumes from antique first editions to present best-sellers, and the staff was knowledgeable about all the manuscripts. From time worn shelves she spotted a new hard covered novel, Isabel Allende's *Paula*. Adina had already read and enjoyed Allende's first novel, *House of Spirits*, and so this seemed like another good choice. Anything to shower her with a few hours of quiet entertainment that evening, or actually a distraction.

But once settled in by early evening, she was only capable of reading a few pages before she placed the book down on her coffee table. She just let her mind tumble around. Her thoughts were like garments of clothing swirling gently and falling back and forth, round and round, as in a clothes dryer.

She thought about Alice and wondered if she was truly as happy as she wanted everyone to think. It was obvious Daniel was having affairs, and Alice had to know, it seemed. She had to sense it. Could Daniel be so crafty in covering his indiscretions? Adina had seen him out with women in the city enough times to surmise that he was not the faithful husband. Yet Alice painted a rosy, happily-ever-after life to her friends at every opportunity. She delighted in creating a home worthy of any *House Beautiful* magazine spread. Every item so strategically placed, every room purposely furnished from their formal dining room, to each of their kids' bedrooms, all reflecting their unique personalities or rather the personality Alice aspired for her children. Alice's home was highly polished, while Alice's relationship with Daniel was tarnishing with the passing of time, without her even realizing it was happening.

Then Adina thought about Anna. As close and comfortable she felt in Anna's company, Adina still thought Anna always had something burning inside of her. She was always on the run, moving away it seemed from her own true self. It was obvious that even at this middle stage of her life, Anna was not yet comfortable in her own skin. Peter seemed to only add activity to Anna's life allowing her to flee from one location to another, always searching. Anna and Peter appeared to have such an amenable relationship, but that partnership somehow did not bestow Anna with any significant inward contentment. What Anna truly wanted was a mystery to Adina.

All of these thoughts spinning around in Adina's head saddened her a great deal. But then, she would think about Amelia. Now Amelia was the embodiment of contentment. She was still deliciously in love with Vinnie, and also so full of joy for her daughter, Angelina Rose. Adina remembered the past year when she and Amelia took Angelina Rose to see a performance of The Nutcracker Suite. It was so gratifying to observe the love Amelia bestowed on Angelina, and how Angelina showered such affection on her mom. It was difficult to imagine that if Amelia had been able to give birth again, that there could possibly be any more room left for another child in Amelia's loving heart.

Then Adina thought about herself. Was she right in defending her relationship with Tristan to Alice all the time? Should she have tried to pair herself off with someone living at least in the same country? She couldn't explain away her deep feelings of love for Tristan. He was just there, much like the air around her that she needed to feel alive. She had acclimated herself to the situation as it unfolded year after year. Adina never thought of herself as alone, because she carried Tristan in her heart all the time. The sense that Tristan loved her, even when he was far away from her, comforted her and in her aloneness, she never felt truly alone. She didn't need elaborate sparkling furnishings to decorate her soul. Nor did she need to wander the world looking for the one thing, the gratification that her heart already held. The time for having a child had passed and she didn't feel particularly sad about that either. Maybe later in her life she'd have some regret about that, but she didn't need a child to fill a void. Adina never felt a void. Adina had much love to give, to spread around besides the special love reserved only for Tristan. She loved her family with deep devotion. Her nephew Joshua, was totally showered with her affection, as was Angelina Rose, who occupied a special place in her heart. Adina also had a warm relationship with Fiona, Alice's daughter. She was fulfilled by all these connections and the daily rapport she enjoyed with her students each year. How wonderful she felt to be occupying her days with a profession she so richly loved.

A few moments later she picked up the book she had bought, and her mind took a different mental trip into someone else's life, a practice the she found very satisfying as she turned each page.

CHAPTER 13

THE NEXT FEW years slipped by and Adina was living her life in the city and taking her life to Paris for the summers. With the looming technology of the nineties, Adina and Tristan resorted to emailing each other often every week, although Adina did miss his handwritten letters. Those letters were a tangible affirmation that she could hold in her hands.

Astrid had blissfully accepted the Baron's marriage proposal, and they were as Amelia had imagined, living in a lovely villa in Sweden. According to the photos Astrid sent to Adina, it was more like a grand estate then merely a house. But most important, Astrid seemed incredibly happy, and very much in love. She and her Baron spent much time traveling, mixing with many of Europe's elite. Astrid, though, still kept her apartment in Paris, and insisted Adina stay there when she took her summer excursions abroad. This offered Tristan and Adina more privacy than spending their time exclusively at Tristan's family home.

Alice continued enjoying her suburban lifestyle and unfortunately Adina suspected Daniel was still living a questionable life in the city on his weekly rotations. On a number of occasions, Adina ran into Daniel at various Upper East Side posh restaurants when she was out for a meal with other teachers from Dalton. Some of those times she greeted him, but seldom did he offer an introduction to the woman he generally was attached to at the bar. Adina only mentioned these run-ins to Amelia, when they spoke on the phone.

By the time they were all approaching their fortieth birthday it was evident that the time for all baby making had passed. Alice never added a fourth addition to her crew. Anna seemed content with her son Benjamin and didn't feel the need to complicate the ease of traveling around Europe with more than one child to look after. Benjamin clearly, was going to be an only child. On their yearly visits to her parent's home, Benjamin was doted upon and continued to relish the attention his grandparents bestowed on him. Amelia was quite satisfied lavishing her endless love on Angelina Rose. Her dream of a home full of children was easily revised by the ultimate pleasure that Angelina Rose delivered. Everyone was content.

On Tuesday, April 5, 1994, the actual day of their collective fortieth birthdays, each of them; Anna, Amelia, Alice and Adina all received a small international parcel at their homes. In each package was an elegantly printed invitation that read as follows:

My very special friends,

I am requesting that this year we break from our tradition of celebrating our mutual birthdays meeting at Grand Central Station, New York. Instead, I am inviting

*you all to spend a long weekend here in Sweden. I am looking forward to you all vis-
iting for a few days in our home. It will be my absolute pleasure for you all to accept
this gift from me. I've enclosed first-class round-trip tickets for each of you departing
Thursday, May 4th in the afternoon and returning to New York on Monday. Let's
make this happen.*

Much Love to all, Astrid

PS…A car will be at the airport to transport all of you to our villa.

It didn't take long before phone calls were being made, as each reacted to
this invitation. Anna was immediately on board with the plan. Adina too, was
open to take the days off from work and accept the invitation. Once Alice was
assured her housekeeper would spend the nights at her home, she also enthusiastically agreed. Amelia's arm needed twisting. She had never been away from
Angelina Rose other than when Angelina had a sleepover with her grandparents. Adina then enlisted Vinnie's help to persuade Amelia to agree this very
generous gift, and that was the key to Amelia's acceptance.

Their longest discussion pertaining to the trip was the debate over
wardrobe and hair dryers. Each day their excitement grew as they anticipated what Astrid had planned for them once they arrived in Sweden. It
was Amelia who first suggested they bring some special gift for Astrid, for
arranging this extravagant opportunity for these longtime friends. So, one
night, on a conference call with each other, Alice suggested an idea that met
with immediate approval from the group. Alice thought she might be able
to find a miniature replica of the clock at Grand Central Station. Year after
year they had all met there for their annual birthday celebration lunches.

Alice, with all her home furnishing expertise, volunteered to secure such an item, if it existed.

A few days later Alice found a small gold replica of the clock in an antique jewelry shop in Manhattan. Alice called each of them with the good news. She had asked the proprietor of the shop to hold the clock until she received approval to purchase this lovely item. The clock sat on a six-inch base of antique gold. Amelia suggested they have something special engraved somewhere on the base. Anna suggested the mutual date of their birth which was acceptable, but then Adina had another idea which everyone quickly agreed upon as the better option. On the back side of the base of the clock they had engraved,

For Astrid,

With Love from

Adina, Alice, Amelia and Anna

4.5.54

The jeweler promised he could have the engraving completed by the Tuesday of the week they were scheduled to leave. Adina and Anna met at the store to pick up the clock in the late afternoon. Both were in awe of the beauty of this small but precious gift. The engraving on the back was flawlessly inscribed. It was definitely worth over the one thousand dollars price they gladly paid. Adina was charged with wrapping the gift and she knew exactly how she was going to perform that task. In the little bookstore in her neighborhood, she had noticed some interesting gift wrap sheets. On her way home, she stopped in the store and purchased a package of white gift-wrapping paper with red hearts and under each heart was the logo *I Love New York*. Perfect, she thought. Adina added some red curling ribbon to the package and *voilà* the gift was ready to be bestowed on Astrid.

Their flying time seemed to pass very quickly, as they were conversing with each other during the entire flight, in anticipation of the fabulous adventure they knew awaited them all. Any apprehension that Amelia or Alice felt during their first flight out of the country, was quickly subdued after they downed a few glasses of the airline's Chardonnay. They easily managed the baggage claim as Anna and Adina, the seasoned travelers, led Amelia and Alice through the airport. As Astrid had written, a tall blonde-haired man was spotted holding a small sign with the words, Astrid's Friends. They all laughed as they approached the driver.

The trip to Astrid and Henrik's villa only took about forty minutes, and the scenery along the way was enchanting, especially for Alice and Amelia who had never ventured out of the States. Anna and Adina sat back and smiled at each other, as they witnessed the excitement of their two friends' first adventure into a foreign land. Astrid and Henrik were standing outside the front of their beautiful home set against the backdrop of a lovely inlet showing off the glistening waters of their part of town. The scene was beyond their expectations. The country-styled white manor was a site to behold, with its black wrought iron trim on all the windows and railings. The brightly colored flowers in full bloom on this early afternoon in May, created a vision of sheer splendor.

Hugs and kisses and more hugs were exchanged before they entered the very charming residence that at last housed Astrid's true happiness. They were

139

each shown to their rooms upstairs, and Viktor, their driver, delivered everyone's luggage. Astrid gave them a little time to settle in and then they met outside in a beautiful space overlooking the inlet, where a table was set on a huge brick patio. Astrid suggested that they could relax for the rest of the day while everyone had a chance to casually sample delicious delicacies. Later, a special birthday dinner, prepared by their cook, would be served in the evening.

Then Astrid announced, "Tomorrow we will sightsee and the next day we will relax at the spa all day. I've arranged special treatments for each of you."

Alice quipped, "Swedish massages no doubt?"

Astrid replied, "Of course, and much more," as the others sat back and laughed.

The Baron, Henrik, excused himself to attend to some business, and to leave the women alone to enjoy each other's company. From the patio, they could see such lovely greenery and breathtaking views of the town that Astrid called home. They were all so comfortable, and feeling wonderful to be breathing such fine air that was definitely not at all like the exhaust fumes that infiltrated New York City.

An hour or so later, Anna, the body conscious member of the group, decided to go for a jog around the estate grounds. Alice went upstairs to call home and check on her kids, and Amelia decided a nap was in order for her. Astrid and Adina lingered, enjoying the late afternoon, sipping some tea on the terrace as Astrid inquired about Tristan.

"It must be so difficult for you, Adina, not to be with him all the time, yes?"

Adina responded, "We manage, and yes, it is difficult when we are not together, but it does make being together all the more pleasurable I suppose." She continued,

"I plan to leave for Paris at the end of June this year, and I'll stay till the first of September."

Astrid then asked, "Is his father any better?"

"Not really. And Tristan is so invested in his work at the Institute, I fear he will never leave Paris again, other than when he comes for my winter breaks."

"You are very strong my dear friend. And I can tell you still are very much in love."

Laughingly Adina responded, "As are you, Astrid. What a wonderful life you have found. I am so happy for you and Henrik."

"Yes. He is such a kind man, and best of all he adores me, and I get to enjoy all of this."

For the next few minutes they sat in silence, simply enjoying the familiar nearness of each other.

Later, after everyone had showered and changed from their travel clothes, an elegant dinner was served in a beautifully appointed formal dining room. The cook had prepared a sumptuous meal of some typical Swedish dishes; meatballs with lingonberry sauce and a delicious potato casserole made with gravlax. They enthusiastically tasted all that had been prepared in their honor. But the pièce de résistance was the most exquisite dessert presented to the table. Astrid referred to the prinsesstarta as "princess cake". It was a white cake with raspberry cream filling and a light greenish marzipan icing. Along one side of the cake was a delicately placed fondant red rose. Just before the cake was served in celebration of their mutual birthday, Adina presented the package she had been hiding under the table, to Astrid.

Adina announced, "It's from all of us."

Astrid admired the wrapping with her usual wide smile. The shiny gold replica of the Grand Central clock was amazingly striking. Alice was bursting with joy at her find. Astrid, for the first time ever was speechless for a few moments, and then with a tear slowly passing down her incredibly high cheekbones, said to Henrik sitting across the table from her, "It's our spot. It's where we meet when I am in New York."

Amelia spoke, "And now you always have us with you."

Anna added, "Turn it over."

Astrid read the inscription with all their names and their birthdate and said,

"I will treasure this always."

Then she got up and each one of her friends received Astrid's grand hug expressing her sincerest thanks. As soon as Astrid sat down, she nodded to their cook and another huge cake was brought into the dining room with forty multi-colored candles all lit. The women laughed once they recognized that this cake was a simple traditional New York cheesecake, that the cook prepared for this special occasion. Together they blew out the candles. Henrik sat at the table with such a delightful grin. Adina assumed he was finally realizing what Astrid's friendship with these women had meant to her.

The next few days passed all too quickly, and these friends all had a truly memorable time. They arrived home late in the day on Monday, all feeling tired and exhilarated at the same time. Anna and Adina shared a taxi back to the city, while Alice and Amelia left in car services back to their homes.

The calendar was still approaching the middle of May and Adina had a month left to finish the school term before traveling back to Paris. In the taxi

Anna had commented that Adina was returning to a nice quiet apartment, free from the mundane chores of parenthood, while the rest of them were returning to laundry, preparing dinners and the responsibilities of keeping their households in order. Adina, glancing out the taxi's window, told Anna that sometimes the silence of an empty apartment can be quite deafening. Then Adina smiled and added, "Other times it can be sheer heaven."

A few moments passed and Adina turned towards Anna and asked, "Astrid seems completely happy now. Do you think that is true for the rest of us?"

Anna turned to Adina and answered, "I think Amelia and Alice have chosen to be happy with their lives, and so they are…at least for now."

"What about you and me Anna?"

Anna then stated with much certainty, "Everyone struggles to be happy, to find some joy in their own little world. I just think our struggle is a journey that both you and I have not yet finished exploring."

Adina placed her hand on Anna's shoulder, and smiled, and said, "I suppose you are right."

Anna said, "Alice and Amelia really enjoyed their time visiting the Royal Palace in Stockholm. Alice is probably ready to redecorate again having seen the striking interior of the palace."

Adina could not contain her laughter. Then she said, "Amelia loved shopping for those Swedish dolls in such lovely folk costumes for Angelina Rose. I also bought a stuffed Red Dala Horse to give to her, as well."

Moments later the taxi arrived in front of Adina's apartment building, and Mr. Brooks took her luggage out of the taxi's trunk, and welcomed her back home. Life had returned to its familiar rhythm.

Once in her apartment, Adina called her parents letting them know she had arrived home safely, and would call them again later in the week. Then she sat at her desk in the little alcove where she did her school preparations, and turned on her computer. There she sent an email message to Tristan letting him know she was back in New York, and about the lovely retreat she and her friends enjoyed, visiting with Astrid and Henrik. She unpacked only a few essentials, and finally was ready for bed. It took a few minutes listening to the quietness of her own private world before her eyes closed and sleep gently welcomed her into a calm reverie.

When summer arrived, Adina was off to Paris and into Tristan's waiting arms. Every year that followed they managed to meet each other with the unrelenting passion that their separations engendered. Their times away from each other, only served to make their reunions all the sweeter.

Tristan was a man who immersed himself in study. He was determined to make progress in order to relieve the pain he observed in the eyes of the children in his care. The eyes of his young leukemia patients affected him greatly. He devoted himself to the goal of searching for a cure, or at the very least, making inroads that would eventually lead to a cure. To this end, hours and hours of research were necessary, and it was more than apparent to Tristan that he would never have the inclination to reconcile himself with a regular nine-to-five work life. Maybe that was part of the reason he was so attracted to Adina.

Given the nature of their relationship, and the vast geography that was planted between them, Adina became a most welcomed alternative to an every day, every week, every month, kind of relationship. She did not clamor for his attention all the time. She was, by his appraisal, so capable of occupying her time with her many other pursuits. He knew how much she enjoyed teaching. He knew her days were fulfilled by the delight of being with young adolescents, although he never heard her speak of having her own in order to fulfill some maternal need, much like other women he had dated. Tristan recognized that she had internalized a different blueprint for how she envisioned her life. It was that independent nature that so attracted him to her. She was loving with him at her side, but also completely adept at enjoying her life when they were apart.

Physically, she was tall but slightly shorter than Tristan, with the longest legs her frame could splendidly support. Even at forty, she exuded a posture similar to that of a dancer, always with her head held high. Her long brown hair with a slight auburn tint was as shiny as a copper tea kettle, and fell just below her shoulders. In the summers her expression glowed with the appearance of tiny freckles on her cheeks, which Tristan still found completely disarming.

Adina had a mysterious quietness about her. Although she displayed a vivacious manner when alone with Tristan, in a crowd she succumbed to a demur calmness, never needing to be the center of attention. This, Tristan found to be undeniably attractive.

Tristan had told Adina that he always remembered the day he had first met her in Paris. She was wearing a pair of jeans, a cream-colored turtleneck sweater, showcasing a long gold chain with an oval locket, and a pair of bright red Swedish clogs. When he inquired whether the locket contained a picture, Adina nodded affirmatively. He imagined perhaps it contained a boyfriend's picture, or maybe some ancestral relative. She had bent closer to him and opened the locket for Tristan to view the tiny picture. Much to Tristan's amusement, it revealed a small photo of a powder blue parakeet. Tristan laughed heartily until Adina told him it was her childhood pet named, Happy, whom she loved dearly until he met with an untimely death. He had been in her family for thirteen years.

A few years later, Tristan admitted to Adina, it was probably at that moment when he had fallen under her spell. He often recalled that memorable encounter to her. He could not ever imagine some other women carrying a picture of a parakeet in such a lovely antique locket. It was a pleasing memory for Adina to recollect, whenever she was in one of her thoughtful, introspective moods. Returning home from a trip always aroused her memories of the many pleasant times shared with Tristan, and brought to the surface her longing to spend even more time with him.

CHAPTER 14

AFTER THEIR FORTIETH birthdays, their lives began to present some challenges that the passing of time inescapably brings. Before they were all about to reach the age of forty-five, two of them had witnessed the loss of parents. Amelia's father was the first funeral they all attended together, followed a year later by Alice's dad's passing. Amelia's mom insisted on remaining in her home, and so did Alice's mother, even though Alice persisted in trying to have her mom move in to Alice's Long Island home. Mrs. O'Connell was not ready to abandon her Brooklyn neighborhood. Somewhat surprisingly their mothers became even closer friends. One day, much to Amelia's and Alice's surprise, their mothers announced that they were going on a cruise together to the Caribbean. These two ladies who were both well into their seventies, hadn't ever ventured anywhere without their husbands by their side, until now. They were both ready to strike out on their own, or at least accompanied by a longtime acquaintance. Amelia slowly warmed up to the idea of her mother embracing some degree of independence. But Alice had a far more difficult time seeing her mother make the trip "alone," even though Mrs. Vernola was not only going to be on board, but was sharing a cabin with Alice's mom.

Naturally, Anna and Adina both agreed that it was wonderful for these two women to be venturing out into the world, or at least to the Caribbean, which was as good a first step as any other destination. When they returned home, they were full of delightful stories and memories from their trip. They had been pleased to meet other widowed women, and all of them were already planning their next cruise the following year.

It demonstrated to Adina and her friends that any woman left on her own, regardless of age, can function quite nicely. Certainly, they both missed their husbands, but it was not only possible and necessary, but also exciting to construct another kind of life for themselves; an independent kind of life. However, at least once a month, Alice pleaded with her mother to move to Long Island, but Mrs. O'Connell would not succumb to her daughter's monthly appeals. She was now volunteering her time at the neighborhood elementary school, reading to children in an afterschool program, and thoroughly enjoying herself.

Shortly after their forty-fourth birthdays, in late June, Tristan's father suffered another stroke. It was not unexpected but, nevertheless, truly sad, as he had begun to make improvements in his ability to walk and speak. Adina flew out a week earlier than she had planned to be with Tristan and his family. Her presence was a welcomed distraction not only for Tristan, but also for Tristan's mother, Juliette.

By now Tristan was working at the Institute seeking young patients for his research project. He was established, and his work was getting international attention. Adina could not help but wonder what changes, if any, might lie ahead. Would he now consider coming back to New York if a position was offered to him, or had he adapted to this relationship with Adina, that brought them together once or twice during the year and during the summers?

Adina also wondered if she was so totally comfortable with their continental divide that existed each year. When the summers ended she flew back to the States. The first couple of weeks she desperately missed Tristan, but eventually resumed her life, and the yearning for him dissipated. The time passed quickly until they were reunited once more. When Adina left Paris this time, it was apparent that both Tristan and Adina were questioning the impact of being apart, while still being very much in love with each other. Despite the many distractions in her life, she always found time to brood over these questions of the heart.

When she was in Paris, Tristan seemed completely devoted to her. But Adina could not help but wonder, if he actually met other women in Paris that he became attracted to, without that intention when Adina was back in New York. Those thoughts terrorized her. Tristan was a very handsome man, and Paris was filled with beautiful women in pursuit of such a man.

Once, at one of Alice's dinner parties, Richard had been in attendance, and Adina was able to introduce him to Tristan. She openly explained that she had showed Richard some of the city's sights. They had also seen a Broadway show together, a while ago, when Richard first arrived in New York. Back at home that night, Tristan asked Adina how often she saw him. She was surprised by his curiosity, as she knew her feelings for Richard were nothing compared to her feelings for Tristan. But nevertheless, she was glad to realize that he might be a tad jealous of her friendship with Richard. Adina chose not to mention to Tristan that she in fact tried to fix up Richard with one of her fellow single teachers at school. A little jealousy, or concern, she thought, was good for their relationship, as long as it was Tristan, and not her, who might feel the pangs of jealousy.

On Saturday mornings, Adina would usually find herself at the New York Public Library, along with many essays her students had written during the week. They always had an assignment to write a one-page essay, in French, of anything that they found to be interesting during the week. It could be a television show, a conversation with a friend or just some random thoughts that engaged their minds. When Adina left school on Friday afternoons, always, in her tote, were these essays for her to review over the weekend. On Saturdays, Adina would read and grade the content of the essays in a non-judgmental manner, focusing only on the French grammar. Adina found some of their chosen topics fascinating. She usually sat at the same table in the New York Public Library each week.

After grading a few of her students' papers, she would just sit back and glance at the other people in the library, and wonder about their lives. Some were clearly college students working on papers, and some were older. Some came to read a newspaper and some came for the gentle quiet embodied in this long-standing structure. Every individual, each depicting the city's vast multi-cultural, multi-ethnic population was what Adina found so fascinating about living in this metropolitan location. Here they all were, a representational sample of a colorful tapestry that was embodied in this library, all sitting silently together, exploring their own particular interests.

Sometimes when Nathan and Joshua were out together for a game of catch in Central Park, or visiting some new museum exhibition, Emma would meander into the library around noon. She and Adina would go for some lunch across the street. There were times when Anna would join them as well. Both Emma and Anna knew they could most always find Adina in the library on Saturday mornings. They were both pleasant distractions for Adina, who came to realize that distractions are how one's life is measured. When one's life runs off course, in a small or significant way, the manner in which one approaches these distractions, revealed one's true character. The way she and each of her friends acclimated to their aging parents' needs, for instance, demonstrated well how they each chose to cope with those particular disruptions of their daily lives.

One of the pleasant distractions in Adina's life was her relationship with Alice's daughter, Fiona. Fiona, having been the first born to the group, was doted upon by all the women. Adina, was always sending her little gifts and always brought a souvenir home for Fiona from her trips to Paris. When Fiona entered high school, she opted to take French as her language choice, which delighted Adina. Now Fiona was entering college and even though she was accepted to many universities, she opted to attend NYU. She wanted to major in biology, and eventually enter a pre-med program. Fiona's aspirations were to become a doctor and work in underdeveloped countries, much to Alice's dismay, who thought her daughter should settle on becoming a nurse, and not aim quite so high. But Alice and Daniel had raised quite a sensitive and caring child, and her dreams were not to be denied. Fiona also opted to live on campus in a dormitory room, traveling back home only during holidays and semester breaks.

Adina was in the city, and Alice felt comforted that Fiona had a "go to" person if she needed anything in a flash. Once a month Adina would invite Fiona for dinner at her apartment. Fiona loved spending time with Adina, and loved her apartment with its artsy feel to it, a sharp contrast from the *House Beautiful* style where she was raised. Fiona was simply just taken in by Adina's lifestyle in general. She witnessed only the romantic aspect of Adina's life, but Adina tried to let her know at times that her life was certainly not perfect, and that no one really is free from the obstacles life deviously delivers, sooner or later to all. But Fiona was of a youthful age that didn't believe that, yet. They usually met on Thursday evenings and Adina would often prepare a simple meal. Fiona would arrive by bus around five o'clock. They always spoke about Fiona's classes and about different exhibitions in the city that one of them might have already visited. On occasion, Fiona would confide in Adina about her latest love interest. She could tell Adina things she would never reveal to her own mother. Adina knew that every girl needed someone to confide in other than their parents, so she happily took to that role on Fiona's behalf. After dinner they would curl up on the sofa and watch a romantic movie. Adina introduced Fiona to some of her favorites from the 1960's and 70's. One evening Adina took Fiona to a showing of *Sleepless in Seattle*, which Fiona adored.

During one of Fiona's visits, much to Adina's surprise, Fiona asked Adina if she thought her parents were happy with each other. Taken aback by the question, Adina tried to quickly give a generic response about all married couples having ebbs and flows, then managed to change the subject.

Alice had always told Adina that she was grateful that Fiona had Adina to lean on while in the city. Alice always grilled Adina afterward about her conversations with Fiona, a few days after they had met. Adina merely responded that they had a pleasant chat about her classes and the boys she was meeting. Adina would not reveal anything to Alice that was spoken in confidence. By nine o'clock, Adina would escort Fiona downstairs and put her in a taxi to return to her dorm.

In the spring, the city was so full of sunshine and energy and such unusually pleasant temperatures, that Adina decided to take Fiona out to eat at a local restaurant instead of cooking. After Fiona arrived they began their stroll up a few blocks and settled into a nice new restaurant. In the late nineties many new places were opening, all with modern décor and ultra-modern menus. Bean sprouts were served with almost every selection and buffalo wings were now in competition with the new chicken fingers. Adina and Fiona settled at a table and both ordered a hamburger with the new curly-spiced fries. Fiona was asking how Adina came to spend her senior year abroad, as Fiona was beginning to have thoughts about possibly having that experience as well. Adina was very animated while recalling her experience to Fiona, and all of a sudden Fiona's attention was waning, and she was looking in another direction.

Adina inquired, "Fiona, what's got your attention all of a sudden? Did some handsome guy you know just come in?"

Fiona answered, "Yes, my dad."

From the expression on Fiona's face, Adina was almost afraid to turn around. When she did, she saw Daniel headed toward the bar, and not alone.

"He's with a woman." Fiona said.

Adina responded, "Oh it's probably a colleague from the hospital. Why don't you go over and say hello?"

Adina thought Daniel would immediately alter his behavior once he realized Fiona was in the restaurant. "Fiona, let's invite him to join us."

Still with a startled look upon her face, Fiona said, "Not yet. I want to watch him a while."

Panicked, Adina could not let that happen knowing Daniel's history with these "colleagues". Adina stood up to walk over to the bar, but Fiona held her arm across the table pleading with her. "Wait a minute." Fiona demanded. Adina was determined to reach Daniel as quickly as possible. Before Adina reached the bar, Daniel already had his arms all over the woman he had come in with, and seemed shocked when Adina approached him.

"Hello Daniel," she uttered. "I'm here with Fiona." Immediately his arms fell to his side. "Come join us, or at least say hello."

Flustered, Daniel introduced Adina to the woman, and excused himself while he found Fiona at their table. Meanwhile Adina lingered by the bar for an awkward moment, enough time for Daniel to make some explanation for what Fiona had already witnessed.

Adina settled the check for their meal as she knew Fiona would want to leave right away. When she returned to their table Fiona had tears in her eyes. Daniel looked at Adina, and then at Fiona, and simply said, "I'm sorry."

Fiona looked up at Adina and said, "Can we leave now?"

They walked back to Adina's apartment saying very little to one another. Once they entered Adina's apartment, Fiona said, "He claims the woman is a good friend. Do men always put their arms around a good friend?"

Adina said, "Sometimes, I suppose."

With all her years working with teenagers, Adina was still at a loss for how she should handle this incident. She certainly did not want to get in the middle of this family situation. Adina then asked Fiona if she wanted to spend the night at Adina's apartment. Fiona told Adina that she had an early class the next morning, and would prefer to return to the dorm. She thought that she should maybe go home for the weekend and speak to both her parents about what she now surmised was really the situation between her mother and father. Adina advised her to think long and hard about how to approach them, and not make any assumptions. Adina then handed Fiona a box from Adina's favorite bakery containing Fiona's much-loved brownies, for her to enjoy at the dorm. She walked Fiona downstairs to the building's entrance, and put her in a taxi while shoving a twenty-dollar bill into Fiona's hands to cover the ride.

"Fiona, you can call me anytime if you need to talk," she said. Fiona thanked her for the dinner such as it was, and promised to call soon. That night Adina sat on her couch and wondered whether to call her friend Alice to explain what had transpired.

CHAPTER 15

ADINA DID NOT want to discuss or make any accusations about Daniel's behavior, even though she was fairly certain these indiscretions had been on-going for several years now. While Alice was consumed with decorating their home, and her country club social life, Adina, many times suspected Daniel was having affairs in the city. She decided to let it all unravel without her participation. Fiona could confront her parents from her own point of view, and Adina would steer clear of the entire ordeal.

That Sunday, a few days after the scene with Fiona and Daniel, Adina spent the day with her parents. Both Sophia and David were noticeably aging so much, that Adina tried to visit more and more often. She had spent the entire day with them and did not return home till well after dinnertime. When she entered her apartment, there was a message on her answering machine. The blinking light appeared to be bursting with urgency. She had hoped the message might be from Tristan, but instead, it was from Alice. The message announced that Alice was coming into the city the next day to talk with Adina. She would be at Adina's building by 3:30 p.m. Alice also mentioned that she would wait in the lobby until Adina returned home from school. This was exactly what Adina did not want to hear.

It was difficult for Adina to concentrate on her lessons that next day at school, as she just kept thinking about what Alice was going to reveal to her, or rather what she would not reveal. With no pressing issues at the conclusion of the school day, Adina managed to arrive home shortly after 3:00 p.m. She found Alice already sitting in the lobby. They greeted each other with a quick hug, and headed to the elevator which took them quickly to Adina's apartment. Once inside Adina said,

"What shall it be? Coffee, tea or a glass of wine?"

Alice chose tea, and Adina quickly filled a pot to boil water, and took out two newly acquired ceramic mugs. She had purchased these mugs during her most recent visit to the Metropolitan Museum of Art. Adina filled a plate with some cookies, and arranged everything on a tray. Adina set the tray down on her coffee table. Alice lifted one of the mugs and admired it.

"I bought them a few weeks ago when Anna and I went to the Georges Seurat exhibit at the Met."

Alice half-smiled and said, "You really do enjoy living here Adina, don't you?"

"Alice, you know I always have."

Alice continued her questioning. "You never wanted to have a nice house?"

Adina rebutted, "I think I do have a nice home. I just didn't need to fill it up with things."

"But, didn't you ever want children?"

Adina, with a hint of exasperation in her voice responded, "Alice, did you travel all the way here to discuss my wants and desires?"

"No, of course not. You know that Fiona came home this past weekend. She told me about your dinner out, and that Daniel happened to be at the same restaurant."

Adina told Alice that Fiona had mentioned that she might go home for the weekend.

"So how did it go?"

"Well, how do you think it went? She accused her father of having an affair, and accused me of not caring. She had sensed that we were…how shall I put it, not getting along."

Adina sipped some tea and then asked, "And what did you tell her?"

"Well, I told her that marriage is difficult. That couples go through different cycles. I tried to reassure her that Daniel and I do still love each other in our own way, and that we will always be together."

Adina said, "Did she buy that?"

"When Daniel came home she was somewhat cold towards him, but didn't confront him about what she had surmised about him being in the company of another woman."

Adina adjusted her position on the couch so that she was looking directly at Alice and said, "So... exactly why are you here today?"

"I guess I needed a friend to talk to about all of this, and you already know some of the story."

"Well that's nice that you feel you can confide in me. You know how I adore Fiona, and you, too. I don't want to see either of you hurt."

"I know that when Daniel comes to the city for his rotation, he sees other women. I've suspected it for years now." Adina interrupted, "But you're never said anything before."

"Well at first, I was upset, but I thought long and hard and I really don't want to go through a divorce. I have three kids to think about. I'm content with my house and the life we have. Daniel is a good father and he shows up when I need him to. Adina, you have always been the romantic dreamer, while I dreamed of other things which I now have, and don't wish to relinquish."

"Well Alice, I can't say I understand your point of view, but I am your friend. I will always support any decisions you make, much like I'd appreciate your understanding of my choices as well."

"Adina, do the others know that my husband likes to chase skirts all over town?"

"I only know that once, a few years ago, Amelia and I saw him at a bar while we were having dinner. It was before Angelina Rose was born."

"But you never said anything."

"It wasn't our place and certainly, we did not want to hurt you."

"Thank you for that. I think as time moves on and we get older, this will all pass. He can't be a playboy forever, and I will still have my nest and my kids."

"Alice, I hope you are right about that, if those are the things that bring you happiness. I'm glad you came into the city and shared all this with me."

"Well, I figured you were wondering what was going on since Fiona told you she would come home over the weekend. You know Adina, Fiona absolutely adores you and your apartment, and frankly everything about your life. And I must tell you, that it worries me a lot."

They both laughed, and Adina hugged Alice as she said in a consoling tone, "Actually, I have a very nice life."

Alice asked, "So what's going on these days with you and your prince charming?"

Adina said, "Oh Alice, like you explained to Fiona, none of us ever gets it all. It's difficult at times but I do love him, and I believe he loves me too, and that sustains us through the years. Sometimes I even think our separations actually contribute to heightening the passion and love we feel for one another. We appreciate each other all the more. Who knows, maybe absence does make the heart grow fonder. I never believed that when I was younger, but I've come to appreciate that premise."

"Well then, as long as you are happy."

"I am Alice, most of the time. And I suppose that's all we can ever hope to attain in our lifetime."

Shortly after their very personal conversation, Alice got up and announced she had to leave to get downtown to catch the train back to Long Island. Adina walked Alice out to the building's entrance, where Mr. Brooks hailed a taxi for Alice. Adina waved goodbye and returned to her apartment, sat on her couch, and just tried to absorb her own thoughts concerning the conversation she had just had with her dear friend.

She wondered if Alice was not unlike many women who stay in marriages for what the relationship might procure for them. To the outside world, Alice and Daniel seemed like an extremely happy couple. And in fact, Alice did seem happy with her garden, her country club, the tennis lessons, and her overly decorated house. The connection, that special connection, when Adina and

Tristan were in each other's company, and the world could pass right by while they were enraptured with the inexplicable delight of merely being together, clearly was not the case for Alice and Daniel. Perhaps, Adina wondered, if the passing of years changes the way a husband and wife react to one another. Maybe, Adina was just a dreamer, and certainly a romantic. She could never imagine bartering passion for comfort. Adina would always remember with such delight, the morning Tristan came to Adina's hotel room on the school's trip to Paris, and the day they had spent together, or the many weekends during the summers she visited him, when he exposed her to all his secret haunts in his city of lights. He was a master of romance, and she was a willing recipient of all the sensations his amorousness nature bestowed upon her. With each visit, each year, their feelings for one another continued to weave a tale of love that Adina could not abandon. And apparently, neither could Tristan.

These were the memories Adina recalled whenever she was riddled with questions regarding her own life choices. For to continue on this path with Tristan, now in her mid-forties, was an active decision on her part, even though it seemed that one year simply and effortlessly, danced into the next.

CHAPTER 16

ADINA AND HER friends had celebrated their forty-fifth birthday on May 4, 1999. The day bestowed much sunshine providing warmer temperatures, a wonderful departure from April's soggy, rainy season. The day begged for them to enjoy their annual gathering outdoors. After meeting at Grand Central, arm in arm, they took a stroll to Bryant Park, where they found a table for all four of them. Astrid, this year, was not in New York.

Eventually the conversation turned to the coming new year...a new millennium. Everyone had a theory about what might happen other than a simple change in the calendar. All kinds of celebrations were already in the works in anticipation of this once-in-a-lifetime event.

For Adina, simply having Tristan by her side at the new year as they entered the new century, would have been more than sufficient. He always arrived in New York during her winter break. This meant he would be with her, as the world turned the page onto a new century. Alice was already planning a grand and glorious bash to welcome in the new year, and she alerted her friends that she expected her oldest and dearest friends to attend. In fact, Alice insisted they all commit that very day, that they would be joining her and Daniel's New Year's Eve party, still several months away. Amelia was first to burst Alice's balloon.

"Alice, it is a big night at the restaurant. Vinnie and I cannot leave the restaurant on such a special evening. We'll do a lot of business that night."

A little exasperated, Alice then said, "Well I will expect the rest of you to come."

Adina shook her head and said, "As the song goes Alice, it's a long, long time from May to December…"

They all laughed while Alice's smirk showed her utter annoyance with her group of friends. Adina said, "Seriously, let's talk about it when it gets closer to the time."

To lighten the mood, Anna suggested they all have some ice cream cones, and dragged Amelia up to go with her to get them for all at the table. And so, another birthday celebration was marked by these women, who had been friends for so long. Whether they dined at an elegant restaurant, or even a casual outdoor eatery, they enjoyed the familiarity that resumed on this day, year after year.

Unfortunately, two weeks before the much-anticipated end of the century, Tristan's father suffered yet another stroke. This time he only lingered two days before succumbing to his death. Tristan's usual trip to New York during Adina's winter break was canceled. Adina tried, but could not get a flight out to Paris on such short notice, given all the excitement about the coming millennium. There were many celebratory trips planned so far in-advance by countless people, wanting to see the new century born in exciting places, Paris, being one of them. Adina was heart-broken that she could not travel to Paris for Tristan's father's funeral, and express her deepest condolences to his family, personally.

Adina had many alternative invitations including Alice's grand and glorious festivities, but she declined them all. She knew she would not be feeling in the mood for merrymaking. Adina spent the time alone allowing herself to lament over Tristan's loss, and his absence at this very unique moment in time. This was the emotional price she paid for this kind of relationship. But now their situation was changed with the death of Tristan's father. Tristan had settled at the Institute in Paris where his work was getting much attention. Adina could not help but wonder if Tristan would consider coming back to New York, provided of course, he could continue his work there. Although it was certainly too soon to think about this possibility, Adina could not deny her thoughts.

During the immediate weeks following the funeral, Tristan wrote that he was consumed with assisting his family with the usual tasks a death in a family encompassed. It was the first time he had skipped speaking with Adina on their customary time on Friday evenings. Adina sat by the phone anticipating a call that never came. What did arrive was a brief email message a few days later, with an explanation of how harried Tristan had been. Adina decided to do what she thought was the right thing to do, given the circumstances, and simply responded to Tristan's message with only two words, '*Je comprehend*' and then backed off any further communications with Tristan. In her caring heart, she knew this was a time to give him space, and unburden him with any added responsibilities towards her. As difficult as this was for her to withdraw from her role in his life at this distressing time, she did it with grace and silence.

That January was the coldest month of Adina's life; not due to any drop in the temperatures, but rather to Tristan's complete lack of communication with her for the entire month. Once again, her mind ping-ponged back and forth thinking their relationship was over to thinking he just needed this unfettered time to grieve his father's death. But like most women, Adina would always skip to the worst-case scenario. She was not an insecure woman, except of course, when it came to Tristan. That was the only time in all these years that she considered, if they had been married, there would not be this long disruption in their fond exchanges. But the longer she thought about that, she realized that married people are not always in tune just because they happen to occupy the same home, and are legally bound to some arrangement. Such an arrangement, Adina thought, probably also differed for every couple.

In the many years she was continually taunted by Alice, who insisted she wanted "better" for Adina, Adina remained exasperated by Alice's assessment of the liaison Adina shared with Tristan. What Adina found unacceptable was Daniel seeking the tender company of other women, while Alice aspired to a lifestyle that was rejected by her husband. These thoughts, and many others dominated her mind throughout the long month of January. Waiting, a feminine characteristic, was a woman's most unkind charge. Men just lived their lives, and seldom were aware of the grueling lapsing of time. But Adina knew, each passing day reminded her that he was possibly not bothered by their disconnection.

Adina's longtime colleague, Rhoda, was one of the few women who Adina would speak to intimately, about her relationship with Tristan. Rhoda understood and championed the manner in which Adina followed her heart.

After twenty-five years of marriage, other than their two beautiful daughters, Rhoda's marriage did not generate much else. According to Rhoda, her husband, a history professor, was seemingly a good candidate for marriage when he and Rhoda met during their college days. As it turned out, years into their marriage they began to develop different outlooks on the path their lives should embrace. Rhoda admitted to Adina, that she remained in a passionless, unexciting, but comfortable relationship, until their youngest daughter left for college at UCLA. Rhoda's husband was shocked when Rhoda's attorney delivered separation papers to her husband's university office. Rhoda explained, that he had no idea that she was anything but content with their very predictable life. For Rhoda, that was the crux of the matter. He didn't know her at all, or who she had become, after all their years together. They divorced a year later and Rhoda finally was content, even though she was alone. And in that aloneness, she found out who she really was as an individual, and not merely half of a duet, whose song sounded very much out of tune. Adina was stunned, once Rhoda divulged her personal circumstances to her. It was a moment that sealed their friendship. Rhoda clearly understood how Adina could let go of Tristan for a few months at a time, and still enjoy her life away from him.

Adina and Rhoda spent many a late afternoon in the teacher's lounge after the school day had concluded. Sometimes they attended various lectures together at the 92nd Street Y of mutual interest. Often, they continued their discussion at some new restaurant that they both wanted to check out. By now, Rhoda and Adina had become reliable friends for one another.

When February arrived and Adina turned her calendar of impression-ist painters hanging on the wall near her desk to this new month, she was amused to see the painting *Snow at Monfoucault* by Camille Pissarro. It made her think about the possibility of snowfalls to come during this bitter winter season. Then, she thought about how many more pages of the calendar would be turned until she heard from Tristan. But all the while she knew, she had to give him time. As difficult as that was, she knew in her heart that giving some-one, giving Tristan, the opportunity to stay in his own private cocoon for as long as was necessary, was in fact the most precious gift she could bestow upon him. And so, in quiet solitude, she continued to wait.

Weeks later, on Valentine's Day, she traveled home from school and stopped as always, at the bakery. She bought a box of elaborately decorated pastries, filled with raspberry jams and chocolate icing, to present to Mr. Brooks, and a smaller box of chocolate chip scones for herself. By now she had known Mr. Brooks almost twenty years, and they shared an endearing friendship. He ac-cepted her gift with a somewhat brighter smile than usual. She attributed his overzealous grin to the fact he was pleased that she always remembered him with some special offering. His thank you included an all-encompassing hug, and he wished her a good evening. Clutching the other box of scones, her consolation prize for making it through the past two months without the man she loved so dearly, she headed upstairs to her apartment.

Once off the elevator, beneath her door she found a single red rose. No note, no explanation was visible as she bent down to pick it up. The scent was intoxicating and she thought, perhaps, Mr. Brooks had left it for her, though no other doors on the floor had such a lovely flower. She went into her apartment and there resting comfortably on her couch, was Tristan. Adina was so stunned at first, she could not move. Tristan got up and walked over to her very slowly. Their silence spoke volumes as they fell into each other's arms.

Relationships are certainly not easy to navigate, but time had taught Adina a thing or two. Although she had always wanted to be with Tristan all the time, she had learned that constantly being with one's lover, does not always enhance the desire that only prolonged absences inspired. She observed that with some couples, that day-to-day familiarity may lead to many things, but intimacy and erotic pleasure was not such a result. And what a conundrum that was to contemplate. She knew that constant companionship was an advantageous benefit of a marriage arrangement. But did it provoke the excitement, the hunger, the overwhelming desire that she always felt for Tristan? It was always when they were reunited, even if it was only after a week's separation from each other, that they were on fire for each other. Did she really want to trade that for the comfort of being with him every day?

Tristan stayed in New York with Adina for the rest of the month. But it wasn't until their last evening together that Tristan spoke about the future. He had established his reputation at the Institute and was unsure about leaving his research project. He told Adina that perhaps he might be able to develop a partnership, by collaborating with other doctors in New York. He had an offer from a researcher at Stanford, but thought California was still too far away from Adina, and there was no point to pursuing that opportunity. He told her, "I need more time now to see how I can continue my work outside of Paris. It might take another year or two. Adina, how do you feel about that?"

"Tristan, I want you here with me, of course. I imagine what that would be like all the time. But we have managed to live apart many months of each year and still sustain our feelings for each other. For now, you must do what you need to in order to continue your important research. I understand that. I wish you could acquire the funds to work here in New York, and maybe one day that will happen. That is always my hope. But my parents are aging, and I would not leave them now to live full-time in Paris. I suppose we keep doing what we have done all these years. We have the months together in the summer, and you still come here when you can, and we will continue to endure, drawn to one another by whatever it is that has kept us together all these years."

"But Adina, sometimes I feel that I have not provided you with the life you should be living."

"I do not need you to provide a life for me. I am quite capable of providing for myself. I enjoy my teaching job, and it affords me the opportunity to travel all summer. Tristan, we do not need to see each other every day in order to sustain our feelings. In fact, I've come to understand that our times away from each other serve to enrich our commitment to continue to love each other."

Tristan looked at Adina and said, "You are not at all like most women."

Adina answered, "I've just learned a great deal from observing others, that love takes many forms over the years. My friends tell me that passion fades over time and other forms of love enter the scenario. Personally, I like where our love has taken us. I want always to be passionately, romantically and breathlessly in love with you, for as long as we can be."

Tristan laughed and embraced her and asked, "Even when we are old and what is the English word for I am thinking…?"

Adina shouted. "Crotchety, cantankerous, crabby, take your pick. and yes, even then."

Tristan's face then exhibited a more serious expression. He touched her chin and turned her face until she was looking directly at him, eyes to eyes, and he spoke these words, "Adina, I promise that one day we will find a way to be together."

She smiled and said, "Tristan, we are together."

CHAPTER 17

―――――――――∽∞∾―――――――――

THE MILLENNIUM YEAR 2000 went out as uneventfully as it came in. As far as Adina could tell, the atmosphere took on no significant changes caused by the turn of the century. The universe was calm, and everyone's lives continued on their natural paths. But change, in fact, is inevitable as Adina was to experience a few months later.

Sophia had just celebrated her eightieth birthday in early September. During the year leading up to Sophia's birthday, she had suffered a series of heart failure episodes. That summer Adina cut short her trip to Paris, when she learned that Sophia was admitted to the hospital in mid-August. Upon seeing Adina enter her hospital room, Sophia looked surprised and laughingly said, "Oh boy, I must be really sick to bring you back from Paris, and from Tristan." Sophia made light of her illness, and did not have any desire to be a burden of any kind to her daughters.

Sophia came home for a while as life took on its normal routine, and then she was admitted once more to the hospital, several weeks later. Adina, Emma and David, their father, spent many nights by Sophia's hospital bedside with each attack, until one damp and dreary late October afternoon, Sophia took her last breath.

Devastated, Adina believed that the day you lose your mother is probably as poignant as the day you are born. The limitless love and fondness her mother bestowed upon her, when first she entered the world, was only eclipsed by the moment her mother left her forever. It was Adina's sincere belief, from that moment on, no matter what her age, her life would never be the same. If a person was lucky enough to have lived their life with a caring, self-sacrificing woman, much like Sophia, all future joys would in fact, become less joyful. Adina knew now that she would rarely experience absolute delight, because absent was the person whom not only gave Adina life, but helped to steer her towards the life she aspired. Once that person was gone forever, Adina's heart would never again be totally filled with joy. That was the case, if someone was as fortunate as Adina, to have had such a woman as their mother.

The Sunday that the funeral was held exhibited the coming of colder temperatures. The array of many-hued leaves of gold, auburns and browns on the cemetery grounds, served as a stunning backdrop, as Adina watched Sophia's coffin slowly being lowered into a place very far away from Adina's heart. Tristan had flown in the day before. He had stood closely behind her, with both of his hands tenderly resting on her shoulders. If any comfort could be realized in such a moment, for Adina, it was in Tristan's quiet presence. Even Alice, admitted later that week when she visited Adina, that Tristan's kindhearted attention to Adina's every emotion, was illuminating to observe.

Adina realized the totality of her loss quickly after her mother's passing. As the days and months followed, she knew that eventually her heart would know gladder times, and the void her heart now experienced would not always remain empty. But it would never again be filled in the same way, once she navigated the world without her beloved mother. That, Adina knew, was the nature of things.

On Saturday afternoons, Adina would spend more time with Emma, as together they both grieved their mother's passing. Emma would call Adina on the phone more often now, as Emma seemed to want to establish a new kind of relationship with her younger sister. Emma felt more concerned now with Adina's welfare. She refused to allow Adina to ever feel like she was alone in the world.

In the few years that followed, Adina would be shocked when those in her circle of friends would occasionally complain about the times they needed to attend to their aging mothers' care. Inside she cringed with every complaint aired, when Alice or Anna needed to take their mothers to a doctor visit, or assist them in other ways. Adina would always listen to their grumbles with a sullen look on her face, hiding the annoyance she felt at that moment towards her friends. It was an issue she could never comprehend.

Adina could never imagine feeling so separate from her parents, or even from Emma. They were a family, and those bonds, she always assumed were eternal. Maybe for some those bonds loosened once you got married, but then she thought about Emma. Her marriage never altered her unwavering concern for her parents or for Adina. There was a connection that had been nurtured throughout their lives that nothing could impede. Yes, Emma had a husband and a son, but their status in Emma's life did not diminish the devotion she retained for her parents, and her sister. But Adina's family was not necessarily like that of all of her friends. Although Adina did realize that Amelia's family was much like Adina's. Amelia's devotion to her family and theirs to her was resolute. Her brothers had treated Vinnie as if he was truly a brother to them. They had helped him with the restaurant and argued passionately with him when they had disagreements, as if he was another one of their siblings.

But Alice kept her distance from her family as soon as she had moved to Long Island, only to gradually reconnect with her mother after her father had died. Anna was never emotionally attached to her parents. Adina wondered whether that emotional distance would translate to her son, Benjamin. Would Benjamin treat his mother with the same detachment as Anna displayed toward her own parents? Astrid never lived geographically close to her parents, who had made their home in New York City for many decades. But Astrid was always in touch with them, and often surfaced back in New York for several visits every year, not out of obligation, but out of natural fondness for her parents, and the life they had afforded her.

Adina though, did manage to live her life with her absent mother. Her relationship with her father became even more engaging, as she spent many weekends keeping him occupied. As summer approached, Adina could not bear to leave her still grieving father, and so she had an idea to bring him to Paris for a few weeks with her. She first spoke to Emma about this proposal, and

Emma thought it might be worthy of consideration. Emma assured Adina that once their dad returned from Paris, she would attend to all his needs, while Adina stayed on in Paris for the remainder of the summer. Although it was not easy for Adina to convince her father to take the trip, she eventually wore him down, and he grudgingly decided to go. Tristan was on board with the idea and knew Adina's father would occupy Adina's time, when he was at work during the day. Tristan's apartment, that he had moved into after his father died, was not large enough for them all, so Adina rented a flat for the month of July. It was large enough for Tristan to also stay there on the weekends.

It was a special time. Adina was more cheerful then she had been in months at the prospect of escorting her dad all over Paris, and seeing all the sights. When they arrived in Paris, Tristan was at the airport to meet them, and take them to the flat Adina had rented. It was in a nice neighborhood only a block from the Metro. It would be convenient for all the daily excursions Adina had envisioned with her dad. But no matter where Adina took him; the Eiffel Tower, the Louvre, the opera house, David Saville's most pleasurable experience was to sit at an outdoor café. He would spend hours there with a copy of the *New York Times*, and linger over several cups of coffee and an almond croissant. Afterward, he preferred to return to the flat for an afternoon nap.

Tristan's mother, Juliette, invited them one weekend. She and David got along so well. Both being widowed, they seemed to have much to chat about as they sat comfortably in Juliette's lovely garden. It was a beautiful sunny day and a long dining table was set outdoors near the shade from the Horse Chestnut tree. Jules was there, and Eleta's family arrived late in the afternoon along with Cleo. It was a lovely day and Adina's father was so full of pride as he listened to Adina converse in French with Cleo and Eleta. Juliette invited them to an art show the following weekend that was displaying some of her more recent sculptures, and David was looking forward to that already.

At the end of July, Adina's dad left Paris feeling so much better than when he had reluctantly arrived. Adina waited at the airport until his plane departed, and was at ease knowing hours later Emma would meet his plane in New York. Emma would make sure he arrived home safely. For the remainder of the summer, Adina returned to Tristan's apartment to savor each day and night they had, until it was time for her to return to New York, and her other life, the life away from Tristan.

When Adina arrived home from Paris she felt renewed and refocused. She still in her own quiet way, grieved the loss of her mother, but the routine of going back to school would certainly distract her from dwelling on those thoughts all the time. However, shortly after she had been back to school for only a few days, the horrendous bombing of the Twin Towers in New York City altered every aspect of daily life in the city. Nothing was the same after the early morning announcement by Dean McFarland. Everything was suspended in time, and Adina sat with her students in her second period class, and tried to comfort them, when in all actuality she didn't know if they were going to be safe inside that building. Many parents arrived at the school to personally take their children home. Some of the faculty wanted to leave to take their own children out of school and just be with them. Adina volunteered to stay with the students that were not sure where their parents were. Some phone lines were down and calls were not easily made.

Some of her students had lost parents and other relatives on that dreadful day, and the massive clouds of grief among those who Adina spent her days, could not be diffused. It was a difficult school year. Misery was everywhere and took hold of everyone, but with the misery came kindnesses, too.

It took two days for Tristan to be able to get in touch with Adina. When the phone lines were finally functioning, his call came through late one night. He said,

'*Adina, tu vas bien?*'

"Yes Tristan, I am okay. The phone lines were not working for a while."

"I was so worried when I could not get hold of you. The pictures on the television here are so awful."

"Here too. I think everyone is still in shock."

"What about the rest of your family, your father and Emma, Nathan and Joshua?"

"They are all safe."

"*Bien,* I am so relieved."

They spoke for a little while longer and then Tristan realized how late in the evening it was, and he promised to contact her again in a few days. Although Adina was glad to have spoken to Tristan, she was not able to shake off the feelings of sadness and distress, that she and the city's other residents shouldered.

As time went by in this new century, Adina and her friends saw less and less of one another. The passing of months tended to diminish the slots of

time they had hoarded for blissful, carefree hours that were so plentiful when they were younger, and had fewer individual obligations. Months after the 9/11 attack, when they met in May of 2002, everyone was still in a kind of daze, all sharing stories about others of their friends or colleagues, and their heart-breaking narratives wrought by the city's catastrophe.

To add to the still depressing atmosphere in the city, in January of 2003, Amelia notified Adina that Vinnie had suffered an accident in their restaurant's kitchen. He was severely burned. Adina had rushed to the hospital to be with Amelia and her family. Eventually Adina contacted the others, and each offered their help for whatever Amelia needed. On occasion, Adina met Amelia at the hospital, if only to share a meal. Some weekends she kept Angelina Rose busy for an afternoon while Amelia sat with Vinnie. No one, other than Amelia, was encouraged to visit, as Vinnie was in a sterile environment. But Amelia did appreciate the small breaks she afforded herself when Adina arrived at the hospital in the late afternoons, even if it was only to share a cup of coffee in the hospital cafeteria.

When they finally all met in May of 2003, at their usual birthday celebration, Amelia informed her friends that Vinnie's burns were slowly healing. Amelia had taken on more and more responsibilities at their restaurant, while he underwent a series of several surgeries. She explained that her family had been more supportive than she could have imagined, particularly when her brothers took turns managing the restaurant and cooking during Vinnie's absence. They stayed whenever Amelia needed to leave, and insisted she continue meeting her friends for random lunches. Her mother went to work part-time in the family bakery that her sons had totally taken over, since their father had died. This gave

Amelia's brothers the time to assist Amelia and Vinnie with the needs of their restaurant. Their devotion to each other was quite gratifying to witness.

Alice was particularly quiet, and they hesitated to inquire about her son, Jeremy. Two months before their annual lunch, it was discovered that Jeremy was under the influence of a variety of drugs. Alice's housekeeper was first to come across the many pills he had stashed in his bureau drawer, when she was replenishing the drawer with newly laundered socks and underwear. His behavioral changes had been observed by members of the family as well, but Alice attributed it to male adolescent issues, and often made excuses for him. It was obvious to their housekeeper, as well as Fiona, that Jeremy was exhibiting mood changes much too often.

When their housekeeper showed Alice the pills that had been stored in Jeremy's bureau drawer, Alice was stunned. She took the plastic bag of pills and waited for Daniel to arrive home that evening. When he examined the variety of pills in the bag, his look of concern was one Alice had never seen before. He told Alice that they had to confront Jeremy, and get him help. Daniel was furious when Alice admitted that Jeremy had been displaying a variety of moods, and that she had been attributing it to the behavior of teenaged boys.

Alice wanted to just talk to Jeremy, but Daniel was insistent they be sterner and after a few weeks of Jeremy's continued erratic behavior, they placed him in a drug rehabilitation center. Daniel had consulted with some colleagues at the hospital who recommended some facilities that had some success with adolescents Jeremy's age. At Daniel's insistence, Jeremy was shipped off to a center in Connecticut for a period of four months. Alice was filled with worry and guilt for not acknowledging the problem sooner.

Amelia was the first to begin the conversation about Jeremy. She asked Alice, "How are you and Daniel coping with all that has happened?"

"Not very well I am afraid. I brought up the possibility to Daniel of us going to marriage counseling, but he is not enthusiastic about that, at this point in time."

Anna said, "How do you feel about that Alice?"

"I feel like I don't know what to do. Daniel is spending less and less time at home it seems. I feel like it's all my fault. It's as if our life is crumbling into bits, and I don't know how to stop it."

Adina said, "Alice, it's not your fault. You cannot take on all the responsibility for what is happening with Jeremy. Maybe Daniel is feeling helpless too."

Alice said, "I just hope the rehab center can make Jeremy well again, and help him to kick this habit. Then maybe Daniel and I can move past this. Let's talk about something else."

Then Anna began to bring everyone up-to-date on her mother's condition. Her dementia had progressed. Anna's father refused to consider placing his wife in a facility to see to her needs. Anna told them she would only call once every other week, and did not visit very often. Adina could not understand how Anna could maintain her life so completely separated from her parents' lives. When she did start to visit more regularly, at least once every few months, it seemed like Anna's confronting her mother's condition was an unwelcomed intrusion to her own well-ordered existence. But this was nothing new. Once Anna had married Peter, she managed to separate her life from her parents. From that moment on, the connection between them was fragile at best. Adina could not fathom this ability Anna had to move on with her life, with little to no regard for her parents. Adina thought something in Anna's past must have had to happen for her to be left so devoid of feelings for her mother, and especially for her father. Adina was sure there was some secret that Anna held on to, that allowed Anna to dissociate herself from them.

For Adina, it was unimaginable to have such an emotional distance towards one's parents. Adina would do anything for her parents, and Emma would as well. But for Anna, a trip to Lancaster was more problematic, then any of her travels all over Europe with Peter, and Benjamin at her side. Anna did not have the capacity to understand her father's point of view concerning her mother's care. Despite Anna's harsh view of him, he did love his wife and would not separate himself from her, at least not at this time. Love triumphed over convenience, a concept Anna was unable to grasp.

Adina listened to all her friends' problems with a sympathetic ear. She acknowledged as time insisted marching on, life does indeed get difficult. Adina understood that when she lost her own mother a few short years before this meeting. When the conversation turned towards Adina, Alice asked if she was going to Paris that coming summer. Adina responded that she would only go this time for the month of July. She did not want to leave her father for so long a time. Emma and Nathan were taking their vacation in August, and neither wanted their father to be alone, without either of his daughters to rely on. Predictably, Anna thought that was ridiculous, but Amelia smiled in agreement with Adina from across the table.

Alice then asked, "What is our friend Astrid up to these days?"

Adina answered, "Well, she is off to Kenya on a safari. It is an anniversary present from Henrik."

Anna thought that was wonderful, while Alice insisted that she couldn't consider staying outdoors for any length of time in the wilderness. Adina then addressed the group.

"Astrid always had the ability to know how enjoy the life that sits beside her. I've always admired that about her."

Amelia then asked, "How can anyone be that open and free? I'm glad for her though. Whenever I think about Astrid, I always feel so light-hearted."

Adina agreed, "That's the affect she has on people. Always did."

Once the last morsel of cheesecake was devoured, the group dispersed after several rounds of wishing each other well with respect to each other's present circumstances. Alice reminded them that the following year they would be celebrating their fiftieth birthday, and that they should plan some grand gesture to mark the occasion. Amelia laughingly suggested they meet at some spa for a group massage considering the increasing stress their lives were all beginning to confront. Anna suggested they all fly off to some exotic island for a long weekend, allowing only the ocean breezes to keep them relaxed. When Adina was asked, she hesitated to respond with any ideas. It was as if she had some premonition of what the next year would hold in store for them all, considering the struggles some of them were already tackling.

"Let us decide next year when we meet again, what we want to do once we have crossed over to that next decade." They agreed, they said their good-byes, and each went their own separate ways.

When July rolled around, Adina left for her planned month's visit to Paris. Once she arrived, Tristan met her flight at the airport, and she found him in an unusually good mood. On the ride back to his apartment, he conveyed to her that he had made a huge breakthrough in his research, and was so excited to tell her all about it. She listened with delight how he explained about stem cells and their potential, and even more obscure scientific conjectures that she really did not understand. She listened with the utmost enthusiastic attention to his every word. Adina was thrilled to find Tristan this engaging about his work. To add to this glorious greeting, Tristan announced that he had made arrangements for them to spend a week together in St. Tropez. Another doctor had a villa there and offered it to Tristan for a week to use while he visited the states on business during July. Adina was thrilled beyond the pale at this wonderful surprise.

Tristan explained, "You are only here for one month, so we must enjoy our time together, and a week by the ocean will be good for both of us."

Adina threw her arms around him and asked, "When do we leave?"

This was their way when they came together. Like young lovers, they remained, ignoring the passing of time. It was the magic they provided for one another. Their rationed time was an escape from the rigors that life presented, as it naturally brought the rude intrusions that time bestows eventually on everyone, transforming the joys of youth to the sorrows of aging lives.

When they dined at the cafes in St. Tropez, they were just as they were when Adina first arrived at the Sorbonne. This was a rare gift that they provided for one another, while the world around them grew old and laden with responsibilities. They remained as they were, when they first met, frozen in a time that they continued to be able to thaw, whenever they had the opportunity to be together. It was a unique way to live their lives. It had worked for them all these years. Both Adina and Tristan were willing participants in this romantic drama that set them apart from everyone they knew. Not many could understand their mutual desire to continue to live in this manner. But year after year, it brought them both a distinct quality of contentment, that few are fortunate enough to experience over such a long period of time.

The month of July provided such a pleasant interlude for both Adina and Tristan, but Adina was adamant about getting back home to be near her dad for the remainder of the summer. Before long, what was left of the summer ended, and Adina was back at school, meeting with a new crop of eager students, and looking forward to the subtle appearance of the change in seasons.

CHAPTER 18

———————— ꝏ ————————

ON OCCASION, ADINA would think about her approaching fiftieth birthday, especially when she was getting ready to take a shower. She scrutinized her body to see what time had surreptitiously modified. The number seemed to denote a rather aged creature, but in her mind, she still felt so youthful, and her energy level had certainly showed no signs of decline. She thought about a fitting celebration too, as she knew the other women would want something fun. Her thoughts of amusement always would have taken place abroad. A celebration in May could find them visiting Switzerland or the canals of Amsterdam, or even spending a few days in Rome feasting on delicious Italian dishes, which Amelia would enjoy. But in her heart, she knew that was impractical, given the dubious circumstances of Alice's life and Vinnie's recovery. Maybe a weekend at the Jersey shore being pampered in one of the hotels, and an evening of gambling would be a more reasonable solution. But it was fun to imagine all the possibilities they might pursue. It was only October, and there was still plenty of time to think about a fitting celebration for this coming May.

Adina was entering the shower readying herself for school, and in one horrifying moment, her soapy hand moved across her breast. Panic visited, as she felt an odd bump on the right side of her right breast. She immediately shut off the warm water, and moved her fingers again on the spot, the spot that would hold her life in its grasp. Something was there that hadn't been there before. Maybe, she thought, it was nothing, a swollen muscle from banging into something.

She got dressed, left for school, and aimed to move from one activity to the next with the usual routine of her daily schedule. During her lunch break she phoned her gynecologist's office explaining her morning discovery. She was given an appointment for a late morning visit followed by an afternoon mammogram the following day. Adina felt good about taking action. She wanted to know as soon as possible, if this bump was something serious. If not, she could begin to feel at ease again, knowing there was no reason to be overly concerned.

That evening she mentioned it to Emma on the phone, and Emma insisted on accompanying Adina to her mammogram in the afternoon. The visit with her doctor only elevated Adina's concern, as he was undecided whether this "small mass," as he referred to it, was suspicious or not. Later in the afternoon, Emma met with Adina in the suite, in the same building where the diagnostic mammogram would be performed. Adina had had many mammograms during the past ten years, but there was an air about this time, that simply did not reflect anything routine as the others had been.

After the pictures were taken, Adina was asked to wait before changing back into her clothes. Soon a technician told Adina that the radiologist wanted her to have an ultrasound to examine the mass more closely. The technician went into the waiting room to apprise Emma of what was occurring. The ultrasound did not take that long, although to Adina it seemed like an eternity. A few minutes later the radiologist, a tall man with greying temples who looked like he had been doing this for decades, entered this small darkened room. Adina took one look at his facial expression, and realized the words he was about to utter were not necessary. His concerned and serious demeanor told the story. She only recalled hearing words like *malignancy, treatable, biopsy and oncologist*. She could not recall his full sentences. It was like a carousel of horrific words trying to penetrate her brain.

After she got dressed, she met with Emma in the waiting room, and they were escorted back to her doctor's office, where a nurse was awaiting their arrival. It was in this small office that the nurse explained the results of the ultrasound. The nurse told them that a biopsy was necessary to determine the nature of the mass. She provided a list of breast surgeons for Adina to select to perform the biopsy. The nurse also volunteered to make the appointment for Adina. Even though several hours had passed since she had first arrived in the building, it seemed like everything was happening at rocket speed. An appointment was made for the end of the week.

Once Adina and Emma left the building that housed all these offices on Lexington Avenue, Emma suggested they stop in one of the restaurants, as they hadn't eaten much throughout the day. Adina could only manage to get down some soup, and Emma insisted she take out a sandwich for later in the evening. It was at the restaurant that Adina told Emma that the radiologist had told her he was fairly certain the mass was malignant. Emma tried to be so supportive, assuring Adina that whatever the biopsy revealed, it could be treated. They agreed not to mention this to their father until the results of the biopsy were established. Emma then offered to stay with Adina that night, but Adina refused. She would go to school the next day.

In her apartment, alone, all that kept echoing in her ear was the radiologist telling her that the mass *was probably malignant*. She thought it was inconceivable that she could be sick. She had felt fine. There had been no evidence that she was anything but healthy, except for that bump. If her arm had moved in a different direction, none of this would be happening. Maybe the radiologist was wrong, and the biopsy would prove there had been a huge error with the films. But his words kept echoing. She thought that maybe Tristan could allay her fears, by convincing her that there was a chance the mass was benign. His reassuring voice might diffuse her apprehension.

That night she emailed Tristan and apprised him of the situation. With her written words, she tried to downplay her worry and concern. About twenty minutes after she pressed the "send" key on her computer, Tristan phoned her. Just his voice alone had the most calming effect on her. He tried to assure her that whatever was found, could be treated. "But Tristan, I know I'll need some kind of operation to remove it."

Tristan then said, "You will do whatever needs to be done. I know you have the fortitude to see this through."

"But I will look different."

"As long as you keep that smile when we are together, nothing else matters."

Adina immediately felt better. Tristan told her, that if the biopsy was positive for a malignancy, he would recommend an oncologist, one of his esteemed colleagues, for her to see at Sloan-Kettering Memorial Hospital. He also would make the appointment for her as well. He assured her that when she needed him the most, he would surely fly out to be with her. When the phone call ended, Adina felt so empowered knowing Tristan would not turn away from her, and indeed see her through whatever was forthcoming.

At the end of the week, Adina met with Dr. Michael Aronow. He was probably in his mid-forties and had such a kind manner about him. He very slowly explained Adina's situation to both Adina and Emma. From the ultrasound films, he too was fairly positive that the mass *was malignant.* But he performed the biopsy, and said he would call as soon as the results were available. He briefly spoke about mastectomies and lumpectomies, and how the choice would be Adina's once the pathology reports were analyzed. When he uttered the word *cancer* during his explanations, Adina felt like a sword was piercing through her chest. She tried not to show her utter fear and revulsion, listening to Dr. Aronow's assessment of the situation. She didn't want to upset Emma any more than she assumed Emma was already experiencing.

It took four days for the results to be returned. Dr. Aronow phoned Adina with the news that she indeed had *breast cancer.* He asked her to come into his office the following afternoon, and she immediately agreed to see him then.

During the office visit, Dr. Aronow explained the pathology report. He spoke about staging issues and phrases Adina had no knowledge of, but was sure to learn about in the coming months. He did recommend she consult with an oncologist before any decision about her surgery was made. Adina mentioned that Tristan wanted her to see someone at Sloan Kettering. Dr. Aronow was agreeable and thought it was a good idea. She was at a loss for a word to describe who Tristan was to her. After all, he was not her husband, nor did they live together, and she felt peculiar using the word *lover* to describe their relationship. The word *friend* was not intense enough to describe their connection.

That afternoon Adina emailed Tristan with attached copies of the report that Dr. Aronow provided for Adina. A few hours later, Tristan phoned Adina, and told her she had an appointment the following Monday afternoon with a colleague that he had much respect for, and who was well-known in this field. His office was on the third floor in the Evelyn Lauder Breast Center on East 66th Street. Her appointment was at four o'clock in the afternoon, with Dr. Alexander Hoffman. Tristan assured her she would get the best treatment and that Alex, as he referred to him, would keep Tristan up-to-date on Adina's care if she signed papers giving Tristan access to her medical records, which Adina would certainly do.

The day of the appointment was in early November, and a slight chill was already felt as the afternoon temperatures began to drop. Emma met Adina in the lobby of the building, and together they went to meet Dr. Hoffman. After a short time in the waiting room, they were led into Dr. Hoffman's office. The doctor rose to shake hands with both of them as he introduced himself.

"I am so pleased to meet you Adina. Tristan has always spoken about you through the years."

For the moment, knowing that Tristan had mentioned her to one of his colleagues, during his time in New York, was very pleasing to her. It almost felt like Tristan was in the room, right there with her. She responded,

"And I am grateful that you agreed to see me on rather short notice."

Adina introduced Dr. Hoffman to Emma and both of them got comfortable in the lush aqua and brown upholstered chairs in the doctor's office.

"I received all your test results from Dr. Aronow, who by the way, I am acquainted with, and I have reviewed all the data. Also, quite coincidentally, while setting up your profile for my records here, I noticed we have something else in common besides knowing Tristan."

"Oh, what might that be?" was Adina's response.

"It's that we not only have the same birthday, but we were also born the same year."

Adina gave Emma a look that expressed Adina's disbelief, and her amazement at the same time. Adina then asked in what hospital he was born.

"Well my family is from Brooklyn. I was born in Kings County Hospital."

Adina and Emma for the moment were rendered speechless. Dr. Hoffman continued typing into his computer, and once he finished he looked up and considering the expression on Adina's and Emma's faces, asked if anything was wrong. Adina then proceeded to tell him the story of her birth along with Amelia's, Alice's, and Anna's, and how they all eventually met one another.

Dr. Hoffman looked at Emma, and she said, "Yes, it is true. They've been together as the most devoted and dearest of friends. They are like family to one another."

Adina sat there stunned, thinking that this man, who she was now placing in charge of her life, and her survival, had come into this world the very same day she had. A minute later her stunned expression transformed into one that demonstrated Adina was now completely at ease and confident, that this was the physician meant to be her healer.

"This is nothing short of remarkable," he said. Then Adina told him there was more to the story. "During my time at the Sorbonne, I met my roommate Astrid, who was also born on the same day, but in Sweden. Astrid and I have been close friends ever since. That was actually around the time I first met Tristan, when I was studying in Paris."

Dr. Hoffman appeared to be amazed as he heard this story unravel. He looked at Emma seemingly for agreement to his dumbfounded expression. Emma reiterated, "Yes, it is all true, just as Adina said. Amazing, but all true."

Then he looked at Adina and said, "Well, I suppose from now on you should call me Alex. After all, apparently, we've known each other for many, many years."

The three of them laughed, which made the next part of their talk a bit more tolerable.

Dr. Hoffman explained the type of *cancer* Adina had, and told her it was certainly serious, but treatable. He asked if she had made her decision yet as to have a mastectomy or a lumpectomy. Adina told him she would prefer the lumpectomy, if possible. He told her it certainly was, but she would need to go through several rounds of chemotherapy followed by a few months of radiation, if she chose a lumpectomy. He also communicated in the most honest approach that it would be a very challenging treatment. He explained that she would be very sick on some days, but at the end of chemo, it would prove beneficial for reducing or eliminating the tumor. Because there had been much success with a particular new therapy, he suggested that she first have six rounds of chemo to shrink the tumor, and then the lumpectomy. After that she could have radiation treatments.

It was almost all too much for Adina to absorb. She had nearly stopped concentrating on Alex's remarks after he uttered the word *cancer*. She still could not believe she was actually there, in real time, listening to him speak of something pertaining to her. Cancer happened to other people, not to her. She wondered why this was happening to her. Why was she singled out? What had she done to be forced to travel on this terrible path? What was she being punished for? What was the reason that this was happening to her? There had to be a reason.

Emma could sense Adina's reaction and placed her hand on Adina's. Adina felt immediately comforted and smiled at Emma.

A few moments passed and Adina then reacted, "Alex, I appreciate the complete explanation of my condition, and your plan to see me through this journey."

He looked down momentarily at the paperwork that he had generated for his proposal to oversee her medical condition. Then with the most serious look on his face, with his sparkling green eyes, looked directly into Adina's eyes he said,

"I need to make you very sick, in order to make you better. Will you let me help you?"

Adina looked back at him and was only able to murmur, "yes".

Alex then countered, "Are you sure Adina? It is a difficult treatment, especially for a woman. You will lose your hair, and that seems to be a particularly tough issue for most women."

She glanced at her shoulder that was covered by her shiny brown locks and simply said, "It will grow back eventually, right?"

"Yes, it will, in time."

Alex then phoned for a nurse to come into the office. Ms. Martinez entered and greeted Adina and Emma. Dr. Hoffman quickly summarized Adina's treatment plan to Ms. Martinez. He explained that he would set up a schedule for Adina's first infusion, and contact Dr. Aronow with the plan as well as Tristan. Ms. Martinez then ushered Adina and Emma into another office to discuss the effects of the chemo, what foods she should and shouldn't consume, and also gave her several prescriptions to fill prior to her first infusion. She also gave a brief explanation as to how each pill would provide relief from certain ailments that were sure to arrive at some point. Ms. Martinez then escorted them to see the infusion room where Adina's chemotherapy would be administered. Ms. Martinez explained it was now empty, as infusions were administered on other days of the week.

Emma could tell that Adina was overcome by just the look of the room. She placed her hand on Adina's shoulder and whispered, "We will get through this." Several reclining leather chairs were lined up against a pale blue wall. Next to each one was a metal holder for intravenous meds, and a small cabinet with all the supplies that were required to administer the drugs. Next to each recliner was another chair which Adina assumed was for anyone accompanying the patients while they were being infused. It was all so much for Adina to take in her stride. It was all so much for anyone to absorb. At least the room was filled with large windows, she thought, which would allow for some sunlight to make the room a bit cheery. But her optimism quickly faded.

Adina turned to Emma and whispered, "It's like a medical prison."

Emma shook her head, "Well if I know you Adina, one of those chairs you'll cover with a bright, colorful throw."

That made Adina laugh, and then she said, in a mocking tone, "I wonder what sort of outfits I'll wear when I come here? What's the latest style for having poison pumped into one's veins?"

Ms. Martinez laughed and said, "Miss Adina, you just keep that sense of humor. It will get you through the rough days."

When they returned to Dr. Hoffman's office, Adina was informed that she would need to have a port surgically implanted in her chest, for the chemo to be infused into her body. He had already contacted Dr. Aronow, and made an appointment for Adina the following week for the surgical procedure. After that, some time would be necessary for the incision of the port implanted in her chest to heal, and then her treatment could be set in motion. Her first chemotherapy would be administered in early December.

CHAPTER 19

DR. HOFFMAN HAD told Adina that most of the side effects she would experience would appear about three weeks after her first round of chemo, and that her side-effects would become more acute, progressively with every round. Ms. Martinez told her that her hair would begin to fall out about three to four weeks after her first infusion. So, with that schedule of events in mind, Adina made her first three decisions.

The first was in regard to her professional life. Adina decided that she could continue teaching until the winter break in mid-December, and then she would request a medical leave of absence for the remainder of the academic year. Having taught at Dalton now for over twenty years, she had accumulated the equivalent of several months of sick leave to see her through most of the treatment, while still being salaried. Her personal disability insurance policy would cover her through the times after her sick leave was exhausted. Having been conscientious about her work obligations, and not squandering days off all these years, certainly proved to be a sensible judgement on her part. At least there was no need to worry about finances during this approaching period of managing her care. The Board of Trustees at Dalton granted the leave, and were most gracious in wishing her well, and would be looking forward to her return to school.

Her second decision was to contact her hairdresser, Kaleb, who owned a salon on 65th Street. Adina had been going there for over ten years, and Kaleb had been cutting and styling her hair all that time. When she arrived at the salon, one day after school, Kaleb took her into his small office in the back of the salon so that they could have some privacy. Adina explained her situation, and the scheduling of her first chemo. She also needed a recommendation about purchasing a wig. He listened intently to her exchange of information about her situation. The first thing he did was move from his chair, and offered a friendly supportive hug. Then he said,

"Adina, I have had many clients like you. You will be fine. We will get you in for an appointment soon so that I can give you a short hairstyle, a short sassy style."

Adina managed a smile although inside she was dreading the new look Kaleb was describing. She never thought she looked all the great in a short hairdo. She wondered if she would still appear attractive to Tristan. But then she realized she only needed to have it short until it all came out. Suddenly, a shorter hairdo was viewed by her as better, than no hair at all.

When she inquired about a wig, he directed her to go to a salon on Madison Avenue, where she would be taken care of by a friend and colleague of his, Jessica Michaels. He would call her first and make an appointment for Adina to see her. After the wig was ordered and delivered, Kaleb would make any adjustments so that it fit her face perfectly. He called the front desk of his salon, and had them give Adina an appointment for her haircut. Kaleb also called Jessica's salon, so that he could send Adina over to see her right away, and Adina could select a wig. It could be ordered and delivered in time for Adina's haircut appointment with Kaleb the following weekend. He would be able to make any adjustments so that it perfectly framed her face.

Kaleb said, "Adina when you come back I will create a lovely hairdo for you. Bring your friends. That's what many of my clients with *breast cancer* do. We can all celebrate your new look."

Adina knew she would not mention it to her special group of friends. She just wasn't ready to broadcast this news. Too many things were about to be changed. She was desperate to hold on to her old self, the self before *cancer* invaded her life. If she kept her friends in the dark about this, they would relate to her as they always had, before she became a victim. It was enough that Emma knew, and was unwavering in her support for her. Rhoda was also someone she would be able to unburden herself to when that became necessary. And of course, Tristan. She knew he would be the one she could turn to for whatever difficulty was yet to come.

Everything was going according to the plans Adina had orchestrated. Up to this point she still felt that she was in control. She was taking charge during this frightful circumstance she found herself forced into. Maintaining some semblance of control was the most essential ingredient in order to not fall apart and slide into utter despair.

The third decision, perhaps the most challenging, was to inform her dad of this grim situation, that up until now had only been known to Emma, Tristan the administration at school, and her hairdresser. Finally, it was time to divulge the nightmare to her father. On Saturday morning Adina took a taxi to her father's home. She was to meet him for a typical weekend breakfast. Later in the afternoon she would return to the city for her appointment with Jessica Michaels. The morning hours were designated for explaining her condition to her dad. It was a delight, as always, when David Saville greeted his daughter with his usual welcoming smile. His table was set much like it always had been when Sophia was still preparing the morning breakfast. The table was filled with all the family favorites: bagels, cream cheese, smoked salmon, herring, sliced tomatoes and onions, and smoked white fish taking the center stage. Adina had stopped earlier at her favorite bakery, and brought several of her father's much-loved cheese Danishes. Their conversation began as they sat down at the dining room table.

Her father said, "I was surprised that you wanted to visit today. You usually come on Sundays. Are you busy tomorrow with something special?"

"Well there is something I needed to talk to you about, and I didn't want to wait any longer."

David Saville gave his daughter a quizzical look and said, "Are you in some kind of legal trouble?" And then he laughed.

"No. It's more like medical trouble." Suddenly her father's expression became quite serious.

Slowly she explained what had been going on the past month with all her tests and told him the results. She was quick to mention that she didn't want to worry him until she knew for sure, what the findings would reveal. She explained that she would have her first chemotherapy the following week. Holding back tears with all her strength she said, "Daddy, I will get through this." For a moment he was quiet looking down at his plate, and then he looked up at Adina and said,

"Yes, you will get through this, and I will be with you for all of it. No more keeping these secrets from me. I will go with you to the chemo thing."

"Daddy, it will be a long day, several hours of infusions. Emma can come with me."

"No, I won't hear of it. I will come with you. I'll bring my newspaper. We can do the crossword puzzle together."

Adina realized there was no use trying to talk her father out of coming with her. She agreed he could come, as long as he took a taxi to her apartment and not come by subway. Adina always worried when her father traveled the subway by himself. He was pretty spry, but he was still eighty-four.

Adina forced herself to eat a bagel with some cream cheese and lox to show her father that she still had an appetite, and wanted him to eat as well. The doorbell rang and Adina got up to see who was at the door. Standing there were Emma and Nathan.

Emma said to Adina, "I thought it might be a difficult time for you to deliver the news to daddy, so we decided to come and help lighten the mood."

They all sat around the table eating and talking about anything but Adina's *cancer* diagnosis. After another hour had passed, Adina announced she had to leave for her appointment to order a wig.

"I'm having my hair cut short next weekend, so that when it falls out it won't be such a shock, but first I am going to order a wig today from some fancy-shmancy place on Madison Avenue. Then I will take it to my hairdresser next week to tweak the style for my face."

David Saville despondently looked at Adina and asked, "Are you going to lose all your hair?"

She said, "Yes daddy...but it will eventually grow back."

Adina could see the extreme sadness in her father's eyes. It was almost too much for her to bear. It was at this moment that Adina realized the magnitude of her father's distress, at hearing the news that she delivered. It was one thing for her to comprehend her diagnosis, but quite another for her father, or any parent, to shoulder the news of their child's dismal condition.

Emma offered to go with her, but Adina felt she needed to do this by herself. She needed to maintain what little control and independence was still left to her.

Jessica Michaels, the proprietor of the shop that sold the wigs, was most gracious and kind. She provided Adina with a preview of what she should expect to happen, and when it would occur. Jessica knew that Adina would be seeing Kaleb for her haircut the following Saturday to cut her lovely shoulder-length hair. Adina selected a wig similar to the style she usually wore, in a color that seemed to match her own shade perfectly. In the shop on display, was a navy-blue baseball cap with long straight hair that was attached to it. It had a casual, friendly look about it and Adina ordered one in her shade as well. Jessica was willing to show her several head scarves but Adina seemed to know that was not a look she would aspire to wear outdoors. Besides, Adina already had an extensive collection of scarves she could use to wear around the house. But Jessica did insist she purchase an oh-so-soft sleeping cap.

"Your head will be cold at night and you will need this." Jessica insisted.

Adina could not imagine that, but agreed to make the additional purchase. It was all so bizarre to be experiencing this hair saga, but she kept plowing through every suggestion Jessica made. With everything ordered, she thanked Jessica for the time she spent with her. Jessica gave her a hug and said,

"You will be okay Adina. And your hair will come back in no time. I will call you when the wigs are delivered, but I am sure they will be in before you see Kaleb next weekend."

The following Saturday Adina left her apartment in the mid-morning headed to Jessica's shop on Madison Avenue. Jessica showed the wig and baseball cap to Adina, and indeed the shade of chestnut brown with copper colored highlights was so close to Adina's color. Jessica packed all the merchandise and also gave Adina a bottle of special shampoo to care for the wigs. She wished Adina well and told her to come back for whatever else she might need. Adina thanked her for all her invaluable assistance and left the Madison Avenue shop on route to Kaleb's salon for the haircut. He greeted her and placed her immediately in his chair. He took out his scissors and he chatted away about mindless stories of his various clients and celebrities he knew personally, all the while leaving a mass of her hair strands falling to the floor.

Adina tried to be relaxed and open to the notion of a shorter style. Most of her life she had worn her hair long, and this new look would take a while for her to settle upon. As she looked at herself in the salon's huge mirror, she realized how much of her identity had been wrapped in those long strands of her hair. But now she had a new persona, that of a woman with *breast cancer*. As hard as Kaleb tried desperately to convince Adina that she looked dazzling in this new sassy style, Adina was not persuaded, but was so appreciative of Kaleb's efforts.

He said, "Adina, all you need is to wear a turtleneck and a pair of big earrings and this haircut will look stunning on you."

He then placed the new wig on Adina's head, which immediately eased her skepticism. Kaleb made a few small nicks here and there, until it was a picture-perfect facsimile of Adina's former coiffure, before she lost what was to become a symbol of the disease that had invaded her body, and almost every aspect of her life.

When she went to her classes that last week before her medical leave began, her students were very complimentary of her new look. Tyler, a charming fourth-year French student who had been taking her class every year that he had been at Dalton, and bared a slight resemblance to Tristan, said with a wink and a smile,

"Ms. Saville, you look hot."

Adina managed a grin as she wished she could harvest the optimism her students so easily imparted to her. It was the first time ever that she realized how far away her buoyant frame of mind had traveled. She had been shattered by the diagnosis that took her so far away from the joyful disposition she had always exuded.

Other decisions were made when Adina felt they were necessary. It was not an easy thing to spout out the words, *I have breast cancer.* Just the word *cancer* alone, in regard to oneself, becomes an appalling word to articulate. Adina had to muster much courage whenever it was necessary to communicate her fate to others in the various circles of her life. Sometimes it was easier to convey the message on the phone, or by email, so as not to see the look of sadness, and sometimes pity on people's faces once Adina revealed her message. Adina tried to be nonchalant in delivering these messages, as if the tumor was like one's appendix, that just had to be dealt with by a treatment that would simply remove it. In public she was optimistic and cheerful, in her apartment, alone, she was overcome with dread and uncertainty.

Adina had told Rhoda about the *cancer* on the phone hoping to be spared any sad looks, and surprisingly enough, Rhoda became Adina's most positive ally and confidante during her journey. She would not abandon their friendship, and innately knew when Adina needed her to hover, and when she needed to be alone.

Adina told Mr. Brooks, and he was his most charming self as he stepped out of his usual formal doorman posture, and simply embraced Adina. No words were offered, just the comfort of his embrace accompanied by his consoling smile. That meant the world to Adina. Finally, Adina said, "You're going to see a lot more of me in the next few months, now that I'm not teaching."

"Whatever you need, you have only to contact me on the house phone. I can bring you whatever you need Adina."

She thanked him. His gentle demeanor was always so appreciated.

Emma and Adina would speak about how the various people in her world reacted. The generous compassion from the many individuals Adina knew became a welcomed gift.

Emma continued to ask Adina if she had told her friends yet. Adina told her she was still not ready to tell most of them. She made excuses that they all had their own difficulties now, and that she didn't want to burden them with her news. Emma knew this was not the case, but would not press the issue.

Maybe she could not bring them into the ring of her highly personal wrestling match with *cancer* as her formidable and powerful opponent. She didn't want to be told how to feel or how to fight. Adina wanted that loving circle of friends to remain suspended in a time, where she was full of her usual vitality, instead of being plagued by the gruesome effects yet to come. It just didn't feel right, and she didn't feel the need to justify her decision, for whom she told, and for whom she did not.

Adina did decide to email Astrid, not only because she was a dear friend, but also because she knew Astrid was geographically far away. Astrid would not drop in unannounced, and thereby attempt to choreograph Adina's days by regulating her activities and such, well-meaning as it would be. Adina also mentioned to Astrid that she was not, at this time, telling her other friends about her circumstance, and would appreciate Astrid not communicating with them about her situation. In fact, she insisted that Astrid keep her situation private.

For some unspecified reason, Adina continued not to tell Anna, Amelia and Alice, that which was transpiring in her life. Although they would all be benevolent and act from their hearts, the need for Adina to retain control of her every move was fundamental. Maybe she just wanted to keep a part of her life preserved where her *cancer* was not a focus of communications. There had to be some normalcy when any of these three friends called or chatted on email with Adina. She planned that she would feign a cold or speak about other engaging appointments, when any of them would invite her out for dinner or even just a coffee.

Emma and Adina's father understood this, and allowed her to pick and choose when they could stay with her during the very devastatingly ill moments chemo thrashed upon her. The only non-negotiable was David Saville's insistence on accompanying her to the infusions. Her eighty-four-year old dad was feisty as ever, and was determined to not have his daughter confront the treatment alone.

Adina's first infusion in early December was uneventful. Her dad sat in a chair next to her, but out of the way of the IV stand, where bags of meds were changed every sixty to ninety minutes. The tubing contained the liquid meds that slowly dripped into her body through her port. The port had been surgically implanted about ten days prior to this first infusion. She tried to remain cheerful so that her father would not know the absolute revulsion she felt inside, just sitting in that room.

Around noon she insisted he take the elevator down to the building cafeteria and get himself some lunch. He would only acquiesce if Adina would agree to have him bring her something as well. He came back about twenty minutes later with a large bag filled with a roast beef sandwich for himself and a tuna sandwich for Adina. There was also a bag of potato chips and a box of donuts to offer the nurses when they came to change the IV bags. Coffee and water were always available in the large infusion room at any time. Water had become her salvation and her enemy. She needed to drink a lot of water to remain hydrated, but Adina found it difficult to continually drink. It became her father's mission every half hour to remind her to drink water while they were in the infusion room. When her day of treatment ended, and he arrived at his home after the taxi first dropped off Adina, he would phone her periodically, and remind her to drink some water.

When Adina did arrive home after the long hours of the infusion, Mr. Brooks greeted her and told her she had a large package that had been delivered earlier. He insisted on carrying it to her apartment, and she let him. The package was from Astrid, all the way from Sweden. She took out a knife and split the package open. In it were three individually and beautifully wrapped boxes with traditional Swedish Dala Horses in red against a white background. Just looking at the packages brought a smile to Adina's tired face. The first large box Adina opened contained a beautiful Klippan wool throw in a grey and cream color. The design had a delightful sheep motif, which Adina thought that Astrid imagined would help her sleep. She laughed at the sight of it. The next box she unwrapped contained a new pair of Sandgren's Swedish clogs in red patent leather. How thrilled Adina was to have these clogs. They had been her favorite choice of footwear, back in her days at the Sorbonne, when she first met Astrid. To have Astrid remember her in this way was so touching. She immediately put the clogs on and for a minute, she forgot all about the *cancer*. The last smallest package contained a box of Dala Horse chocolate candy, a genuine, delicious Swedish treat.

Adina sat down to immediately send Astrid a note of thanks, but instead went to the phone and called her. She was thrilled that she was able to reach her, and that Astrid was in fact in Sweden and at home. Their conversation was like a soothing balm that Adina found so tranquillizing. Astrid was happy to know the package arrived intact, and that Adina was thrilled with its contents. Astrid promised to call Adina the following week to keep up with her progress. When Adina hung up the phone she felt confident and encouraged, but not enough so to call her other close friends.

A week later, her last day of school ended and the winter break began. She was touched by all the concerns expressed, not only from the faculty, but also from the students who were aware that she was beginning a leave of absence for the remainder of the year.

Rhoda came into Adina's classroom as Adina was packing up some of her belongings. Rhoda put her arm around Adina and said, "I'm not saying good-bye, because I plan on seeing you every week. I will come by and check up on you whether or not you want me to. When you feel up to it, we can still continue our weekend searches for new restaurants that satisfy both our palates."

Smiling, Adina said, "Thank you. You are such a dear friend. I will look forward to you keeping me up-to-date on all the goings on at school."

"You can count on it," Rhoda replied as she left Adina's room.

Adina beheld her classroom one last time, then shut the lights off, and exited the building where she had spent every day of her professional life. When she arrived home, there was a huge bouquet of flowers waiting for her from the language department, that had been delivered with a lovely note of well wishes from her very compassionate colleagues.

CHAPTER 20

TRISTAN ARRIVED IN New York about two weeks after Adina's first chemo treatment. She had already experienced only minor discomfort a few days after the first infusion. Adina had begun to utilize the drugs that had been prescribed to relieve the side-effects she had started to encounter.

Mr. Brooks called Adina on the house phone to alert her that Tristan had arrived. Excitedly he said, "Adina, Tristan is here and he is on his way up to your apartment."

"Thanks for letting me know, Mr. Brooks."

A moment later he was knocking on her door. Their reunion, in her apartment was marked by an overwhelming array of feelings that both had separately been experiencing. Tristan's concern was masked by his smiles and embracing hug when he first saw her. But his eyes could not hide the worry as he observed Adina's look of apprehension even though she was so overjoyed to see him, and have him so near.

He said, "Adina it is so good to see you. You look wonderful."

Just then he touched the tip of a few of her hairs and said, "Your hair is short, and looks so adorable. I love it."

She moved her head under his chin and clung to him for what seemed a very long time, and then she finally spoke and said, "I am really glad that you are here."

Adina was relieved, and more than willing to abandon the courageous façade she had been forced to muster during the weeks of testing, worry, anxieties and the onset of treatment, by simply falling into Tristan's arms. For the first time, she allowed herself to surrender her need to be in control of all that was happening to her as a result of this dreadful malignancy. Tristan understood well, Adina's need to allow herself to be piloted by him, at least for the next two weeks of his visit.

He complimented her again on the attractive look of her new impish hairdo. Adina told him to enjoy it while he could. They were able to laugh as Adina tried desperately to maintain her sense of humor throughout this time of new tribulations challenging her fortitude. The last thing she wanted to do was to succumb to misery and depression, at least certainly not while Tristan was with her.

Before Tristan arrived, Adina had the opportunity to speak privately to her nurse, Ms. Martinez. It was during Adina's first round of chemotherapy. Ms. Martinez was changing the intravenous bag of toxic chemicals that were slowly dripping into Adina's body, the powerful liquid charged with the challenge of eradicating the *cancer*. Ms. Martinez looked at Adina's curious expression and asked, "Adina, do you have some questions for me?"

Adina glanced at her father, then back to Ms. Martinez and instinctively Ms. Martinez knew Adina needed to speak with her in private. She asked Adina, "Do you need to use the restroom?"

"Yes," Adina answered.

Ms. Martinez said, "Let's unhook you for a few minutes and you can wheel the IV stand in with you. I think you've done this before."

Soon they were headed out of the area. Ms. Martinez led Adina into an empty examining room where there was room for both of them to sit comfortably. Then she asked Adina what was on her mind. Adina took a deep breath as she attempted to muster enough confidence to inquire about something that had been occupying her thoughts.

Finally, Adina said, "What about having relations?"

That was the word she preferred to use instead of asking whether sex was on or off the table during chemo. Ms. Martinez displayed a look of surprise at the question Adina had posed. After a brief hesitation, and with a bit of a grin, she told Adina that that was one question she had never been asked. A moment later she told Adina,

"Well if you feel like it, that is if you're not too tired, go for it."

They both laughed, and any awkwardness disappeared. Then Ms. Martinez added, "It's probably best not to engage in any sexual activity for forty-eight hours after the infusion, but after that, you are free to have at it."

Adina explained that she was anticipating a visit from Tristan, and just wanted to know what the acceptable practice was, even though Tristan would already have that knowledge, given his profession.

Ms. Martinez said, "Most women never ask that question. It is a good sign that you have such concerns, but as I said, if you feel like it my dear, then by all means, go for it."

They both stood and Adina returned to her spot and re-hooked herself back to the machine to continue the flow of the meds. Her father looked up from his *New York Times* and asked. "Need anything?"

She answered "No, everything is fine." From across the room she shared a smile with Ms. Martinez who then walked into the workspace where several nurses were updating patient charts. There was half a glass wall separating that office from the infusion area so that the staff could see and monitor the patients at all times.

Looking at Adina, Ms. Martinez said to another nurse, "That is one gutsy lady over there. She's going to be okay, that one. The chemo can't do it all but I think she has the one other drug that will get her through."

The other nurse asked, "What's that?"

"She's blissfully in love."

"Really, at her age?"

"Yes, kind of gives us all hope, right?'

And with various charts open in front of their computer screens, the nurses resumed their job of recording patients' data.

The first night they crawled into bed together Tristan was particularly sensitive, unsure what Adina was desiring. But Adina was a willing partner, and he made love to her slowly, lavishing warm kisses all over her body. With such sweet tenderness he caressed her breasts, and she reacted to his touch as she always had, wanting more and more. Adina felt so alive in his embrace, and with his body against hers. At the moment when their bodies locked togeth-er in sheer ecstasy, Adina's *cancer* had been propelled far, far away from her awareness. These precious moments spent under the silky sheets in Adina's bed, banished all the obstacles in her world, and brought her to a place where it was impossible for the *cancer* to reside. Making love to Tristan was the best tonic. For in these moments of heightened passion, she was the woman she had always been before this utmost, unwelcomed intrusion into her life, and ultimately into Tristan's as well.

During Tristan's visit they did manage to fill their days visiting many of the marvelous places that Manhattan so generously offers to all who can seize its rich cultural haunts. They managed to visit MoMA, the Museum of Modern Art, that had a wonderful exhibit of the sculptor and print-maker, Kiki Smith, on display. They were both so moved by her work, that Adina suggested they purchase the volume *Prints, Books and Things* that featured Ms. Smith's work, to take back to Paris for his mother, Juliette. Tristan had already begun to notice how tired Adina looked, and they went back to her apartment stopping only at a local deli for take-out to enjoy later. That evening he ate a full-sized corned beef sandwich that he had developed an affinity for while he had lived in the city so many years ago. They also brought back a large container of chicken noodle soup for Adina as her appetite for food had already began to slack off.

Tristan was well aware that Adina was trying hard not to give into the fatigue as a result of the chemo drugs piercing through her body. He was content to stay in the apartment with her when the tiredness overpowered her yearning to be out enjoying the city's offerings with Tristan. They watched Adina's favorite black and white movies in the evenings, while Adina sat curled up alongside Tristan on the couch. He had brought some recent French movies from Paris for them to watch together as well. He surmised from her increasing bouts of exhaustion, that this trip would not be a time for "painting the town red," but rather for indulging Adina, with the hope of making her feel as comfortable as possible. Tristan did that with such panache and of course with his endearing love for her.

Before he returned to France, Tristan was able to accompany Adina to her second round of chemo at the very end of December. David Saville allowed Tristan this one time to take his place beside his daughter for this appointment. First, they met with Dr. Hoffman in his office.

"Tristan, it's wonderful to see you again."

"Same here Alex. I know you have been taking good care of Adina."

"Yes, she is doing well. Isn't that right Adina?"

Adina nodded and said, "Yes."

Adina left the office momentarily to have some blood drawn, the usual procedure before the chemo could be administered. When she returned to Alex's office, he and Tristan were discussing what she assumed was her condition, using words whose meanings she was still unaware. *Metastatic, hemoglobin, neutrophils, hormone receptors*, and others, all linked somehow to this jigsaw puzzle of Adina's treatment and prognosis. It was doctor talk of the highest degree. Finally, a nurse brought in a sheet of paper with the results of the blood work, and Alex shared it with Tristan as Alex pronounced, "You can go into the infusion room now."

As she and Tristan were getting up, Alex asked, "Adina, if you don't mind, I'd like to consult with Tristan a little later in the day on a case study I know he would like to review."

Adina responded, "Alex, for you, anything."

She and Tristan got comfortable in the infusion room. He had brought his filled briefcase to work and some of his patient files. Adina brought the French novel, *Hôtel Splendide* by Marie Redonnet, that Tristan brought for her from Paris. He had also given Adina a burgundy-colored velvet journal, suggesting she write about this journey that she had embarked upon, not by choice, but by necessity. In the center of the journal's cover was a small replica of the Eiffel Tower in silver threads that was so striking against the burgundy background. He also gifted her with a silver pen with circular swirls etched all around its casing, filled of course with black ink, which she had always preferred using to write her letters to Tristan. Adina loved the exquisite design of the pen. It felt so good in her hand, but more importantly, it had come from Tristan.

The nurse arrived to connect the tubing to her port so that she could begin receiving the chemo drugs. Tristan put his hand on the nurse's arm and said,

"Please, let me do this."

The nurse graciously stepped aside. Adina smiled as he repositioned her royal blue sweater to expose her port, a few inches below her left collarbone, and connected the tubing as Adina flippantly said,

"Sometimes, I forget you are a doctor."

After gently making the connection, Tristan winked at her before he sat back in the chair and he said,

"Sometimes I forget you're a patient."

Two hours later, Alex appeared in the room and nodded to Tristan and they left together. Adina used that time to phone her dad and tell him all was going well. It had been especially cold that morning, and she was glad that he did not insist on coming since Tristan would take his place on the chair next to her.

Tristan returned about an hour and a half later with a tray carrying two cups of herbal tea and two large black and white cookies and a knowing look on his face that Adina could not discern. After their snack, he returned to his files as Adina napped for a while. Several hours later the infusions ended. As they left the building, Tristan hailed a cab, and instead of going straight home to Adina's apartment, he directed the driver to take them to 59th and 5th Avenue.

He said, "Let's go watch the skaters at the Wollman Rink in Central Park."

Adina was thrilled. They often had gone there when Tristan lived in New York so many years ago. They had even rented skates a few times, and made their way onto the rink. But that was many, many years ago. As the sun went down, they were content to sit on one of the benches and watch the sun's parting, deliver a spectacular view of the Manhattan skyline while Adina sat content, watching the skaters make their way around the rink. Adina turned to face Tristan and said,

"You know Tristan, when I am with you, I still feel so young and so open to the world around me. Hard to imagine this year coming, I and my friends, will all turn fifty. And Alex too. It's still so amazing that our paths crossed. And to think, you knew him for so many years."

"Yes, it is always so incredulous how the universe brings people together. When will you tell the others about Alex?"

"I'm not sure. I'm not ready to mix these two parts of my life just yet."

"You know your friends will be angry that you have not let them be part of helping and supporting you through this time of your life."

"Well I want to tell them when I feel the worst is behind me. Maybe by May I can feel emboldened enough to tell my tale."

Tristan looked deep in thought, and then said, "Well, at least you told Astrid."

"Yes, and I must tell her about Alex as soon as I speak to her again. She will think it's a miracle. You know, it is a miracle. It is the only redeeming aspect of this entire nightmare."

After a few minutes, while both of them sat quietly enjoying the graceful swirls of the skaters, and the closeness of each other, Tristan spoke.

"Adina, I have been thinking a lot ever since your diagnosis. Maybe we should not live so far apart from one another. Fifty is not old but it's a different time in our lives. I am a few years older than you, already into that decade. Alex thinks I can get a position here in New York either at Sloan or Weill Cornell Hospital to continue my research, as well as practicing pediatric oncology. If I can work that out, would it be good for you? I mean, what do you think of that?"

The first thing that entered Adina's mind was that she was even sicker than she thought. Her swift analysis immediately raised the question that perhaps she was dying or that she had very little time left, and nobody had wanted to tell her. With a bit of anger and frustration, Adina responded.

"Is it because you think I'm so sick and I need you to be here until…? Is there something about my prognosis that you and Alex have been hiding from me?"

"*Non, non, ma Chérie* It is because we have been presented with a situation that has reminded us that time is not guaranteed. I felt like a loud horn, a loud French horn was blown in my ear, causing me to re-evaluate what direction I think we should choose for what is left of our lives, both of our lives. I don't want to only be with you in the summers and for two weeks every December. My research has been a lifelong commitment, and it's been very gratifying, but I think now we can alter our direction and share a life together. Maybe *ma Chérie* you getting this disease was a shift for me as well. I realized how time is passing by, and we mean so much to one another, and it's our moment to grasp another version of the life we both could live."

Adina listened and ingested every word he uttered. After a while, he said, "What are you thinking?"

"I think it is time that I choose to take hold of the life that sits beside me."

Tristan smiled and kissed her on the forehead.

He said, "I don't know if I'll get a position here, but I wanted to know that you would want me to try. I'll concentrate on securing such an appointment, and I want you to do everything Alex suggests regarding your treatment. It will be difficult for you Adina, but you must stay focused and you will endure."

"I know. It's going to get a lot worse before it gets better."

"Yes, Adina that's true. I know you can bear those nasty side effects. They will get worse after each round but, you will handle it. Your father and Emma will help you to persevere."

She turned toward him and said, "Tristan, I do not regret any part of our lives that we've had. Although at times I certainly missed being with you, I think I became the person that I am today. Oddly enough, our separations only drew us closer, and allowed us to appreciate one another more fully. Maybe we are ready to be together again…as long as we still keep our lustful lives thriving under those silky sheets you love so much on my bed."

Tristan laughed and responded, "I wouldn't have it any other way. You forget, I am a Frenchman and we speak and act the language of love and romance."

Adina, now all smiles, stood up and Tristan followed her lead. Together, hand in hand, they walked up one block before they hopped into a taxi back to Adina's apartment.

It was almost New Year's. Adina knew she would have at least three decent days before the effects of the chemo would strike. Tristan was leaving on New Year's Day as usual, and in that regard, she was not so upset this time. She knew with each infusion she would become weaker and weaker with each passing day. When Alex had told her, "*I need to make you sick in order to make you better*," she knew it was a matter of days until her overall health would be victimized by the harsh reality that chemotherapy dispensed. For that reason, she did not want Tristan to see her in that condition.

She had always felt attractive around Tristan and wanted to remain so. Adina was afraid, even at this late stage in their very meaningful relationship, that if her appearance was altered, he would not see her in the same light that he always had. She knew that was a shallow assessment of his association with her, but nevertheless she could not help feeling that way. After all, he was not bound to her legally by a marriage contract, so the thought he might not remain with her, was something she could not purge from her thoughts.

They planned for a quiet evening on New Year's Eve wrapped up in the throw Astrid had sent and sipping on some champagne and delicacies that

Emma had had delivered to her apartment from Dean & DeLuca's, the upscale grocery store on Madison Avenue.

The first morning of this capricious new year, after Adina had showered, she started to blow dry her hair. That was the day her world shifted once again. As she ran the brush through her hair, some of it began to fall out and landed on the bristles of her beautiful antique brush. She put her hand upon her head and many strands fell onto her hand. It was at that very moment she realized that what she was told would happen, actually did. The more she brushed the more hairs fell out. Adina felt horrorstruck, as she confronted the wretched evidence of the assault her illness now delivered. Even though her wig and cap with hair bouncing out of it, had been at the ready in her closet, a part of her didn't think it would really happen, until now. And so, it made Tristan's departure all the more palatable. She didn't want him to see what was sure to occur in the next few days.

When they sat having coffee and some breakfast he immediately noticed that she was upset. He asked, "What's wrong? Are you feeling poorly?"

"My hair…it's falling out."

"It happens, Adina. It will come back. Show me the wig you wrote me about that you bought."

Adina went into her bedroom, took the wig off the Styrofoam styling head hiding in her closet, and positioned it on her head. It did look so much like the longer style she wore before she had her hair cut short. She walked back into the kitchen and Tristan's eyes opened wide.

"Ah, my sexy Adina. Come here." He hugged her tightly and told her how lovely she looked. She decided to keep it on for the rest of the day. Tristan suggested they take a short walk on this very first day of the new year. After several blocks he realized that she was slowing down her pace and he hailed a taxi for their return trip back, only having gone four blocks away. It exhausted Adina. A few hours later it was time for Tristan to leave. In the lobby they waited for the cab that would take Tristan to the airport. She thanked him for all her gifts, and for being with her for this slice of her ordeal. Then he leaned in so close to her and said,

"Adina, you are a courageous woman, and you will be able to handle what lies ahead. If I can return in a few months I will try to do that. In the meantime, take good care of yourself, as you are so precious to me. I will call you when I arrive in Paris.

Tu es mon amour pour maintenant et toujours. Au revoir Adina, mon amour."
Meaning,

"You are my love for now and always. Till we meet again Adina, my love."

He kissed her once more. When their lips parted, all she could muster was a trace of a smile as he entered the taxi that would take him so very far away from her side.

CHAPTER 21

WITH TRISTAN GONE, and also, most of her mane of hair, by the third round of chemo, Adina's fatigue was overpowering. It was unimaginable that her biggest challenge was to remain standing in the shower for the few minutes it took to wash off all the debilitating memories of the previous day, in the daily hope that this new beckoning day would deliver some strength to survive.

The task of simply repositioning oneself from the cave-like existence under Adina's soft comforter and migrating over to the living room couch was an enormous accomplishment. She refused to remain under the covers all day, fighting death's unkind invitation. Adina propelled herself on these most difficult days to move, always pretending that Tristan was waiting at her destination, the living room couch. Some days this journey was devastating, but she had to get through the seven or eight days of crushing side effects in order to emerge into a feeling of temporary well-being, a memory that was more and more difficult to retrieve from Adina's exhausted mind's eye. Day after day, she would not surrender to the *cancer's* wrath. Whether she was selecting a colorful scarf to match the top she would wear on a particular day, or putting on lipstick, or applying some blush to camouflage her dulled pallor, she would feel victorious having completed just these simple tasks.

Besides Emma visiting often and helping with all household tasks, every Saturday afternoon Rhoda arrived at Adina's apartment with a large container of her home-made chicken soup. When Adina was up to it, they chatted about all that was going on at school. When Adina felt strong enough, they would walk around the corner to Starbucks, where Adina would order some hot tea while Rhoda guzzled a Frappuccino to help relieve her stress after a week at work.

Although Tristan was not at her side, the mere idea of Tristan, the notion that she was a person who was loved by such a man, catapulted her into the ability to endure these ruinous days, month after month until the rounds of chemo would finally conclude.

By the end of Adina's fourth round of chemo, Dr. Hoffman sent Adina for an ultrasound of her breast. The findings verified what he had already suspected, that the tumor had shrunk significantly, and was now undetectable by the human eye. He was so pleased to find his suspicions validated by this test. Adina, though, was feeling so weak she was unable to grasp the significance of these findings. Alex insisted she complete two more rounds of chemo as a precaution, but at the same time altered the combination of drugs so that the side effects would not be quite as debilitating as the previous rounds.

Adina took the information in stride, even though by now she was so devastated by the physical and emotional damage of the past three months that the *cancer* had hurled upon her. It was difficult for her to absorb this positive news with even a modicum of joy. By mid-March she had been totally ravaged by the treatment. When Tristan phoned for their once a week Friday night chat, she could barely make conversation. When he told her that he was planning to fly into New York City on the first of April for an interview with the current department head of pediatric oncology at Sloan Kettering, she knew that was good news, but was unable to express the gladness to Tristan that this promising news warranted.

By the time Tristan arrived in New York, Adina was feeling better overall since her chemo treatments had been modified to less toxic dosages. Although Sloan provided accommodations for Tristan at a nearby hotel during the three days of interviews with various doctors and research directors, Tristan opted to stay with Adina at nighttime. When they slept together, she kept her wig on throughout the night, never wanting to show Tristan what the *cancer* had taken from her. Even in the depths of the disease, Adina would not succumb to exposing the evidence of *cancer's* cruelty to her lover. This was one victory she refused to allow the *cancer* to win. There was much Adina had to surrender while the disease declared war on all aspects of her life, but forfeiting her feminine sense of self was not going to be *cancer's* triumph. If there was one thing she could safeguard, it was her womanly stylishness, and the pleasurable manner in which she related to Tristan.

Lying beside Tristan throughout the night, she was determined to preserve her sense of femininity even though she knew Tristan would never be affronted by the appearance of her now hairless head. After his three days of intensive interviews and meetings Tristan was offered a position that would commence four months later, on the fifteenth of August. He stayed for another day, and Adina basked in the possibility of a new future with Tristan at her side, instead of fretting about the malignant tumor, especially since Alex had assured her that most of it had been completely eradicated. When Tristan again exited from her apartment, their parting was filled with joyful optimism in anticipation of his return in just a few months. It was the day after Adina's actual birthday on April 5th, and knowing Tristan would be returning in a few more months was the best energy boost she could have received.

By the end of April, Adina had completed her six rounds of chemo. Her lumpectomy was scheduled for the middle of May. It would be an out-patient procedure. A month after that she would begin radiation treatments, all this to remove any malignant microscopic tissue that might still be present in her breast. During the past two weeks Adina had been trying to reclaim her strength. She began by taking short walks around the neighborhood. She even managed a taxi ride to her father's home to resume their usual Sunday breakfast together. Even her taste buds were starting to return as she munched on her favorite everything bagel, cream cheese and lox. Slowly her taste buds which the chemo had made dull from thrush, were slowly making a comeback. She even felt poised to meet her friends at Grand Central by the clock, for their annual time-honored traditional birthday lunch on the fourth of May.

She had last seen them in December just before her first round of chemo, when they met for coffee, and to see the tree all lit up at Rockefeller Center. Adina said nothing to them about her situation. Since that time, she had only spoken to Anna once, back in February, when there was a snow day and all schools were closed. Amelia and Alice all kept in touch by email messages which was easy for them all to manage, as their lives became so hectic. That made it comfortable for Adina to fabricate upbeat messages explaining that she was simply very busy during the winter months. Technically, Adina thought, she was very busy.

When May 4th arrived, she sat at her dressing table and applied her make-up carefully and effectively. Her Lancôme blush in the shade of Peach Petals gave her face a nice glow. She lifted the shoulder-length chestnut brown wig off the Styrofoam form and positioned it on her head. It was amazing to her still, how natural the wig looked. Kaleb definitely had known where to send her for the perfect hair piece which looked as good today, as it did the day she first brought it home. The special cleansing lotion for cleaning the wig kept its shine, and soft style over the past four months.

Adina wore a long pale blue top with matching slacks that Emma had bought for her at Bergdorf Goodman, Emma's favorite place to shop for special occasion gifts. Emma had bought it wrapped in a lovely pink box with a large pink satin ribbon and gave it to Adina on her last day of chemo. It fit perfectly even though Adina had dropped some pounds during her ordeal. Adina sat quietly for a while trying to decide what words she would use to tell her friends about what had happened to her, and why she had kept silent about it these past few months. She hoped the words would come once she began speaking to them.

When Adina arrived at Grand Central Station, Alice and Amelia were already there, at the usual spot under the clock. Anna arrived shortly afterwards. Astrid was not in New York, so it was just the four of them meeting this time. It had already been decided from their email communications, that they would dine at a restaurant at the station much like they had done the very first time they met there so many years ago. Sentimentality was always a consideration in any decision this group made.

The past year had visited many troubles on all of them, which was why they were eager to settle on a simple lunch at the station for celebrating their collective fiftieth birthday. Once they were all seated at the lower level at the Grand Concourse Oyster Bar & Restaurant to mark this special occasion, Alice began talking almost immediately about her persistent problems with Jeremy. He was back in rehab again having resumed taking drugs several months after he was released the first time. Alice seemed more angry and fidgety than usual. She explained,

"Daniel is no help. He's often never home although he keeps in close contact with the doctors treating Jeremy. We have become strangers. Fiona is working now in LA at some free clinic trying to decide if she wants to apply to medical school. And Liam, my youngest, wants to study drama in college but hasn't yet decided which university he wants to attend. Daniel is not too happy about Liam's choice of study as you can imagine."

Exasperated, hearing all of Alice's complaining, Anna then cut in and asked, "Are you getting a divorce?"

"What? Hell no. I'd never give up my house and be put on a smaller budget."

Anna said, "But if you're not happy, why continue?"

"I'm happy with my house, my country club friends that I play tennis with and of course my lovely garden."

Adina and Amelia, sitting across from each other just sat quietly, neither willing to enter into this dialogue exploding between Anna and Alice.

Alice then asked, "Anna, so how are things with you?"

"Oh, very well. Peter has a project in London so I'll be staying there for almost the entire summer. I'm looking forward to the trip."

With a snide expression, Alice looking directly at Anna said, "I suppose even your marriage has its problems."

Anna responded, "What do you mean? Why would you say that Alice?"

And then Alice let loose on Anna. "You stay with Peter because he takes you out of the country all the time. Peter is like your lap dog always trying to please you. He even once told Daniel that he volunteers for these projects in Europe because it's what you want. He'd prefer to stay in the city but he has to follow you all around as you run away in search of who knows what."

Anna quickly answered, "That's not true. Peter loves to travel."

"Peter loves you, Anna. Probably a hell of a lot more than you love him."

Adina felt so badly hearing Alice unload on Anna. Adina had always thought that Anna had long been deeply troubled about her relationship with her parents, and didn't need Alice barking out an accusation about her marriage to Peter. However, Alice's account about why Peter accepted those faraway assignments was intriguing to consider.

A few moments of awkward silence fell around the table and then Amelia entered the conversation asking, "But Anna, how is your mother? Can you leave her for that long a time while you're in London all summer?"

"Of course, I can. When I go to see her, she only recognizes me for a few minutes and then she is off in her own world. She won't even know I'm gone."

Amelia asked, "But what about your father? It must be such a burden on him taking care of her, alone."

Adina thought this was so true to Amelia's form. She had such a soft heart, and there she was worrying about Anna's father.

Anna replied, "It's his wife and his choice to keep her at home. She'd be better off in a facility, but he still won't hear of it. That's his choice, and my choice is to spend the summer in London."

Although Adina sat quietly, now she was getting inwardly enraged. She thought that Anna knew her mother was approaching the end of her life. Any moments that Anna could see her, even if her mom didn't know her, were still so precious from Adina's perspective. It was unimaginable to Adina that Anna behaved so selfishly. It was so evident now, that something in Anna's past had driven her so far away from her parents. Not geographically far, but emotionally so distant. She viewed Anna as a somewhat cruel person for the first time. Adina had been through a lot medically, and so it was inevitable that she had been thinking much about relationships, and evaluating her life, what was important, and what held little significance.

What Adina learned during the many hours of introspection when she was receiving chemo, blood transfusions, her endless hours of body scans, and lying on her couch depleted of all energy, was that personal relationships were of the utmost significance in one's life. No matter how many trips Anna took, she still needed one more. For Alice, it didn't matter how nice a room was furnished, she still needed to re-decorate often. Neither woman found fulfillment in their human relationships. They were always looking away from the people that could bring them contentment, if only they would make the effort. Anna and her parents, and Alice with her husband, both seemed like frayed garments, too damaged for either of them to mend.

In an effort to redirect the conversation, Anna then asked Amelia how Vinnie was feeling after his most recent surgery, since he had now returned to the restaurant.

"Vinnie has healed well from all his surgeries, and is finally back in his beloved kitchen."

Alice added, "It was a rough time this past year, but it was good that his brothers helped out."

Amelia said, "Yes, my family means the world to me. We all take care of each other. But Vinnie is happy now to be back in his kitchen in our restaurant."

Adina couldn't help but smile adoringly at Amelia. Adina always viewed Amelia as the most kind-hearted person she had ever known, and always admired the strong bond she shared with her siblings.

Then Alice turned towards Adina and said, "Adina you have been so quiet since you arrived. Anything new going on with you, or are you just getting ready for your usual trip to Paris this summer?"

Adina chuckled at the question posed by Alice, as if going to Paris was such a tedious and insignificant aspiration. Alice would never understand what brought Adina to Paris every summer, and indeed that was Alice's problem. Adina took a deep breath and kept her eyes focused in Amelia's direction, as if she were only speaking to Amelia, and responded to Alice's question.

"I have been on a difficult journey these past few months. Back in October, I was diagnosed with breast cancer."

Amelia took a breath and raised both hands to her mouth. She said nothing verbally but Amelia's eyes communicated a somewhat look of surprise and concern at the same time. Alice's and Anna's expressions both communicated that they were obviously surprised by this announcement. They began spouting out questions simultaneously.

"Are you okay?"

"Are you losing your breast?'

"Is it treatable?'

"Does Tristan know?"

"Why didn't you tell us?"

Then Amelia spoke, and in her calm soothing voice said, "Tell us about what happened, and how we can help you."

Adina composed herself and began to deliver a condensed summary of all that had occurred leading up to her diagnosis and through to her treatment. She told them that she had recently completed her chemotherapy, and was soon to undergo a lumpectomy. Once that is healed, she explained, she needed to have several weeks of daily radiation.

Alice, examining Adina's head closely, then interrupted and said, "Is that a wig you're wearing? I thought your hair looked a little different."

Adina continued, acknowledging that she was wearing a wig since she had lost her hair during the treatment. Anna raised her eyebrows in disbelief. Then Alice said,

"I thought your hair looked just so perfect. I've been jealous since we met under the clock."

Adina said, "This is nothing for you to be jealous of, that's for sure."

"Oh Adina, I didn't mean to make you feel bad, I just thought your hair looked really nice today."

And Adina answered, "Well Alice, you can get one just like it in any color you prefer."

They all laughed as Adina continued to tell them that Tristan knew about the diagnosis from the beginning, and had been with her during one of her infusions back in December, and also for a brief visit in April. She also revealed that Tristan would be moving back to New York, and would continue his research at Sloan.

Alice interrupted again, "Will you two finally get married?"

Amelia just kept smiling, almost giggling, as Adina seemed ready to barrel back at Alice. For as long as they knew each other, Amelia had always witnessed on multiple occasions, Alice's quest to push Adina into a marriage. It really didn't matter which man Adina would choose, as long as Adina was married, like Alice, and the rest of them.

Adina looked directly at Alice and said, "Why would I do that when we are so happy and still so much in love with each other, and still content with the arrangement we have always enjoyed?"

The sarcasm from Adina's remark was not lost on Alice as she looked away from Adina, and simply took the napkin from her lap and placed it on the table, displaying a trace of irritation.

Then Anna piped up and again, clearly frustrated by what Adina had revealed, again asked the most complicated question of the day.

"Why didn't you tell us? We could have helped. You know we would have all helped you."

Momentarily Adina laughed to herself thinking and wanting to respond to Anna with the words, *like you help your mother?* But instead answered,

"It's not that I don't value our friendship. You all know I do, but I think I needed to keep a part of my life untouched by the *cancer,* and I chose this part. Although I want you all to know I did tell Astrid, and made her promise not to tell any of you."

A slew of angry, judgmental remarks directed at Adina, continued to be tossed back and forth by Anna and Alice. Adina realized they were just disappointed that their cherished friend did not share something so serious with them. Amelia kept silent and that was almost the giveaway as Adina listened to both of her other two friends vocalize their displeasure for having not been informed at the onset of Adina's diagnosis. As soon as there was a pause in these regretful remarks, Adina simply said,

"I'm sorry."

Anna continued, "I just don't understand. We've been friends forever."

"Yes Anna, I know that. You see, everything was changing for me. I was losing so much…more than just my hair. In the medical centers I became someone else, a wounded creature. None of the personnel or technicians, or even some of the doctors, knew me and my life. They only knew I was suffering from a disease. They didn't know I spoke French fluently, or that I loved to visit art museums or that I had four very special friends that were all born the same day I was born. Their focus was solely on my treatment, nothing else. I needed to keep being the person I had always been in some compartment of my life, and I chose all of you to keep me being that person."

There was a long silent pause as everyone wiped a tear or two from their eyes. Adina then assured them that her prognosis was good.

After she composed herself, Alice said, "Well, we will help you with that radiation thing. You will let us at least to do that Adina, won't you?"

"Of course, whenever you want to meet me there. I will be going every day. Maybe by then more of my energy will come back."

Amelia continued to sit calmly not badgering Adina at all. And that's when Adina glimpsed at Amelia and the expression on Amelia's face disclosed that somehow Amelia had known all along. Adina just knew, and decided she would wait to confront Amelia about that prospect when the two of them were alone.

Then Adina said, "Oh, there's one more thing I should share with all of you. It's about my doctor. Tristan had recommended I see a colleague of his when I was first diagnosed. His name is Alexander Marcus Hoffman. I call him Alex most of the time. When he was reviewing my records, he noticed that we shared the same birth date."

"No that can't be," said Alice.

Anna added, "That would be unbelievable."

Then Amelia finally chimed into the conversation saying, "Is it possible that he was born in New York?"

Adina answered, "In fact, he was also born in Brooklyn."

Amelia asked, "In Kings County Hospital?"

With a self-satisfied grin, Adina uttered, "Yes! He has taken such good care of me. We think I was born after he was and that we were probably lying next to each other in the nursery, much like the rest of us were."

They all looked at each other, shaking their heads in mutual disbelief. Adina gave them a few moments to grasp the stunning news she had just imparted to them all.

"If we're all finished here with our lunch, let's pay the check and take a walk back to the clock. Alex will be meeting us there at 3. It's almost that now."

Amelia said, "Oh my God, you're kidding."

Adina began to laugh so hard as she watched the three of them simultaneously reach into the purses, grab their lipsticks, and apply a fresh layer of gloss. They all gathered up their pocketbooks and shopping bags, and walked away from the restaurant to the clock where Alex was already waiting. Adina introduced him to everyone and there were handshakes that led to hugs and the widest of smiles. It was just stunningly amazing how these once newborns were reunited, each with their own individual story of the life every single one eventually chose, from that very first day.

About thirty minutes later, Alex had to leave for a meeting and the rest lingered, compelling Adina to promise to call and keep them up-to-date. They wanted Adina to let them help in any way they could. Adina agreed. Amelia told them that she was stopping at the restaurant supply place, and would walk a while with Adina while Anna and Alice left in their usual separate ways. Once outside in the still bright afternoon sun, walking with arms interlocked, Adina said to Amelia, "You knew all the time."

Amelia answered, "Yes. But please don't be mad. Astrid phoned me. She made me promise not to tell you I knew, or to contact the others. But I did contact Emma each week to find out how you were, and then I would email Astrid as to your condition. She wanted updates every week about your progress."

"I never knew. Emma never said a word to me."

"Well we wanted you to have it your way, but still we were worried and needed to know how you were faring. When Emma told me one week that you needed a blood transfusion, I begged her to let me visit you, but she refused, acquiescing to keep you in control as much as she could."

"Thank you, Amelia, for caring about me so much. But wait till I call Astrid."

"Adina, don't be too hard on her. She was so concerned and she felt so far away. She thought you might not be telling her about the really bad times you were experiencing. Astrid was ready to fly in whenever I gave her the word."

"You know Amelia, this cancer journey has taught me a lot and continues to teach me so much."

"I am so glad to see you looking so well, considering what you have been through."

"I am very lucky to be here today. I know that."

"Yes, and Tristan coming soon is also such good news. I am happy for you."

Adina gave Amelia a probing look and said, "Even though we have no plans to get married?"

Amelia snickered and said, "Even though…"

They laughed and Amelia walked back to the station. She hadn't needed to go to the restaurant supply store. She just wanted some time with Adina alone. As they parted, Adina said, "Amelia, I'll call you next week. Give Vinnie and Angelina Rose my love."

Amelia smiled and waved, and Adina got into a taxi to take her home.

CHAPTER 22

THE NEXT MONTH passed so quickly, and Adina had her lumpectomy along with the removal of five lymph nodes under her right arm. A week later when she went to see Dr. Aronow for her follow-up appointment, he happily gave her the good news. The pathology report on the removed tissue and lymph nodes, were now *cancer free!* Dr. Aronow was full of smiles and self-satisfaction for the successful fight he and Dr. Hoffman had waged against the malignant tumor that had invaded Adina's breast. Adina took in the news but was slow to react. The enemy, she thought was surely defeated, but only for the present time. Adina knew all too well, this was not a lifetime guarantee against the *cancer* returning at some point in the future. Because this would always be hanging over her like a cloud that was neither dark nor bright, but indecisive, it was difficult for her to fully rejoice in the news Dr. Aronow delivered.

The next step on her journey began a few weeks later after her incision was fully healed. Alex sent her to Dr. Lowell Moore, an oncology radiologist. All kinds of measurements were taken and her breast was marked in spots with ink so that the radiation technicians would be able to direct the treatment with necessary precision when her sessions began a week later.

Anna had called Adina the night before her first radiation treatment. Anna asked if she could accompany Adina, and suggested that they could go out for something to eat afterwards. Anna had spoken to Adina on the phone several times after Adina's lumpectomy, and was now more understanding of Adina's original decision not to tell her group of friends. They had smoothed out all the misunderstandings. Anna was leaving the following day for London, so she wanted this time with Adina. Adina accepted Anna's kind offer.

The next morning when they entered the radiation center, Adina was abruptly shaken as she observed the other patients in various seating areas waiting for their treatment. Some were in wheelchairs, others looked so pale with only a small amount of flesh covering their frail skeletal frames. Again, Adina was reminded of the revulsion that she always experienced in these waiting rooms. Those waiting rooms, with their newly upholstered seats cushioning patients whose facial expressions and posture reflected their collective fatigue and anxiety. Adina thought she had skillfully managed to camouflage any evidence of the disease in her own appearance, but maybe she was fooling herself. She thought that maybe she looked just as poorly as all these other haggard souls. It was always so challenging for her to remain hopeful when she observed how countless others had been ravaged by the management of their own encounter with *cancer.*

Adina and Anna sat in the waiting room chatting, until Adina's name was called. As the technician approached, Adina observed a small group of people in one corner of the waiting room. Then she heard the sound of a bell being rung. Adina looked at the technician with a questioning expression on her face, and then the technician explained to Adina that the patient standing with the small group had just completed his treatment. He was eagerly ringing the bell on the wall. It is meant to signify the end, the final end to his treatment. The end of treatment, seemed like such a far-off concept for Adina to contemplate. She was just starting her radiation that day, and needed to return every weekday for the next two months. It seemed unimaginable that a magical day would eventually arrive, and she would be done with all the nightmarish experiences that kept being thrown at her day in and day out. She put it out of her mind, and continued walking as she was escorted into a locker room.

There she was given a short medical gown and a key to a locker for all her clothes and personal belongings. After several minutes another woman, one with a Russian accent, appeared and guided Adina into the room where she would begin the next phase of her treatment, the radiation.

It was a large room with a giant machine and below the machine was a long narrow table. Another technician was already in the room waiting for Adina. They all introduced themselves and Natasha positioned Adina on the table, while Robbie worked at the nearby computer. Once Adina's arm and breast were positioned, the technicians left the room as Adina held still. A moment later the very loud sound of the machine came piercing through Adina's ears along with a flickering light on the wall indicating that radiation was being administered. It lasted only for a very short while, but in the stillness of the awfully dark room, so many thoughts flashed through Adina's mind.

Natasha reentered and helped Adina off the table. "All done," she announced and sent Adina back to the locker room. There she would apply some special cream to minimize any burns to her affected skin, and then she got dressed. Eventually this would all become very routine. Compared to the chemo, Adina would describe the radiation clearly as, *a walk in the park.*

Once dressed, Adina went into the waiting room where Anna was sitting reading a magazine. She said to Anna, "It was really easy. Should we just go to the restaurant downstairs?"

Anna shook her head in agreement, and then said, "Adina, you are so brave."

Adina responded, "What choice do I have? Thirty-four more sessions and I'll be completely finished with this evil *cancer.*"

They arrived at the building's cafeteria-styled restaurant and it was early enough for both to order a late breakfast. The waffles looked good to Adina and Anna had a bagel and some fresh fruit. They found a nice table by a glass wall looking out onto the space for outdoor dining. As Adina began sipping her tea, she asked Anna,

"How is Benjamin doing these days?"

That was all Adina had to say to illicit an outpouring of information from Anna. Benjamin was presently working on a Master's degree at Boston University on environmentally designed structures. He was dating a girl from the Boston area and they seemed fairly serious. Anna and Peter had visited them on various holidays throughout the year, as Benjamin never felt obligated to come home too often. But oddly enough, he did find his way to Lancaster once a month, to visit his grandfather and his grandmother, whose dementia did not keep her from recognizing her sweet grandson. Anna could not understand this, but it was more obvious to Adina why this occurred.

On the rare occasions when Anna brought Benjamin as a child to Lancaster, he had been charmed by their country-like home, that was so vastly different from the city apartment where he had been raised. His grandfather had always taken him into the barn-like structure where Anna's father had made his simple Shaker-styled furniture. Benjamin had been enamored by the abundance of tools, and became so curious about the purpose each one held.

When his grandmother, in her more lucid days, served him a slice of her signature apple raisin pie, Benjamin cleaned his plate, and always asked for a second helping which endeared him to his aging grandmother.

Anna learned that Benjamin was making monthly trips from Boston to Lancaster to spend time with both his grandparents, and she was quite taken aback. It was even more of a shock to Anna that this coming summer, Benjamin decided not to accompany his parents to London, and instead decided to spend the summer living at his grandparent's home to help care for his grandmother. Benjamin's girlfriend was also going to accompany Benjamin to Lancaster for the summer.

Anna said, "I have no idea why my son is doing this. We asked him to come to London for some part of his summer, but he has refused. This is so upsetting."

Adina responded, "Anna, you and Peter have raised a compassionate son. You should be happy he is a kind, young man and that he feels connected enough to your parents to offer his help to them. You always told me how much he loved

247

being in your dad's workshop, helping him make those dining tables and chests. He always seemed to have a fondness for your mother as well. This is a good thing, that he is close to them."

"I don't know about that," Anna proclaimed.

"Anna, let go of your angry feelings towards your parents. I know you've kept your past so private, as you have a right to, but let your son be with them, and give them what you apparently cannot at this time of their lives."

"It is easier for you to say that Adina. You had parents that were very different from mine."

"Well I suppose that's true. But we all have some kinds of challenges, and we can choose to always walk away or find a path that is emotionally favorable for all parties. Benjamin has chosen to find that path in Lancaster."

"Geez Adina, that chemo experience has made you a real philosopher."

"Well, sitting for hours in that infusion room did provide so much time to think about how I was going to handle my life from this point forward. We always, I've learned, have options."

Anna smiled, "Yes, I suppose that's true."

Adina remembered the day she first met Anna at the meeting for students traveling abroad. She did not know Anna so well then. Adina now realized that all these years later, Anna still had not revealed what happened between Anna and her parents, that caused Anna to devote her life to always running away, never able to allow herself a quiet contentment; a contentment that her son Benjamin seemed so easily to embrace.

After they enjoyed a second cup tea, Anna thought it was time for her to get back home. She still had a bit of packing to do for the flight to London the next day.

248

Adina thanked her for coming to her first day of radiation, and promised she would email Anna with updates on how she was feeling throughout the summer. What Adina also realized was that Anna had her secrets, her highly personal motivations, that steered her in the way she conducted herself with regard to her encounters with her parents. That was Anna's choice to be so unrevealing, and it was Adina's choice to accept Anna's shrouded behavior, and still safeguard their continuing friendship.

After they parted, Adina decided to walk a few blocks. She was feeling so much stronger and it felt good to be out in the fresh air. Suddenly she found herself in front of the bakery, and realized how long it had been since she stopped in for a treat for Mr. Brooks. And so, in she went and ordered two cheese Danishes to take back for him. Finally, the first feeling of normalcy in these past months where every movement, every gesture had the *cancer* as its focus. What a glorious feeling it was to do something completely unrelated to the journey she had been forced to travel.

When she arrived back at her building, Mr. Brooks was at the door. She handed him the small package from the bakery and said,

"I know it's been a while since I was able to bring you some treats for your afternoon tea, but today I managed."

He seemed delighted as he said, "Thank you Adina. I can tell you are looking more and more like yourself each day. In fact, you are looking wonderful."

"Oh Mr. Brooks, you always say the nicest things to me."

Beaming, with a broad smile, he tipped his hat, bowed and opened the door for Adina. These little encounters with Mr. Brooks always put Adina in such a good mood.

The following week Alice came into the city and to meet Adina for an early lunch after her treatment. Alice had come into the city to shop for some fresh linens to spruce up Jeremy's room. He would be returning from the rehab center the next day. Alice had hoped he would enroll in some classes to complete his degree. He was a few semesters shy of earning a Bachelor's Degree from Hofstra in graphic arts. Jeremy wanted to work for a while, but Daniel was anxious for him to return to school. Alice had said, "I just hope this time in the rehab center really helped him to kick his drug habit. I never understood how this happened. We gave him everything he ever wanted."

Adina said, "I hope he does okay this time. It's never easy recovering from any kind of addiction."

"I think Daniel didn't spend enough time with the children. He was always in the hospital or seeing patients in his office."

"Well Alice, you were always there for your kids. You made a lovely home for them."

"Adina, I'm beginning to think that wasn't enough. They needed more than a nice home. They needed me and Daniel to be together more than we were."

"I suppose you might be on to something there."

"Jeremy needed his father to be home more than Daniel chose to be. Things just didn't turn out the way I had envisioned they would."

"I suppose they seldom do. I hope Jeremy is better and continues to improve his situation. He's still going to continue counseling, right?"

"Yes, twice a week for a while."

"Alice, I hope when he comes home tomorrow, things will ease up and go smoothly, for all of you."

"Adina, I came here today to support you with your radiation treatments and we're only talking about my problems."

Alice then asked her what the treatment was like, and Adina tried to explain as best she could. Adina sensed that there were still some hurt feelings that she had not confided in this particular group of friends earlier about what had happened to her. Alice also mentioned that she had told Fiona about Adina's illness.

"Oh, thanks Alice. I'll write her a note and smooth things over. Has she made any decisions about school?"

"Yes, she has been accepted to Stanford University School of Medicine out in California."

"Oh, that's wonderful."

"Yes, I suppose it is good news. You know she won't come back east. Her relationship with Daniel has never been good since that incident."

Adina asked, "You mean the time Fiona and I saw him in the restaurant?"

"Yes. Ever since that time, her relationship with Daniel has been fractured."

"One day she will come back east. Daniel though, must be so proud of her."

"Yes, we both are. Now if only we can get Jeremy on the right track. Adina you do not know how hard it is to raise kids."

"Oh, I think I have a sense of that. Probably why I didn't have any."

They laughed for a brief moment and Adina went out on a limb and asked Alice if things were getting any better between her and Daniel. Alice revealed that they were living separate lives, but in the same house. Daniel was very dedicated to his career as a cardiologist, and Alice continued to be a cardiologist's wife. She told Adina she was happy enough, most of the time.

Adina felt so sad listening to Alice. She remembered that Daniel and Alice were once so much in love or so it seemed. Maybe in one's twenties, being so much in love wasn't real love. They hadn't yet been tested by life's fluctuating predicaments. Alice never took on anything other than raising kids, and making a home fit for magazine layouts. Even though, Adina thought, raising three children is certainly challenging and filled with a multitude of responsibilities, it didn't help Alice develop a unique personality, based on her inner wants and desires and interests. She was always the wife with the lovely home, and the room mother for her kids' classes. She did it all effortlessly, but never had something that was hers alone. Alice never returned to nursing, or expressed any interest in keeping current in the field. She defined herself only by Daniel's achievements, not hers.

Over coffee and dessert Alice asked, "Adina, isn't it amazing that we are all fifty already?"

"Yes, I had my doubts that I would make for a while, but here I am."

"You must be so excited that Tristan will be living in New York."

"Well, I think we've finally grown to care so much for each other."

Alice asked, "Will you two be living together?"

"It is likely that Tristan will take a studio apartment near the hospital. He will have odd hours many times, and needs to be close to his patients. But I think other times he will stay with me, especially on the weekends. I am trying to rearrange some furniture to make room for him and some of his things. It will be a big adjustment, for both of us, I suspect."

"Will you two ever marry?'

"Alice…not a big deal for either of us right now. I've learned to take things one day at a time. What is important is how we feel for each other today, and tomorrow will take care of itself. I just want to enjoy his company for a while. That's how it was when I traveled to Paris every summer. I hope that it continues. We come to each other because of a feeling we both have for each other, not because some document establishes how we should relate to one another."

Shaking her head, Alice said, "Adina, you never really wanted the house, the kids and all of that."

"No Alice. You did. Or, maybe, I did, but I didn't want it right away. I wanted to travel a bit, and then once I met Tristan things didn't fall into a neat little package. I always loved having my own place, but don't think it was easy. It's hard to be out there on your own, and be your only means of financial and emotional support. I've had to handle everything by myself, the little things like taking the trash to the incinerator all the time, and the big decisions as well, like planning for my retirement. No division of labor in my household. I had to do it all. But I do believe, the experience made me a very strong person. Strong enough to deal with all I've had to lately."

"Yes, I know you must have had a tough time all those months. It is interesting how we all turned out. We all have such different kinds of lives, considering we all came into this world at the same time."

"I know what you mean. I've often thought about that from time to time. It's one of the great mysteries of the universe I suppose."

Their conversation ended, they left the restaurant, and Alice hugged Adina and said, "I'm glad we met today."

253

"Me, too, Alice. Thanks for coming."

"Adina, please call if you ever need anything."

"I will. And Alice, you do the same."

By the end of June, Adina was in a routine. Every morning at around 9 a.m. Adina left her apartment building and hopped into a cab to take her to the Lauder Breast Center at Sloan Kettering on 66th Street. Her daily appointments were scheduled for 10 a.m. By 9:45 a.m. she was already changed into her gown and sitting in the locker room waiting to be called into the treatment room. Adina often sat there with two or three other patients, either waiting for their dose of radiation or just completing their appointment.

After the first week, another woman seemed to arrive at the same time, and was scheduled to receive her radiation right after Adina. Adina soon learned her name was Brenda, and she came every morning already looking exhausted. She was a middle-aged, African-America woman, who always wore a purple crocheted woolen hat covering her head and huge silver hoop earrings. Adina and Brenda would look at each other with a knowing expression, acknowledging the common affliction that brought them both to this locker room. After a few days of this destined meet-up, they began to exchange *cancer* stories in the allotted time they sat together waiting.

Brenda was a single mother of two boys and was maintaining her job as a paralegal at a law firm located three blocks from the radiation center. She had only received four rounds of chemotherapy, before having her lumpectomy and was now in radiation, much like Adina, for the long haul each day. Brenda spoke to Adina about her two sons, one in high school and the other in middle school. Adina couldn't begin to imagine having such responsibilities while undergoing all the treatment this disease required. Brenda did mention that her parents were picking up much of the slack at her home, and with the boys' activities, in an attempt to keep things as normal as possible on the home front. How Brenda managed to go to work every day was a mystery to Adina, who could not envision dealing with anything other than her own basic needs, during the time the chemo waged war on her body.

Another woman, Louisa, was also usually in the locker room getting ready to leave after Adina had arrived. Louisa was an older woman, probably near eighty, having radiation on a second affected breast. She had been through radiation five years prior and was now starting again on the other breast. Day after day these women greeted each other with warm sympathetic smiles. Louisa was always upbeat, and was trying to convince Adina and Brenda to attend a yoga class for *cancer* patients with her at the 92nd Street Y. She caught them again one morning.

"The class is free and there are a lot of nice women to meet."

Brenda easily bowed out, "I have to go to work right after my dose."

"What about you Adina?" Louisa said.

"Louisa, I am happy to just walk a few blocks after I leave here before hailing a cab. That's enough of a workout for me these days."

A moment later Natasha entered the locker room and called for Adina to follow her. She settled Adina on the table and Robbie positioned the machine right above her right breast. He adjusted her right arm and then they both left the room.

And then again, the sound of the machine blasted in Adina's ear. This time she closed her eyes preferring not to see the red flashing lights warning of radiation being administered at that very moment. A few minutes later, it was all over. Natasha came into the room and helped Adina to sit up and they wished each other a good day.

Back in the locker room Adina retrieved her clothes and went into the changing room to perform what was now a routine of applying the cream to her breast and upper arm and she would get dressed. This practice would continue every week day for the next several weeks. Every time Adina left the building she tried to walk farther and farther before succumbing to take a taxi home. All her doctors had cautioned her that her energy would be slow to return and not to expect so much of herself. Her breast surgeon had even told her that some patients take as much as eighteen months until they begin to feel like themselves.

Adina knew one thing for sure. She would never again feel exactly like she had before. This experience had altered the way she viewed the world and *her* world especially. For the first time Adina thought about the finiteness of life. She always thought there was so much time in front of her, but now she felt there were limits set upon her. Although her doctors were pleased with her progress, none of them offered any guarantees of a specific amount of time she would continue being *cancer* free. She did ascertain that the first two years of her recovery would determine whether she would have a reoccurrence of the *cancer*, although a new *cancer* could develop at any time. This information just proved to sharpen her resolve to celebrate each day that she was given as a gift to be prized, and never to see the mundane quality of any day as simply unvalued.

On one of her walks home she passed a Papyrus store. Looking in the window she saw several gift items and note pads and cards. Adina decided to stop in the shop and see their collection of note pads. She decided to order some powder blue pads of various sizes and have Tristan's name engraved in navy blue ink on each pad in bold block lettering. She thought that would make a nice little welcoming gift for when he arrived in August, to begin working at Sloan. While she was there she also bought a birthday card for her nephew Joshua, who was now doing graduate studies at Dartmouth, and a Father's Day card for her dad to include with the gift she had already bought for him. She was going to his home this Sunday with Emma and Nathan, and they were taking him for an afternoon outdoor concert at the Brooklyn Botanical Gardens, after they all enjoyed their usual Sunday brunch.

By the time Adina finally got home, she was tired and decided to just put her feet up and write an email to Tristan about her day.

CHAPTER 23

JULY FINALLY ARRIVED and brought much warmer temper-
atures. Adina's mornings were still fairly routine, as her appointments at the
radiation center would continue throughout the entire month. She would endure her treatments with ease until the end of the first week of August. During
the summer, Rhoda was free to meet Adina every Wednesday afternoon for an
early lunch after Adina's appointment at the radiation center. Rhoda had become such a good friend to Adina throughout all of Adina's struggles, despite
the fact she was ten years older than Adina. They had become much more than
congenial colleagues. Adina would not forget those Saturday mornings when
Adina was suffering from the chemo, and Rhoda prepared her special home-
made chicken soup with little pastas in the shape of Eiffel Towers floating in the
broth. It was such a kind gesture. To this day, Rhoda would not reveal to Adina
where she managed to find such adorable accompaniments for the delicious

soup. Rhoda had always been a master at procuring the most unusual delicacies to complement her homemade dishes. This summer she was taking a class in Spanish cuisine so that she could incorporate some of the recipes into the curriculum for her senior Spanish classes to enjoy. Rhoda always thought that to teach the language is to teach the culture, and a country's cuisine was certainly part of that culture.

Rhoda knew Adina's taste buds were still tolerating only mild foods, so she was amenable for them to meet for lunch at eateries with non-exotic menus along with their more discriminating specialties of the house. Adina was still gravitating towards mushy textured foods, and was happy to order a Belgian waffle with mint ice cream for lunch. This always paled by comparison to Rhoda's usual lunch orders of paella or barbequed ribs, and more often than not, a combination plate of sushi, always containing an eel cucumber roll. Fortunately, in New York City, it was easy to find restaurants that accommodated both their tongues.

Rhoda was developing a new persona since her divorce. She was now full of energy and was enjoying the summer away from the halls of Dalton. She had taken a bold move by cutting her hair into a very short style, and dyed it a flaming red which looked fabulous. It beautifully accented her large green eyes that before this transformation were hardly noticeable. Her Bohemian styled long skirts seemed somewhat shorter now, and her new summer sandals showed off her emerald green painted toenails. Rhoda was reborn into an artful, unique individual in this still unfolding twenty-first century.

When they met for lunch in mid-July, Rhoda always asked about Adina's treatments, and then always wanted to know about Tristan, and his upcoming appointment at Sloan Kettering. Rhoda recalled the first trip that she and

Adina had chaperoned together, when they took several students to Paris, when Rhoda first met Tristan. She told Adina that she knew just how *smitten* Adina was with him, even back then. That was the word she always used to describe Adina's feelings for Tristan.

She asked Adina, "I often wondered why you two never really got together for more than just the summers. But I suppose leaving your family and New York, was too far a journey for you to take. I can understand, I suppose. After all, it took me over twenty-five years to realize my marriage was not filling me with gladness. I kept things status quo because of my daughters."

Adina said, "And that was a righteous decision on your part Rhoda. I think once there are children in the mix, then their stability is more important while they are growing up. That's a commitment one is bound to, once you make the decision to bring a child into the world."

"Yes, I agree. I have no regrets. We did make a nice home for our girls and my husband was good to them, and he was good to me as well. But life is a long journey, and what worked at twenty doesn't always fit at fifty or even sixty."

Adina said, "We have to navigate through the many obstacles life presents us with from time to time. And for the most part we do it alone. I've learned a lot about what I'm capable of these past few months. I was fortunate to have my dad and Emma every step of the way, and Tristan was at a distance, but close in my thoughts, always. It will be another sort of adventure having him so close, and I'm sure it will be an adjustment."

Rhoda smiled and placed her hand on Adina's and said, "It will be a sweet adjustment for you. Open yourself to the joy he can bring you. You've earned your time in the sun."

"I suppose I have. Finally, I am ready for what may come. I've learned how precious time is, and I don't want to squander any more days. I'm removing all obstacles now whenever they appear, at least the ones I can control."

"I am happy for you my friend, and am so looking forward to you returning to school in September. You are planning to do that, right?"

"Yes. That's the plan. And, Rhoda, I have forgotten to tell you that last week I started to notice some fuzz on my scalp. My hair is starting to come back. Maybe by September I can sport a new short hairdo, much like yours."

"Oh Adina, that is such good news. I can't imagine how awful it was to lose your beautiful hair."

"Well to tell you the truth, once I learned I had *cancer*, my only focus was how to survive, and if it meant losing my hair for a while, so be it. I think when we have to face life or death decisions, we begin to prioritize what is truly important and what is not. Maybe next month I'll visit my hairdresser, Kaleb, and see what he thinks. I've been told it will come in with a different texture, and maybe the color might also be different."

Rhoda waved her hand in the air and said, "Small potatoes compared to what you've already handled."

They both got up with the intention of taking a short walk before parting for the day. Just then, Adina's phone rang, and she saw it was Amelia calling. She took the call, and Amelia was sounding frantic. She had some sad news to deliver. Amelia told Adina that Jeremy was found dead of an overdose in the car he was driving to his new part-time job.

"Amelia, this is so terrible. I'm shocked! He was only out of rehab for a week or two. What can I do?"

Amelia explained that Alice had called her a few minutes before, quite hysterical. Apparently, Alice had received a visit from the local police as her name was on the vehicle registration in the glove compartment. They tried to contact Daniel but he was in surgery. Alice had called Amelia right away in a panic. Amelia and Vinnie were driving over to Alice's house to be with her at least until Daniel arrived home.

"Sit tight Adina, I'll call you later after I know what is happening. Alice's mother is already there with Alice, and Liam should be home soon from his summer camp counseling job. I promise to call you later."

Adina sat back down, and so did Rhoda. Adina then explained to Rhoda all that Amelia had just told her. Rhoda said, "I am so sorry to hear this news. This is about your friend Alice, the one you've always said worked so hard to have a well-planned life. And now this!"

Adina answered, "Yes. She always had a vision of how she wanted her life to unfold from the time we were young. This will tear her apart. And poor Jeremy. How could this have possibly happened?"

"Well we all have visions, but we really don't have the power to orchestrate our future. Life gets in the way, no matter how well we plan. We cannot be with our children all the time. We can only hope they do the right thing when we're not around."

"Rhoda, I cannot imagine what it will be like for them, Alice and Daniel, to confront this. It is so sad."

"You've always said Alice was so intent on getting what she always wanted. Maybe Jeremy wanted or needed other things. Yes Adina, it is a very sad situation."

"But Alice worked very hard to construct this picture-perfect life out on Long Island."

"That's the ultimate fairytale. The best we can do is work with what's in front of us. Look at you Adina. You never planned to get *cancer*, but you took hold of the situation and you fought your way through, and pretty courageously I might add. All any of us can do is make the best of what is thrown our way."

Adina looked at Rhoda and said, "Alice will be devastated. Daniel too. What will this do to their marriage?"

"From what you've told me all these years, their marriage was not on such good footing anyway."

A few moments later Adina's phone rang again. This time the call was from Fiona. She was crying and Adina could barely understand what she was saying.

"Fiona, speak more slowly so I can understand you."

"I am flying into New York, leaving California late tonight, but I don't want to go home. Can I stay with you tomorrow night?"

"You want to stay with me? But Fiona, your parents need you home now."

"Please Adina, I can't face them yet."

"But your mother is already devastated."

Fiona was pleading, "Let me stay with you first."

"Okay, okay. Should I meet you at the airport?"

"No. I'll take a taxi to your place. I should arrive around two in the afternoon, your time."

"Will you tell your parents you are staying with me?"

"I'll call them from your place."

Adina rehashed the conversation with Rhoda, and eventually they left the restaurant. Adina stopped at a deli to buy some food for the next day. Amelia called Adina later that night, and filled her in on all that had transpired at Alice's house. She told Adina of the despair both Alice and Daniel were feeling. She and Vinnie left shortly after Alice's priest arrived to speak with them. Adina informed Amelia about Fiona's plans, which they both agreed were not the best decision on Fiona's part. Adina assured Amelia that she would talk to her, and make sure by Friday she left to go home to her family.

Fiona arrived late in the afternoon on Thursday. Adina had prepared some lunch thinking that Fiona might have a taste for, typical New York deli food. They sat at the dining room table, and Fiona asked all about Adina's treatments. She chose to talk about anything, except her family, and Adina humored her for a while. Finally, Adina suggested that she call her parents to let them know she was already in New York. Fiona agreed, but was firm about not traveling to their home just yet.

"Fiona, I spoke to your mother yesterday, and she is in a bad way. Your father too, as well as Liam. I'll give you some privacy to speak with you mother."

Adina left her apartment and told Fiona she was going to get her mail in the lobby, leaving Fiona alone to make the call that would put her in touch with her parents. Adina lingered in the lobby for a while, and returned to her apartment where she found Fiona still on the phone with Alice. Fiona then handed Adina the phone. Adina immediately asked Alice how she was coping, and Alice only requested that Adina would make sure that Fiona come to Long Island the very next day.

Adina said, "I'll do the best I can. She can stay here tonight and I will see you on Saturday at the church for the service. I'll be coming with Amelia and Vinnie."

Alice, whose voice was barely audible said, "Please come early so I can talk with you and Amelia before everyone else arrives."

Adina said, "Of course, Alice. We'll be there for you. Is there anything else you need?"

Alice answered, "Just my daughter."

The rest of the day Fiona told Adina about her life in California, and the work she had done at the clinic. She was looking forward to attending medical school at Stanford. Adina took a leap and mentioned that there were good schools in New York, and considering all her family will be dealing with in the aftermath of Jeremy's death, maybe she should consider coming back home.

With an angry tone, Fiona asked, "How could you possibly think I would want to do that?"

"Because you're old enough to consider what your parents need instead of only what you need. Don't you think they've been punished enough? I won't mention this to you again, but think about how fractured your family is now. And think about Liam. He needs his big sister, and your mom and dad need their daughter, now more than ever. I just promised your mother that you would come home tomorrow. It's what you need to do."

Fiona sat quietly as Adina went into the kitchen and put the left-over food away. She then brought two glasses of iced mint tea and set them down on the coffee table. Adina then suggested they look at some movies, something they had always done when Fiona was a teenager, and spent a weekend with Adina. There was always a collection of DVDs to choose from and they decided on *Sleepless in Seattle*, a favorite of Fiona's. They both changed into their nightgowns, and Adina laid out fresh towels and linens on the couch where Fiona would sleep. When the movie ended, Fiona was ready to go to bed. Adina put the lights out in the apartment and retreated to her bedroom with her laptop in hand. She wrote an email to Tristan describing all that had transpired in the past twenty-four hours. She then picked up a book to read for a while, and about fifteen minutes later Tristan's email response arrived. He was so sorry not to be there in New York to attend the service for Jeremy. He also mentioned that he would phone Daniel and Alice, to personally offer his condolences. Adina wrote back one more time before she resumed reading her book, and eventually fell asleep.

Adina awoke the next morning to the sound of Fiona showering. She got out of bed and made a pot of coffee, and put a few bagels on a platter with tubs of butter and cream cheese. When Fiona came into the dining room she was already dressed.

She said to Adina, "I know I need to go home now. Thank you for letting me stay the night."

Adina smiled and said, "Fiona, you are always welcome here, but today you need to be with your family."

Fiona had a cup of coffee and half a bagel, and then said, "I didn't speak much to Jeremy when he was in the rehab place. I should have called him more often. I knew he was getting high a lot before my parents knew. I should have told them."

Adina put her arm around Fiona's shoulder and said, "Apparently, Jeremy was very troubled. You were not his savior. Drug addiction is a complicated disease. Ultimately only he could save himself. You cannot blame yourself for anything you saw or didn't see. It is a tragedy for your family. The only thing you can do now is help make things better for your family from now on. It's important that you all be together, and close at hand."

"I don't know if I can do that."

"Think about coming back east for school. It would mean so much to your parents, both of them. Life is very fragile Fiona, and time is really not unlimited."

"I promise I will think about it."

Fiona picked up her suitcase and started walking towards the door. Adina asked if she needed some cash for the taxi, but Fiona assured her that she was fine. She hugged Adina, and then Adina told her she was very proud of her, and that she would see her at the service on Saturday.

The next day Adina awakened very early Saturday morning and was dressed and out the door before eight o'clock, in a cab in route to Amelia's home in Brooklyn. As soon as Adina arrived, they got into the car, and Vinnie drove them out to St. Joseph's Roman Catholic Church, not far from Alice and Daniel's home. They arrived around nine-thirty to find Alice, Daniel, Fiona, Liam and Alice's mom already seated in the first pew, facing the open casket where Jeremy's body was on view. The church was mostly dark except for three beams of sunlight creating three stripes of bright light across the pews on the right side.

As Amelia and Adina walked down the long center aisle towards the family, only the sound of their heels against the cold marble floor was heard. Daniel stood first, then Alice. Amelia and Adina where holding each other's hand as they made their way towards Alice. Vinnie walked a few paces behind them. Alice's eyes were raw and red from all the tears already shed. Amelia and Adina embraced Alice in silence, as more tears fell from all of their eyes. Together they walked over to see Jeremy. The three of them stood there without exchanging any words. There was nothing to say to ease the horrific pain they knew Alice was experiencing. Vinnie embraced Daniel and offered his condolences. Adina stood there and recalled the time Alice first told her friends that she was pregnant with Jeremy. It was during one of their birthday lunches. She was bursting at the seams to be fulfilling her dream of having her second child.

Next to Jeremy's coffin was a large arrangement of white roses atop a beautifully sculpted pedestal structure. On top of the elegant pedestal was a bronze vase containing three dozen white roses in full bloom. It stood over five feet tall. As we neared the casket, the aroma of the flowers brought to mind a paradise of some unknown locale. Amelia remarked at the beauty of the unusually tall stand holding the vase of flowers. Alice then told them that the stand, and the flowers were provided by Astrid and Henrik, as a gift to the church in Jeremy's memory. She pointed to a small engraved oval plaque located on the lower half of stand that simply stated *In Memory of Jeremy Luke McDermott.*

Alice said, "It's a lovely gesture. It will be in the church always. We've been told that for the next year, roses will be delivered once a week for our weekend masses."

Amelia looked at Adina and commented on Astrid's kind generosity and exquisite taste. Adina simply shook her head and said, "Yes, that's Astrid's style."

Alice requested that they sit directly behind her during the service, and so they took those seats. Adina noticed that Fiona kept an arm around Liam the entire time. Alice's mother embraced both Amelia and Adina. She was understandably inconsolable.

Adina and Amelia watched as the many echoing footsteps of friends and relatives began filing into the church. Standing together, Alice and Daniel greeted them with stoic expressions of gratitude for attending. Amelia and Alice observed the procession of all these faces, some familiar from Alice's many social events. When they spotted Benjamin and his girlfriend, they were both surprised, and warmly touched by his presence, as was Alice. He came because Anna was still in London and he wanted to represent his mother, in her absence. Benjamin had driven all the way from Lancaster, Pennsylvania. Later Amelia and Adina would comment on the irony of how Anna raised such a sensitive son, given her own ever constant aloofness on so many matters.

The mass ended in what seemed like a blink of an eye. The cemetery was not far, and the heart-wrenching graveside service was almost unbearable for Alice and Daniel. But there was an observable kindness that passed between them, which was encouraging to witness. A late luncheon was served at their County Club's dining room for over one hundred guests.

When it was time to say their good-byes, Alice promised to call when she was ready to meet in the city or have them visit her at her home. In the car Amelia and Adina reminisced about Alice's original plan for a well-ordered life, and how that had taken such a turn over the years. They wondered whether Alice's and Daniel's already shaky marriage would survive such a tragedy. Vinnie kept quiet and let Amelia and Adina exchange their thoughts the entire trip back. The two friends were so involved in their conversation, they hadn't noticed that Vinnie had gone out of his way. He drove straight back into Manhattan to Adina's apartment, before they returned to their home in Brooklyn. It had been a long day, and Adina was visibly so physically fatigued and emotionally wrecked, as well. She thanked Vinnie for the ride, hugged Amelia, as they both promised to call each other in a few days. Vinnie turned around to face Adina in the back seat, and he said, "Now you get some rest." Adina was so moved over Vinnie's concern for her. All she could do was reach over and place her hand on his cheek and thanked him again.

Once in her apartment, Adina immediately went into her bedroom and removed all her clothes, and took a quick shower. She had to wash away the events of the day, including the image of sweet Jeremy lying in his coffin wearing his favorite New York Mets Jersey. Adina slipped into one of her favorite pink nightgowns, and then her phone rang. Tristan was calling to talk to her about the sorrowful time she had just endured. His calming voice seemed to eradicate so much of the gloominess that had visited upon her throughout the entire day.

CHAPTER 24

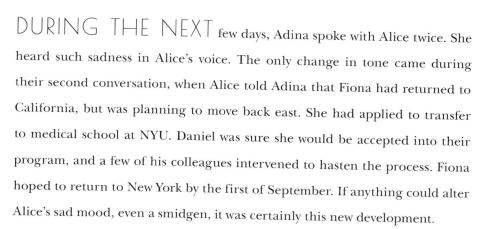

DURING THE NEXT few days, Adina spoke with Alice twice. She heard such sadness in Alice's voice. The only change in tone came during their second conversation, when Alice told Adina that Fiona had returned to California, but was planning to move back east. She had applied to transfer to medical school at NYU. Daniel was sure she would be accepted into their program, and a few of his colleagues intervened to hasten the process. Fiona hoped to return to New York by the first of September. If anything could alter Alice's sad mood, even a smidgen, it was certainly this new development.

On the phone Alice said, "I know you had a hand in persuading Fiona to do this, and I am so grateful that you did. Even Liam decided to change his plans, and he will hopefully attend Columbia this fall instead of going out of town."

Adina said, "I'm glad Fiona made this decision. I know it will help to have her closer to you all."

"It will be good having my daughter back. Getting her eventually settled in the city, while she goes to school there will be a welcomed distraction from the horror of the past two weeks."

They ended their conversation, and Adina was relieved about the news of Fiona's return to the nest.

Finally, the first of August arrived. The past several months had provided Adina with a new filter for experiencing her life's most significant defining moments. Although still restrained, Adina was hopeful that this month might lead to pleasanter times. With only a week of radiation left, Adina could turn her attention to thoughts of Tristan's arrival mid-month, and readying herself to return to Dalton this fall, to the normalcy of her world teaching French again. In the past nine months, since her nightmarish saga had taken over, she had seldom spoken a word of the language, only a sentence or two during the occasional phone conversation with Tristan. There was much for her to study and review.

On the first day of August, Adina left her radiation appointment and re-visited Jessica Michael's salon on Madison Avenue. Jessica was welcoming, and happy to see Adina. Adina decided to order another wig for when she would return to school a month later. Although her hair had begun to show signs of regrowth, it was still too short for Adina to consider going wigless. This time she wanted a wig with a short hairstyle, so the eventual transition when she discarded the wig would almost be unnoticeable.

Jessica helped Adina find an appropriate style, and placed the order for a wig matching Adina's original hair color. Jessica thought she could have it sent directly to Adina's home by the end of the week. When Adina left the salon, her spirit was invigorated. Cautiously, as she now looked at most defining moments, better times were returning. Radiation would conclude on Friday, August 6th. Tristan was due to arrive on Tuesday, August 10th to get ready to begin his work at Sloan on the fifteenth.

When Adina arrived home, she was greeted by Mr. Brooks who told her she had received a delivery in an oversized carton.

"Oh, that must be the desk I ordered for Tristan."

Mr. Brooks said, "I'll have Lou from maintenance deliver it to your apartment and unpack it for you."

"Thanks, that would be wonderful."

About twenty minutes later, Lou came to her door wheeling in the oversized box. He unpacked the desk, and removed all the excess wrap that protected the desk's teak wood finish. Adina was thrilled that it fit perfectly in the small alcove den next to the desk Adina had for herself. Lou removed the carton and its contents including yards of bubble wrap, and was happy to do this for Adina, who always tipped him generously for his services, and for doing it so quickly.

Immediately, Adina made a list of supplies she would purchase to place in the desk drawers, and maybe something special for the top surface. That would take some thought. At last her mind wandered imagining what life with Tristan would be like, instead of her daily grind of fighting the *cancer* and all its baggage. She felt so good that she called Emma and invited her and Nathan to come for dinner that evening. She had all the fixings for a nice salad and as a main course her very popular version of chicken piccata served over capellini, in a white wine lemon sauce. Emma accepted the invitation and offered to bring dessert.

They arrived shortly after six. Emma admired the new desk, and Nathan suggested a couple of shelves on the side wall might be a good idea. Adina agreed, and Nathan offered to purchase two shelves and install them that weekend. He asked what color wood finish she would prefer, and once Adina and Emma consulted on that issue, the deal was sealed, and they sat down for dinner.

Adina announced, "It's the first time I've cooked in months."

Nathan, with his mouth half full said, "You haven't lost your touch. This is delicious."

Adina smiled, and Emma sat quietly thrilled to observe her sister taking these small steps back to a happier time in her life.

Emma said, "I know you just have a few more days left of radiation. Daddy and I want to come with you on your last day, and take you out for lunch afterwards to celebrate."

Adina responded, "Daddy is a real trooper. Sure, that would be nice. Hard to imagine this is finally coming to an end, although it will never be over, but at least it will be a nice change for a while."

Emma added, "Don't think about what could happen, just enjoy what you have now. You're going to be just fine."

"I hope so. I surely don't want to put you and daddy through any more of this."

Nathan said, "That's right Adina. Your sister has been a nervous wreck for months. It's time for a welcomed change...for all of us."

They laughed and Adina went into the kitchen to serve some coffee with the dessert. Emma brought in the box from her neighborhood's bakery, and set it on the table and then removed it from its box. It was a chocolate mocha mousse cake, one of Adina's favorites. Along with the chocolate fondant on top of the cake, there was some pink icing with the words *Almost There*. Adina let out a hearty laugh as Emma set the cake on the table. It had been a long time since Adina laughed so spontaneously. Emma looked on very satisfied with the pleasure she had just brought to her sister. Nathan dove right in and cut himself a good-sized slab, as Adina and Emma looked on and shared a very loving moment.

The sixth of August arrived, and there was not a cloud in the sky which Adina took as a good sign. She left earlier than usual so that she could make a stop at a bakery. Adina wanted to bring a tray of assorted mini pastries for the staff at the radiation center, on this last and final day of treatment. The taxi waited, and within a few short minutes she was at the Breast Care Center. In the lobby, Emma and her dad were already awaiting her arrival. Adina was filled with a variety of emotions that this last day of treatment generated.

They all took seats in the waiting room, and Adina handed the receptionist the tray of pastries with a card she had written earlier that morning. The receptionist smiled and thanked Adina for being so thoughtful. One of the nurses then appeared and called to Adina to enter the area where Adina would have her vitals checked. This always occurred at least once a week throughout her time there. Adina was then escorted into the locker room. The nurse informed Adina, that Dr. Moore would see her in the examining room after she received the radiation, and was dressed.

Natasha came into the locker room shortly after, and they walked into that all too familiar room. Once she was positioned on the table, Natasha and Robbie exited the room. When the jarring sounds of the machine finally ended, Adina became very teary-eyed for the first time. She felt an enormous release of air escape from her lungs. Still alone for those few seconds, she felt oddly defenseless. Up to this point, she was actively fighting the *cancer*. Now she would be turned away, without any ammunition to assist her with the constant assault that the months of treatment had unleashed daily.

Natasha re-entered and helped to lift her off the table, and gave her a tight hug and said, "It's over. It's all over now."

Adina composed herself and thanked Natasha. She went back into the locker room, changed, and went to the examining room to see Dr. Moore, who entered the room in a matter of minutes. He was all smiles and carrying his laptop, as always, to review reports about her progress.

"Well Adina, congratulations. You've done your 35 sessions. How do you feel?"

"Hard to say. Hard to believe it's over."

"I spoke with Dr. Hoffman earlier this morning, and we are both so pleased with your progress. Now we will both follow you every six months or so. I know you are still experiencing fatigue, and that will slowly fade away in the months to come. Every patient is different. You've done everything right, took all the treatments we recommended, and never complained. I will give you written orders to have a mammogram in six months, and then I'll see you afterwards. You may continue to feel some tenderness in your breast or twinges, but that is to be expected after such a dose of radiation as you received. Do you have any questions?"

"No. Thank you for taking care of me Dr. Moore."

"Well then, it's time for you to ring the bell. Come, it's in the waiting room. I've already spoken to your father and sister."

The *ringing of the bell*, the symbolic gesture that a cancer patient performs when one has completed treatment, usually performed in the presence of a patient's healthcare team to signify that an individual is now *cancer free*. Adina recalled seeing that done on her first day at the radiation center, and it seemed like a miracle that she was at that point, in this long journey she had been forced to experience.

When Adina entered the waiting room, she was surprised to see not only her father and Emma, but also sitting next to them was Amelia, Alice and Rhoda. And just at that moment, Alex appeared in the waiting room as well. Dr. Moore ushered them all over to the golden bell hanging on one of the walls next the exit door of the center as Natasha and Robbie joined them. Alongside the bell were the words to the poem, *Ringing Out*, written by Irve LeMoyne that Adina was to recite, and then ring the bell three times for good luck.

Surrounded by her family, friends, technicians and doctors, Adina, with a tear in her eye, recited the words,

Ring this bell
Three times well
It's toll to clearly say.

My treatment is done
This course is rung
And I am on my way.

279

Adina then rang the bell three times. Lots of tears, this time tears of joy and relief, were shared. Many hugs exchanged all around. Adina thanked Dr. Moore again and he wished her well till her next appointment. Then Adina looked at Alex and said, "Dr. Hoffman, thank you for all you did for me."

Alex smiled, and from his pocket pulled out a tiny little package wrapped in a tiny pink satin bag.

"This is for you Adina, to remind you of our special connection. We were meant to cross paths, and know each other for all of our lives. Open it now if you like."

Inside was a beaded baby bracelet large enough to fit an adult. Adina's name was spelled out on the white beads, while pink and baby blue beads, representing them both, adorned the rest of the bracelet. It was a beautiful gift, and Adina put it on her wrist immediately as the others all watched. Alex admitted that it was his mother's idea, and his wife agreed that it was the perfect gift. His mother had reminded him that they had really met when their tiny cribs were side by side in the hospital's nursery, so very long ago.

Finally, Adina's father suggested they go to the restaurant. Emma, her dad, Alice, Amelia and Rhoda all sauntered over to an Italian restaurant on York Avenue, not too far from the center. As they were all enjoying their meal, Adina couldn't help but notice her father's steadfast smile as everyone chatted away. At one point, Adina stood up from her seat at the table, and walked behind his chair. She bent down, placing her hands on his shoulders, and whispered in his left ear, "Thank you for seeing me through this." All he could do was move his right hand towards his left shoulder, as he gently squeezed her left hand. He kept it there for a few seconds. It was a moment that would be carved in Adina's memory forever.

Amelia presented Adina with a small gift bag, containing a lovely message from her group of friends, along with a gift certificate for a day at The Red Door Spa on Fifth Avenue. Toasts were made by all, for better days ahead.

Rhoda gave the funniest toast when she said, "Here's to no more chicken soup for Adina. Time to gorge on some hot wings once again!"

The afternoon slipped by, and finally it was time for everyone to leave. Lots of hugs and kisses were exchanged, and they finally exited the restaurant. Emma and Adina saw to it that their dad took a cab back to Brooklyn, and Amelia went with him sharing the ride. Alice returned to the station to take the train back home, and Rhoda headed up the street to check out some of the shops. Emma and Adina got into a taxi that would drop Adina off first.

Before Adina exited the cab, she took Emma's hand and brought it to her cheek and said, "Thank you so much for being with me every step of the way. I could not have done any of it without you."

Emma smiled as she wiped a tear from Adina's face and said, "Go live your life Adina. You have much to look forward to. I'm in awe of the strength you've shown. Now use that strength to lead you to what your heart murmurs."

It was now just past three o'clock in the afternoon when Adina entered her building. Mr. Brooks gave her a friendly hug and congratulated her on the end of her treatment. From behind his reception desk he retrieved a small bouquet of lovely apricot colored roses wrapped with yellow ribbon, and gave it to Adina.

She said, "Thank you so much. You were always so kind to me, especially whenever I needed your help carrying things and all, these past few months."

"It was my honor to be of service to you, Adina."

Adina kissed him on his cheek, and then took a whiff of the scent of the beautiful bouquet he had just given her, and slowly walked to the elevator.

When Adina unlocked the door, she received the best surprise of the day. Tristan was sitting on her couch. She dropped the bouquet onto the floor and ran to him.

"My flight was delayed. I had wanted to surprise you at the radiation center. I just arrived here about an hour ago."

"Oh Tristan. I am so happy to see you. This is the best surprise of the day, of the year…"

CHAPTER 25

IT WAS MAGICAL. That was how Adina would describe the week that she and Tristan spent together before he began his work at Sloan-Kettering in the Pediatric Day Hospital. There was a warm familiarity having been distant lovers for so many years, at least two decades. And yet there was a sparkle, a new excitement that both found alluring, and that allowed them to easily adjust to living together once more. The studio apartment that Tristan had considered was unavailable, which necessitated both of them to develop a shared lifestyle in Adina's apartment.

It would have probably been more challenging for Adina to adjust to relinquishing her private living space under other circumstances, but what she had endured the past year, steered her in the direction of focusing more on what this new relationship with Tristan would add to her life, rather than what she was giving up.

In bed at night they made slow, sweet love to each other, but in contrast, on some early mornings they simply had sex; a quick, delicious, satisfying start to their day. They often laughed together observing that they could still enjoy this electrifying pleasure in their fifties, as if they were two hungry teenagers. Adina was sure it was born from their constant separations over the years, and they were making up for lost times. Tristan was hesitant to try to explain it, and just continued to enjoy their new partnering.

By late September, once Adina had returned to school, and Tristan with a full patient load of young children, there were many hours they rarely saw or spoke to each other, only recoupling in bed. Sometimes on weeknights when they reconnected, one of them occasionally fell asleep while the other was re-calling the day's events. Tristan's days at the hospital were long, and Adina was still weary from the after effects of her treatment.

Adina was thrilled to be back teaching despite the fatigue that still haunt-ed her every day. By two o'clock in the afternoon she struggled to move about the campus. Once she arrived home, she was spent, and often napped for an hour or two before thinking about a dinner menu. Some nights they were sim-ply content with a tray of cheeses and some fresh fruit, which Adina kept sup-plied all week long. Adina always brought home a fresh baguette every day for them to enjoy as well.

On the weekends they ate well, always trying a new restaurant on Saturday night. On Sunday mornings they often found themselves traveling to Adina's father's home, where Emma and Nathan would also be present, while David Saville was in his glory enjoying their time-honored brunch together.

Once back home, Adina and Tristan would retreat to their corners, Tristan at his desk reviewing his case load, and Adina on the couch reviewing stu-dents' papers. Sometimes for hours they didn't utter a word to each other until the light of day diminished with the official arrival of Sunday evening. Adina would usually order some Chinese food. Tristan had become a fan of the spare ribs from Han Dynasty, a restaurant on the East Side, that would willingly deliver their food in no more than half an hour. Adina loved their vegetable dumplings, and together they both managed to devour a large order of fried rice. It was a delightful way to wind down their weekend.

Most of the time Adina was so content that she began to worry that her good fortune would take a turn. She enjoyed their strolls in Central Park amidst the backdrop of autumn's vibrant landscape. It was during those walks that Tristan would often speak about his father, and the weight of the loss that Tristan sorrowfully experienced. Adina though, was a good listener. And Tristan knew he could easily unload his frustrations, and defeats, when one of his young patients did not respond well to certain therapies. Adina would be a sympathetic audience of one, to Tristan's unburdening banter. She revered his devotion to his patients, and to his research. Some days when he seemed a bit down, she would then insist they visit the zoo, where they would be charmed by Adina's favorite distraction, the seals. That always transformed Tristan's sullen mood, making him a light-hearted, amusing cohort as they both imitated the barking sounds from these entertaining animals.

But once December neared, Adina started to panic during much of the month, in anticipation of the mammogram that was scheduled at the end of

December. She knew her life could change in a moment. Perhaps that was what allowed her to feel joy so intensely now. Tristan had told her that he was entirely satisfied with his position at Sloan, despite the frustration he and his team experienced, when they lost a young patient. These were difficult moments for Tristan, whose relationship to the children was usually so gratifying, when he was able to rid them of their devasting symptoms and the progression of their diseases. As an experienced practitioner, he instinctively recognized the anxiety Adina was having, in anticipation of her upcoming test. With his calming words, and confident demeanor, he tried to be as supportive as possible. But Adina continued to feel worried, despite Tristan's reassuring stance.

Adina's first mammogram was clear. She was told the results immediately after the radiologist reviewed the images. The relief she felt was indescribable. Even before shedding that all too familiar half gown, she called Emma with the good news and then her dad. Tristan had cleared his schedule for an hour while Adina was having the mammogram, and he was lingering in the waiting room. When she emerged with a broad smile, he knew the results were good. He embraced her and lovingly kissed her forehead. He returned to work, and Adina went home, since this appointment had been scheduled during her winter break.

Energized by the results, on her way home, she stopped at the store and bought the ingredients to prepare a nice salad and some French onion soup. She had perfected the art of preparing a sizzling savory soup that Tristan loved. This seemed like the perfect day for them to enjoy such a meal that evening. Although Adina so enjoyed this new stage of her life, she continued to worry that it would disappear at any given moment. This appreciation for the simple joys she found in every passing day, was key to her complete happiness, and it provided a means by which she battled against the fretfulness of any reoccurrence. She often laughed to herself that she could experience such bliss at this stage of her life, as she entered her fifties.

While enjoying the dinner that Adina had prepared, Tristan suggested that they plan a trip to Paris during Adina's spring break. Adina was immediately taken with the idea. They could stay with Tristan's mother, and see the entire family. This was certainly something to look forward to in the months ahead.

That night after dinner, Adina sat down to write an email to Astrid about the good results she had received that day. As usual, fifteen minutes later the phone rang and Astrid was calling.

She said, "Adina, this is such good news. I am so happy for you."

"Thank you, Astrid. I am so relieved."

"I can imagine. By the way, Henrik has some business in New York so I'll be flying in with him."

"That's great. When will you be here?"

"Towards the end of January, just for a few days. I'll send you our itinerary. We will definitely get together. Maybe with the others too."

"Oh Astrid. I will look forward to seeing you. It's been such a long while."

"Yes, too long."

"Okay see you soon." said Adina and on that good note they said their good-byes.

Adina called Amelia, Alice, Anna and Rhoda later that evening with her good news. By the time the calls were over, Tristan asked if she was ready to turn in for the night.

Adina responded, "I just want to do one more thing."

Tristan watched as she took the three wigs, the long haired one, the hat and the newer shorter style from her dressing table, and placed all three in a large plastic storage box. She then placed the box in the back of their closet.

She turned to Tristan and said, "Tomorrow I have an appointment to see Kaleb, my hairdresser. He will give me back my original color and trim my own hair into a style I like, and from this day forward, no more wigs."

Tristan smiled and said, '*oh ma cherie amour, tu es toujours si belle.*'

She glanced back at the antique table whose surface seemed so empty now with all the Styrofoam heads gone. She then went into the living room and lifted the tall pink and magenta orchid plant that sat on the coffee table. She then placed it on her antique dressing table. Adina took a few steps back and then said, "Now that looks better." She then climbed into bed and into Tristan's waiting arms.

Adina had certainly appreciated the words Tristan had uttered. But she knew any woman is beautiful when she feels loved and desired. Such a woman can easily disarm her lover with a simple glance, or by the way she angles her head when looking at him and exposing her own desire. This was a powerful weapon, this feeling of being loved. Their former intermittent relationship only encouraged his desire for her. They were always wanting more, more time to fulfill each other's longings. Their time apart only served to stir up the passion, so that by the time they reconnected, the feelings of love and even lust, were so overwhelming they couldn't be anything but depositories for each of their most basic desires.

In the back of Adina's mind, she was unsure whether she wanted to trade those urgent and unrelenting passionate connections, that might become tarnished by a daily living arrangement, that might only provide comfort and security. Was Adina at a point in her life where she was willing to barter her exhilarating infatuation with the more accustomed routine of days on end? This question held her mind's attention, and added to her mental list of worries and fears, she now confronted in the long quiet of the nights, when sleep would not arrive.

Despite all Adina's worries and fears, she managed to live each day with such joyfulness. By the end of January, Astrid and Henrik arrived in New York. They stayed at the Ritz Carlton at Central Park. Henrik spent the daytime with the Consulate General of Sweden, and Astrid and Adina met, as soon as Adina was out of school. In the late afternoon they watched the skaters at the park as the sun disappeared on this particular chilly day. Sipping some hot chocolate, Adina told Astrid about all that had occurred with her health issues, as well as the horrible time when Jeremy died.

Astrid said, "If it wasn't for Amelia's messages every week, I would have gone crazy worrying about you. I wasn't sure you were being so candid about what happening to you in your emails."

"I understand Astrid, and I'm glad I have friends that were so concerned about me."

"And Alice. How dreadful a time it was for her."

"It still is…it will be a long while till she recovers from this, if she ever can."

The conversation turned to lighter topics when Astrid commented on Adina's *trés chic* hairdo. Adina also inquired about Astrid's parents, since they had relocated back to Stockholm after Mr. Karlsson, Astrid's dad, retired from his position at the United Nations. Astrid was pleased that they now all resided in the same country at the same time.

On Saturday evening, they dined in Brooklyn at Vinnie and Amelia's restaurant. They were joined by Alice and Daniel along with Anna and Peter. Vinnie set up a large table and prepared some of his most outstanding dishes for them all to sample and enjoy. As a gift to Amelia and Vinnie, Henrik had a case of assorted Italian wines and a case of *Moët & Chandon* champagne delivered to the restaurant earlier that day. Vinnie was thrilled with this most generous gift.

Everyone was having a good time, and it was wonderful to see Alice in such fine spirits. Daniel and Tristan could not help but talk about their mutual medical careers. Henrik actually went into the kitchen to watch Vinnie prepare some of the delicious recipes. Henrik had a genuine appreciation for Northern Italian cuisine, and was happy to learn some pointers from Vinnie. Anna and Peter spoke about the possibility of visiting Astrid in Sweden, during the coming summer, and Adina just thoroughly enjoyed being in the company of her dearest friends. When Amelia wasn't seating other customers, she sat with Adina, and spoke about Angelina Rose's newest beau, which Adina found so endearing.

When the evening ended, everyone was in such good spirits and the women were looking forward to their next birthday celebration on their traditional celebratory day, May 4th. Astrid hinted about the feasibility of joining them at that time, and Adina was gleefully hopeful about that materializing.

At home, Adina and Tristan agreed, it had been a lovely evening, and that Vinnie's dinner selections were a delicious feast for all. On this January evening, the weather conditions might have produced such bitter cold temperatures, but the sustaining lifelong friendship of these women, generated such undeniable warmth and comfort and confidence, as they entered this new decade of their lives.

CHAPTER 26

───────────❧───────────

SINCE SCHOOLS WERE closed on President's Day, Rhoda in-
vited Adina to join her to attend an exhibition at the Neue Galerie on 86th Street and
5ᵗʰ Avenue. The museum housed a collection of German and Austrian art from the
early twentieth century, and showcased the work of Gustav Klimt whose work Adina
had always admired. Adina gladly accepted the invitation, and thoroughly enjoyed
strolling through the Galerie's two stories viewing the remarkable masterpieces.

After they surveyed the exquisite works of art, Adina and Rhoda eagerly decided to have a late lunch at the museum's Café Sabarsky, where
they both enjoyed *Kartoffel-Rösti, Räucherlachs, Kräutersalat,* which was a
crispy potato pancake, smoked salmon and herb salad. For dessert with
their tea, they shared a *Klimttorte,* a chocolate and hazelnut cake.

While they were enjoying their tea and dessert, Rhoda asked how Adina's
group of friends were faring. Adina told Rhoda that Alice and Daniel had gone

for counseling after they lost Jeremy. She thought their marriage might just come through intact, despite their family's dreadful tragedy. Adina remarked that maybe in an odd way, it fixed their marriage. Daniel was spending more time at home now. Fiona was attending medical school at NYU, and Liam changed his mind about an out-of-town college, and instead would attend college at Columbia.

Rhoda said, "Maybe they might have a happy ending despite their tragic loss."

Adina responded, "I don't know about happy endings. The word *ending* does not conjure any joy in my mind. I think I'd prefer to have just lived a happy middle. That alone would be enough. I suspect we all come towards the end of our lives with questions or doubts, that may never be resolved."

"But Adina, you and Tristan have your happy ending, right?"

"Maybe. But at what cost? I'm at a point in my life where I worry all the time about the *cancer* snatching the joy again from my life."

Adina sipped some of her tea and continued, "Things change, people change as they move towards their final years. I think the best we can hope for is having experienced intense pleasure during our middle years, when we don't contemplate such things as growing older, and all that will eventually unfold. The endings are ultimately often filled with worry and grief. First, we lose our parents, and then our friends. Our world diminishes. We fight to stay in love with the one person that brings such sweet pleasure to our every day. There is a drifting from friends that we once saw all the time, and whose counsel we once depended on. I see it starting ever so subtly, even at my age, which is not so old. Happy endings are not easy to grasp."

Rhoda then asked, "What about your other friends? Amelia seems happy."

"Yes, Amelia has worked hard all the time for her share of happiness. She knew the secret early on, to choose a simple life. Amelia never reached for the stars, but in a strange way the stars found her. She and Vinnie had a very happy middle despite disappointments along the way. I imagine they will sail through their later years still very much adoring each other. I don't know how prevalent that kind of satisfying longevity is these days in a marriage."

"What about Anna?"

"Anna will always be a question. She strives for happiness all the time, but it alludes her, and I'm afraid until she is able to stop her running, she will never be content. But if there is a happy ending for her, it is in knowing she raised a son who will always know contentment, by being in touch with his desire to connect with the people he so generously loves. That is something Anna, so far, has not been able to achieve."

Rhoda continued with her questions and observations. "Well your friend Astrid certainly leads a charmed life."

Adina laughed out loud. "You mean my friend, the Baroness? Yes, she does. But Astrid always led a charmed life. It must be in her DNA or something. Astrid chose to be alert to the opportunities life presented to her. She always grabbed hold of the possibilities each day brought her. When her first marriage soured, she fled without drama or self-pity. She is an athletic consumer of joy. She pushes hard to live in a state of cherished contentment. Astrid has always taught me these kinds of lessons and I was lucky to be exposed to her very passionate *joie de vie* when I was so young and impressionable."

Rhoda and Adina sat quietly sipping their second cups of tea. Then Adina said,

"One thing is for sure. We cannot look outside for our happy endings. We must look within, and sometimes that might make us sad depending on our circumstances at a particular moment. But I've learned we always have a choice, to choose to embrace the life that sits beside us. The alternative is to become a victim of life's sometimes cruel fate. There is always another option, and if we are fortunate enough to choose a path with grace and love in our hearts, then maybe a happy middle, and a happy ending can be achieved, for those who have the courage to choose and act."

Rhoda looked at Adina and said, "I know I've said this once or twice before, but it's true. The years, my friend, have made you a wise philosopher."

Adina said, "I am not so much a philosopher, but an observer."

"And what other observations have you made my dear friend?"

For a minute Adina stared out the window of the café that had a view of 5th Avenue, and the start of some snowflakes falling on this mid-February afternoon. Holding her gaze was a woman pushing a stroller with a baby girl who looked about a year old. The baby seemed so content pointing to the snowflakes as they fell gently to the ground. She then turned back to Rhoda and said,

"I'll tell you what I have observed. It has to do with our mothers."

"What do you mean Adina?"

Adina leaned back in her chair and said, "I believe that one remains a child until the day we lose our mothers. It doesn't matter how old we are at the time of their passing, but it isn't until we lose our mothers that we truly become a full-fledged adult. I think even my friends, who by the way all still have their mothers, have not yet reached the point of becoming a complete, fully matured, on your own, adult."

"That's very interesting Adina. I must think about that."

"Yes, I'm sure many would disagree with me on this issue, mostly those who have not yet lost their mothers."

Adina then recalled to Rhoda that she in fact did not choose to obtain her divorce until after her own mother passed away. "Rhoda, you fully took hold of the status of your life and fled a joyless marriage, and you did so quite bravely, after your mother died. It was a huge decision to make by yourself."

"Yes, it was." Rhoda conceded.

Adina continued, "I imagine it's like having a child. I can only imagine that when you bring a child into the world, you look at the world differently because this tiny, innocent life that is yours, is now in that world."

Rhoda shook her head in agreement as she said, "Yes, that's true. A parent worries much about their child's welfare, and one does make certain decisions and sacrifices with one's children in mind, all the time."

"As you should," Adina agreed and resumed offering her own points of view.

"And for a woman, your world shifts when your mother dies. You become more of an adult than when you still had your mother. Because no one ever looks after you like the one person who brought you into this world, and once she is gone, you must truly engineer your life without that person. It is like being born once again, this time born into a new adulthood, and now one must become even more capable of making all the challenging decisions that were once clouded by an array of differing emotions. But all that clears, when you are standing tall and alone, and have to become the sole navigator of your life."

Rhoda sat there staring at Adina, and then finally spoke. Rhoda felt the past few months had certainly matured her friendship with Adina. Both women had been through a lot, and their compassion for one another advanced their concern for each other.

Rhoda said, "There are moments in the late of night when sleep won't come, that I wonder if I'm happy or lonely by myself. When I was with my husband, I was not happy. I was numb inside and that was a deeper form of loneliness. So, I took that huge step, and flew away from the marriage nest, and for the most part I found a lightness in that flight. My daughters were already out of the house, and the time finally seemed right."

Adina responded, "You were brave to begin anew at this point in your life. And you waited until your children were of a certain age, able to handle the dissolution of their family, as they knew it. You raised them in a family, and that was a sacrifice for you, but you were a mother, and that's what a mother does. When the time was right, and your daughters were on firm footing, you left. So many others choose to remain glued, as if their feet are forever stuck in a vat of cement. You found your courage."

"Adina, if you want to talk about courage, look at your own life. You managed it by yourself all those years. You were able to collect moments of enchantment from time to time, and that kept your heart aglow, always to the possibilities of love, instead of the slow, torturous, disassembling of love that some couples inevitably must confront. Some pairings do work out gloriously, but that is often not the case."

Adina then said, "It is rare to meet a couple that seems to exude true delight in their connection to each other, after many years of marriage. When I do observe such a couple, I do envy their relationship, but it's not something I see often."

"That's right, Adina. It is difficult to find such people whose magic lasts over time."

"But Rhoda, I'm still not sure which path was the better choice."

"It's what one makes of their chosen path that matters. You will find your way with Tristan, even this late in the game. Better to have such fulfillment at this time of your life, then to come to this time having been weighed down earlier in your life by routine and complacency, with very little joy to anticipate. Go venture into a life now with Tristan, and any clouds you find will gladly and eventually part, and many rays of sunshine will gaze upon you. I promise. You are a wise and loving woman, Adina."

"I don't know how wise I am Rhoda. But I am grateful to be alive though. Whenever I meet up with some challenge or unpleasantness, or when things don't go my way or when someone disappoints me, I recall sitting in that infusion room for all those months, and that gives me the strength to move on. *Cancer* can knock out all your strength to believe in your own future. I had to learn to dismiss despair, and embrace what brings me joy. I am still learning."

"Well that was a lesson well learned then. Adina, I am a generation older than you and I have observed a thing or two, as well. Some of my friends, some already retired, and the friends I had when I was still married, some do tend to vanish once you are divorced. They do not do much with their days other than babysitting their grandchildren. I am sure it is a pleasure to have them, and I look forward to my girls having children as well one day, but that's all their lives have become. They are caretakers yet again, grannies that are now the nannies, perhaps because their own lives have become so dreary and uninteresting and devoid of the captivating passions that never visited their marriages. Instead of confronting the collapse of their marriage partnership, they occupy their time orchestrating their children's lives. I see this a lot. This gives them the opportunity to look away from the life they chose to live. When we fill our days with fabricated obligations, we lose precious time to fulfill ourselves with our own means of joy."

"Well Rhoda, now who's the philosopher?"

"Adina, happiness does not come so easily. But we must run to it with open arms, arms that are not carrying the obstacles that we create for ourselves."

Adina and Rhoda just continued to sit for a moment, as they consumed the last sips of their tea. Once Rhoda looked at her watch and saw what time it was, they decided it was time to leave.

Rhoda smiled at Adina and together they walked out into the streets that already were beginning to collect a soft covering of snow. Adina thanked Rhoda for suggesting they come to the Neue Galerie.

As Rhoda was buttoning her coat, she said, "Well, we certainly covered a lot of territory today. It was a nice afternoon."

Adina said, "Yes. See you at school tomorrow."

"I'll be there," was Rhoda's response.

Adina arrived home, and sat at her desk a while to review some essays her students had written in French last week about a fond memory. Many wrote about a family holiday celebration, and a few wrote about their first plane trip out of the country. One female student wrote a very inspiring essay about the day she was reunited with her biological mother. Her adoptive mother had accompanied her to the restaurant where they all chose to meet. How courageous all three of those people were to confront one another. Adina found that particular essay so moving. She still had an hour or two before Tristan would be home. Adina was anxious to tell him about the beautiful artwork she had seen on this most splendid day.

In a few months all Adina's friends would assemble together once again. On May 4, 2005 all five women, Adina, Alice, Anna, Amelia, and Astrid met under the clock at Grand Central. They had all recently reached their fifty-first birthday, and all were ready for a nice, long chat and a piece of New York cheesecake.

ACKNOWLEDGEMENTS

———————— ⋈ ————————

MY FIRST ATTEMPT at writing was a poem about the sea, and it was featured in my high school's literary magazine. From that moment on, I found comfort in the practice of writing poems and filling up journals relating my life's daily tribulations. After retiring from a teaching career, I endeavored to write a novel. This is my second story in novel form.

When I received Honorable Mention in the Tortoise and Finch writing contest for my essay, "Into the Box", I had the great pleasure of making the acquaintance of Chloé McFeters, a writer, personal historian and documentary film director. During a phone conversation, we became long-distance friends. Chloé has been an inspiration, and has provided me with such kind support for my most recent literary endeavors. Chloé was a reader of this novel, offering me countless and invaluable suggestions. I cannot thank her enough for all the kind guidance and assistance she has given to me, and for being such a cherished friend.

I also want to offer my thanks to a former colleague, Patricia Underwood, an English and Latin educator, who was an early reader of the draft of this novel. Pat's expertise helped in making my written words more succinct.

For all the French phrases found in my novel, I would like to thank my cousin Stephanie Wolkin, a world traveler, who reviewed and revised my attempts at remembering my comprehension of high school French.

I am eternally indebted to Dr. Ashot Bapat, a hematology oncologist, and Dr. John Wilson, a radiology oncologist, who were both instrumental in steering me through my own personal cancer journey. Their kindheartedness and skilled expertise was crucial for my own recovery.

Lastly and most notably, I have been very fortunate in my life to always have had one person to happily encourage me to pursue many of my dreams, from the small ones to the rather grand ones. This person stands by me, and celebrates my accomplishments as well as making my disappointments more palatable. That person, is my dear sister, Dr. Rochelle Sandra Cohen. She was the first reader of this story, providing valuable feedback, along with unwavering support, and she remains the most knowledgeable person of my heart. I thank her for always being my most enthusiastic devotee.

ABOUT THE AUTHOR

MARION COHEN WAS born and raised in Brooklyn, New York. She earned a BA in mathematics from Kean University and an M. Ed. from Rutgers University. She enjoyed a gratifying career as a mathematics teacher for thirty-six years. Her first novel, *What the Heart Murmurs* was published in 2015. Two of her essays appear in the coloring book journal, *C is for Cancer* by Chloé McFeters. Her essay, *Into the Box*, received Honorable Mention in the Tortoise & Finch Writing Contest, "On Courage".

She currently resides in Cherry Hill, NJ.

Contact at mcohen.author@yahoo.com